Sasquatch Serial Killer

An Ele Carmichael Novel

M. Sparks Clark

Loophole Books

Copyright ©2023 by Melissa Dawn Hancock

All rights reserved.

No part of this publication may be reproduced, distributed, or transmitted in any form or by any means, including photocopying, recording, or other electronic or mechanical methods, without the prior written permission of the publisher, except as permitted by U.S. copyright law. For permission requests, contact Loophole Books, P.O. Box 1, Guthrie, OK 73044.

The story, all names, characters, and incidents portrayed in this production are fictitious. No identification with actual persons (living or deceased), places, buildings, and products is intended or should be inferred.

Book Cover by Shawn Hancock

First edition, 2023

To Billy and Sheri—for "setting me free" and believing I could fly.

To the *real* Nate the Great—thanks for all the inspiration! Love you, little brother.<3

CHAPTER 1

I'd rather be getting a root canal by a drunk dentist than be at a funeral this morning, but someone mysteriously murdered Sheriff Sam Struthers last week and they found his body deep in the Kiamichi Mountains near his home. Someone broke his neck and tore his heart literally out of his chest cavity. I was not the biggest fan of the sheriff and I pretty much detest his wife, Dorothy, with whom I am on the Annual Bigfoot Fair Planning Committee, but it doesn't matter how much you like or dislike someone–when something like this happens, you show up and support. And a grizzly murder like this is not something I would wish on anyone, not even Dorothy.

I was sitting with Bert, Nona, and Vance—three of the four other members of a secret bigfoot protection society called 5S which I recently joined. (Shoot me now, but it's true. Yes, you read that right–a secret fucking bigfoot protection society. Sounds cracked, I know. But what can I say? When I made the move from my cushy urban NYC writer life to southeastern Oklahoma, I jumped right into a goddamn loony bin of natural wonders and mythical beasts. Of course, I know now there is nothing mythical about them.) Our fourth member, Dr. Ahmet Pamuk, is a hermit who lives in a cabin in the woods like me, his property adjoins mine. His growing PTSD from having been a frontline doctor during the 9/11 attack caused him to take early retirement/disability. Even though he had been an emergency room doctor for several years, something about the magnitude of that event had pushed him over the edge. I also suspect there's more to his story that we don't yet know, but the fact that he has even come out of his hermit-dom to join our little group at all is significant. All of us, in fact, (except Nona) live in cabins deep in the woods of the Kiamichi Mountains near Oklachito, Oklahoma—a town that's name is the Choctaw word used by some to refer to the giant furry beasts (its literal meaning is "people big")–but I didn't know that before I came, okay? I didn't mean to fall down this fucking rabbit hole, but now that I'm here, I'm finding it kind of cozy.

Like Dr. Pamuk, I moved here from New York City, well actually from Hoboken, New Jersey, where I lived with my cheating bastard ex up until the point I discovered he was a cheating bastard. I kinda lost my shit and randomly bought a cabin deep in the backwoods of Oklahoma, hoping to hide from both Doug and men in general for the rest of eternity. I am the author of a best-selling series of thrillers based around Detective Rainey K. Moody, who never leaves a missing person missing, or a case unsolved. My move was about four months ago, so as you can tell, a lot has gone down in a short amount of time. Not two months ago, the recently deceased sheriff was interviewing me after my kidnapping from which I narrowly escaped my own untimely demise (thanks to Bigfoot Bob) but that is another story.

An elderly woman began playing "Onward Christian Soldiers" on the church organ and we all rose. They rolled Sheriff Struthers to the lobby of the First Southern Baptist Church of Oklachito and Dorothy followed the casket down the aisle. She was all dressed in black, down to a hat with a veil. I would have called it overkill, but the poor thing was sobbing into her hankie, and I may be a cynical hard-ass sometimes, but I'm not a bitch. Nemesis or not, my heart really went out to her. One row at a time, we exited the building, rising from our seats and walking down the aisle along the same path Dorothy and her dearly departed had just traveled and we took one last look at Sheriff Sam Struthers who looked like a weird waxy quasi-replica of himself and then hugged Dorothy's neck.

"Dorothy, if you need anything, anything at all, you just let us know," Nona said as she pulled out of the embrace. Dorothy nodded, tears streaming down her face. I took Dorothy's hands between my own and said sincerely, "I'm so, so sorry for your loss, Dorothy." She nodded at me, her lips trembling. Again, the cynic in me was fighting to come forth and say she was playing the role of a grieving widow to the hilt, but her open mourning outweighed my critical spirit and I again just felt terribly sorry for the poor woman. They say she was the one who found the body. Nona and I stepped out the front door of the church into what was already a hot, sunny day. It wasn't even 11:00 AM yet, and the thermometer had just crept above the ninety-degree mark. I could hear Vance and Bert giving their condolences to Dorothy behind us. My damn pantyhose were slowly sliding down my ass and the crotch was now midway between my actual crotch and my knees. It was starting to make me walk funny. Why the hell had I decided to wear them, anyway? I hadn't worn hosiery in over a decade. I had to go out and buy some for crying out loud. My complete lack of knowledge on what is appropriate here often screws me over and these damn hose were a perfect example.

PSA #16: If you think you should maybe wear pantyhose to a funeral in the boiling heat of an Oklahoma summer, DON'T! (You are welcome. I'm spouting off some serious fucking wisdom here, heed my words.)

"So, what now?" I asked Nona, trying to ignore my slowly descending undergarments. It had also been years since I had been to a funeral and that was an old school wake, so this was very different. I didn't quite know how the Southern Baptists of Oklahoma did these things.

"Well, most of the people here will follow the hearse out to the cemetery for the graveside part of the service," said Nona. "They will lower his casket into the ground and then those close to Dorothy will go back to the church fellowship hall for a meal. She asked us to come to that, so I guess I'm just gonna keep the coffee shop closed for the day." Nona had recently hired backup and weekend help, but Chloe Clark was not yet fully trained, so Nona had no choice but to close down for the day. Truth be told, most of the town would be at the sheriff's funeral anyway, so it probably wasn't much of a loss. About five or so years ago, Nona had bought the old bank and converted it into a destination coffee shop called Coffee O'Clock. Using her skills from her previous life as a high-dollar interior designer in Austin, Texas, along with her love for coffee and baking, Nona had managed to create a coffee shop that people actually took road trips to come and visit.

"Wait. She asked *me* to come to the dinner at the church?" That couldn't be right. I had known Dorothy for all of four months, tops, and there had been no love lost between us. I could not fathom why she would invite me.

"Well, she said her fellow fair planning members were all invited, so that would mean you too," Nona explained. When I first moved to town, Nona had tricked me into attending a town meeting where they were selecting the newest member to the planning committee for the Annual Bigfoot Fair, the biggest tourist event—well, the only tourist event—the town put on each year. Unbeknownst to me, Nona could no longer bear the idea of another year as the only other woman besides Dorothy on the committee. Also unbeknownst to me, one did not have to put their own name in the hat in this race. Instead, the townspeople would all write names on a scrap of paper and put them into Bert's literal hat, and whoever had the most votes would be the newest member. Bert had strategically introduced me to the whole town directly before the vote and since my name was so fresh on everyone's mind, they voted me in. Needless to say, I was spitting mad when I realized what had happened and had no plans of letting them trick me into servitude, but somehow, Bert and Vance had been so welcoming that I ended up participating in spite of myself. Nona had apologized profusely for setting me up. Apparently, the same thing had happened to her when she moved here, but she confessed she just couldn't face Dorothy another year on her own so she had led me like a lamb to slaughter so that I would have to face Dorothy each week at the planning committee meetings alongside her.

"Yeah, but I think she only said that because—well, how do you politely say, 'Everyone, but Ele?' You don't. And we both know how Dorothy likes things to be proper. I'm afraid I will be more of a nuisance than a welcome guest."

"Or she might think you are snubbing her if you don't show. Just come with us, Ele. It won't be that bad. The four of us will stick together." This, of course, meant that Bert and I would spend the afternoon watching Vance and Nona make eyes at one another. Vance and Nona had officially become a couple when I had been kidnapped and they partnered up with one another in the search party. They were still in that phase of the relationship where they were smitten with one another, and I would find it utterly repulsive if I didn't like both of them so much and wasn't so damn happy for them to get together. Unbeknownst to either of them, they had been mooning over one another for over two decades, so needless to say, this relationship had been a long time coming and it kind of restored my hope in humanity to see their love blossom.

"You all wanna ride with me?" Bert asked and our collective unspoken answer was to follow him to his forty-year-old Land Rover. It was in impeccable condition and was now considered a classic. Vance insisted I take the front seat with Bert under the guise of being gentlemanly, but we all knew it was just that he wanted to sit in the back and hold hands with Nona on the way out to the cemetery.

"Avert your eyes, fellas. I gotta take these pantyhose off." Bert stammered in disbelief and looked out his side window. Vance turned red and stared into his lap, and Nona laughed. I kicked off my shoes and shimmied out of the blasted things. "All clear!" I announced as I slipped back on my shoes. "Ahhh! Much better."

Bert started up the Land Rover and got in line for the procession of cars that would be following the hearse out to the cemetery. "What I can't believe is that Sam was out there without his gun," Bert said. "I mean, it doesn't even make sense."

"Why not? Surely you don't always have your gun on you? *Do you?*" I asked, bewildered.

"Of course. I usually have three on me." Holy shit. Well, I hadn't been expecting that.

"Like now? You have three guns on you right now?"

"Well, of course not, this is a funeral," Bert said, shocked that I would suggest such a thing. "I only have the one."

"So, you think it is strange that he wasn't packing heat?" A smile threatened to escape my lips, but I held strong. I couldn't help myself. How often, in my real everyday life, do I get to use the expression "packing heat"? I could tell I was teetering on a line and Bert was trying to decide if I was making fun of their ways. I wasn't. Well, mostly I wasn't. I thought it was ludicrous that the man would need to wear three guns just to go into the woods, but maybe I was naive.

PSA #17: Never EVER miss the opportunity to use the expression "packing heat" in everyday conversation, should it arise. A wasted opportunity like that may haunt you forever.

"Yes. I do. You know Ele, the last time I was out scouting property, I shot a six-foot rattler. Goddamn, I swear that thing was as big around as my forearm." Bert held out his arm. Bert was a stocky guy, relatively short but built like an ox, and I for damn sure did not want to meet up with a rattler as big around as his forearm. "Time before last, I came across a mountain lion. These woods seem so peaceful and they are, but they are also full of dangerous creatures and I'm not talking about the bigfoot."

"Point taken," I said seriously. "I wasn't trying to make fun. I am just not used to people needing to carry weapons." I glanced over my shoulder to see Nona and Vance were holding hands and listening quietly to our exchange.

"Things are different out here, Ele. Sometimes it's a matter of survival and if Sam had had his gun on him, he would have likely survived. I just don't understand why he was out in the woods unarmed." Bert was somber and for more than just the fact that we were at the funeral of a man whose life had been cut short by violence. The murmurings around town were getting louder. People were blaming Sam's death on bigfoot. Some folks were buying into the idea that the bigfoot population was now attacking the humans of the area and while those of us in 5S strongly suspected that it wasn't true, we didn't have any way to prove it. The loss of the county's sheriff was sure to get hunting groups out looking to pick off any bigfoot they could find. The good thing was that these creatures had millennia of experience at not being found. But the tension was growing, and it was getting harder and harder to ensure the safety of the bigfoot community.

Vance had done a little sleuthing of his own after Sheriff Struther's murder. He had reached out to some of our bigfoot friends, but the whole interaction was less than conclusive because of the complexity of the nature in which Vance "talks" with the bigfoot. You see, it's not a verbal language like we're used to, it's a telepathic communication of ideas, feelings, images, and intentions. Asking a question like this could be tricky. First, Vance had to project the impression that the sheriff had been killed, which, of course, the word "sheriff" was impossible to translate as it was a foreign concept to them, but Vance tried to communicate that one of our honored members had been found dead. Then he tried to project that his neck was broken and his heart ripped out. That image really upset JoJo, the pregnant bigfoot that had recently befriended me and whose mate had saved my life. Then, after Vance had upset her thoroughly, he had to try and inquire whether a bigfoot had committed the crime. It was tricky and at first, JoJo didn't get what he was saying at all.

"You know," Vance started as we drove slowly in the long processional from the church to the cemetery. "At first, when I was trying to talk to JoJo about all of this, I think she thought I wanted her to kill someone for me. She was mortified. I finally got her to understand that someone had already been killed, and I was just asking if any bigfoot had been involved and although she seemed shocked that I would even ask, I could tell that, in truth, she did not know if they had or not. But that didn't stop her from still being a little offended."

"I know," said Bert a bit forlornly. "Even though we don't believe any bigfoot were involved in the murder, it's just not at all conclusive. And just because JoJo and her mate don't know about the killing doesn't mean another creature didn't do it and keep it a secret. Humans live next door to other humans who are killers without knowing it, so it would stand to reason that bigfoot could have committed the crime without the others knowing. This is a stumper."

The real zinger was that Sheriff Struthers was the third killing of its kind in two months and it was becoming clear that a serial killer was plaguing the Ouachitas, the larger mountain range of which the Kiamichi mountains are a part. At the second killing, some in law enforcement became concerned that it was a serial killer and not just a copycat killing, but with a third victim, even the biggest skeptic now had to consider the possibility that a serial killer was on the loose and whether on purpose or coincidentally, he had killed one of their own. Of course, serial killers were not something local law enforcement officers were used to dealing with and if rumors were true, the FBI would be stepping in if they hadn't already. It seemed that more and more of the locals were being persuaded into believing that bigfoot was behind it all, based on the nature of the wounds. There was no obvious use of weapons involved, which was certainly unusual in crimes of this nature. Two of the victims had died from broken necks and one from blunt force trauma, and all three victims had had their hearts removed in such a way that they appeared to be literally ripped out of their chests. It was unlike anything any of them had seen before, and the crimes would take an incredible amount of strength to pull off, not to mention barbaric behavior. Now that they had killed a member of law enforcement, things had become even more personal and I imagined the search for the killer by the authorities would intensify, which meant that our search for the killer had to intensify as well. If we didn't find a way to solve this, the entire population of bigfoot in the area could be at grave risk.

"Well, hell's bells!" Bert exclaimed.

I was about to ask what was wrong when I saw it and by the collective gasp in the vehicle; I knew everyone else had as well. There was that fucking billboard again, and it wasn't in Arkansas this time, it was right here in our own community. Our eyes were all locked onto a giant billboard that stood right before you got to the cemetery and on it was the face of an illustrated bigfoot depicted to look like a vicious monster. The artist had overlaid a target over the bigfoot's face and the bullseye would mean a bullet right between the eyes. Across it were the words, "Bag the Biggest Game of them All!" and "Boutique Bigfoot Hunting Adventures" and the line that really made my skin crawl, "Guaranteed to get a shot at the beast!" The web address made me want to puke. It was a dot com—w w w dot kill the beast. There was an addition to this sign that hadn't been on the one in Arkansas, in swirly golden script were the large words, "Coming at you this NOVEMBER!"

"Son-of-a-bitch," Vance muttered under his breath.

"My sentiments exactly," I sighed and Nona nodded, commiserating the misery. We sat stuck in line, forced to stare at the sign before us.

"Who the hell is this, anyway?" I asked. We had looked it up the first time I saw one of these billboards in Arkansas and the website only had a landing page with the same information as was on the billboard and the words, "Coming this Fall!" but there was no information as to who was behind it. "You think it's the Crawleys?" I wondered aloud.

"I can't imagine them having a solid enough business plan and finances to put up billboards and a website, but I could be underestimating them," Bert answered.

"I can't imagine them keeping their yaps shut about it if it was them," pondered Vance.

"Or using the word boutique," added Nona, and this may have been the most compelling point of all against the likelihood that the Crawleys were involved.

"That's true enough on both counts," agreed Bert. The line had finally moved enough that we were no longer looking at it, thank heavens. The long procession began to pull into the cemetery and a highway patrolman was blocking traffic coming from the other direction so that the long line of cars could make it safely into the cemetery. I once read an article in the newspaper about a funeral in which a motorist crashed into the limousine carrying the family of the deceased as it turned into the cemetery and three more members of the family had died that day at their own father's funeral. It was so morbid, it had become part of the plot in Rainey K. Moody's book three. Of course, in my story, the crash had been intentional because one of the family members had been about to reveal that there had been foul play in the death of the father. With all witnesses except one dead, it had been a hell of a tale as Detective Moody unearthed the killer. There were no missing persons in that book, as in most of my thrillers, just twisty family secrets and a betrayal to unfold. Most of my books include a missing person, as my own mother still resides on the missing person list of Boone, Iowa, where I grew up.

A popular theory among the press is that I write my books in a metaphorical effort to solve my own mother's missing person case. I don't know if that's true or not, but I do wish with all that is in me that someone had found answers to her mysterious disappearance. She simply vanished one evening after leaving two-year-old me with my Aunt Becky. Although there was no evidence of foul play, my mother's car, or her remains, Aunt Becky strongly believed that something terrible had happened to my mom. Aunt Becky's reasoning was simple; she said my mom would never, in a million years, abandon me otherwise. And since Aunt Becky was my mom's younger sister by all of thirteen months and probably knew my mother better than anyone else in the whole world, I believed her.

Thankfully today, all the vehicles made it safely into the cemetery to lay Sheriff Struthers to rest. Dorothy took her seat in the front row of folding chairs that were under the canopy by the hole in the ground that had already been dug. She had cried all of her makeup off during the service and looked gaunt and afraid. Dorothy's mother sat beside her and held her hand, and a few of Sam's siblings joined Dorothy in the front row. Sam and Dorothy's one estranged son had surprised everyone by showing up for the funeral but apparently had no interest in reconciliation as he kept his distance from his mother and stood at the opposite end of the row from where his mother sat weeping. He looked like a linebacker and wore an icy stone expression, staring straight ahead, not even glancing toward his mourning mother. Somehow, this made the whole thing even more tragic and depressing. It was as hot as Haiti and I could feel a trickle of sweat run down my back as I stood in the Oklahoma August sun, only half listening as the pastor once again droned on. This part, however, moved quickly and ended in a literal bang. Since Sam had been in the Navy, there were seven retired military men in full regalia who shot their rifles three times into the air in a twenty-one gun salute. I had never seen one of those in real life before, but it was fascinating and set a real tone of reverence. After this, they lowered the casket into the ground as a single bugler in full military regalia played Taps. I looked around at the masses of somber faces. As a long-time sheriff of the county, Sam Struthers had his fair share of both friends and enemies. The question was whether his death had anything to do with his life at all or if he was simply at the wrong place at the wrong time. One thing Bert and Vance believed, however, was that no bigfoot had been involved in the murder. Now the trick was going to be how to prove it.

CHAPTER 2

Bert was glad Ele had backed out of the funeral dinner at the church. The Crawleys were giving him, Vance, and Nona the stink-eye something fierce throughout the whole dinner. When Ele remembered the Crawleys were cousins with the Sheriff, she had her out. She told Nona, "Well, I can't go to the family dinner when I have a restraining order against part of the family. I shouldn't even have come to the funeral. I wasn't thinking." Then she bolted.

It was a relief to Bert. Ele didn't know that Bert had once again just refused to give the Crawleys a booth at the Bigfoot Fair. This time using her restraining order against them as an excuse, so it would really be bad if she had ignored the restraining order entirely. She also did not know that the Crawleys had been threatening to sue the Bigfoot Fair for discrimination if they did not allow them a booth this year, but Bert was stubborn. He knew the Crawleys would try to sell their own "Bag-a-Bigfoot" hunting trips in their booth and he simply would not allow it. If the Crawleys weren't the ones behind these billboards, Bert could only imagine how they were taking someone moving in on their territory.

The reason Bert had gone to the trouble to run the fair all these years was to prevent booths from people like the Crawleys from popping up, so he sure as heck wasn't budging on it now. Besides, Rob Abbot, his attorney and friend, told him not to worry about it. They had written the bylaws of the fair's nonprofit in such a way that the Crawleys didn't have a snowball's chance in hell of winning if they ever sued, which neither he nor Rob could imagine they would actually do. Unfortunately, Bert had inadvertently re-aroused their anger towards Ele by citing the restraining order as the reason they could not have a booth this year. He had told them it would be too difficult to ensure that they stayed a hundred feet away from Ele at all times if they were all working at the same festival.

There were a lot of things Bert hadn't told Ele. He felt an incredible responsibility for her safety, not because he had been the one to sell her the cabin. He sold property all the time free from feelings of any future responsibility for the well-being of the people he sold it to. But with the cabin Ele bought, he knew that his refusal to sell the property to the Crawleys had presupposed her to their hatred. He hadn't been unethical, but he knew he had been walking a fine line during that sale. Still, the Crawleys hated her because she had won and Ele's complete unawareness of this truth ate Bert up inside. Ele didn't even know that the Crawleys had ever made an offer on the property she bought. In actuality, they made an offer the first day it was on the market and had upped their offer on the fourth day. Bert had refused both offers because they had not been full-price offers and the clients had left the decision up to him, wanting to have as little to do with the property and its sale as possible. Bert knew that if he'd told his clients of the Crawley's offer, they surely would have taken it. But because they had left the decision up to him and he could not bear for the Crawleys to get their hands on the property, therefore increasing their chances of capturing or killing a bigfoot, he had taken the liberty of promptly refusing the Crawley's offers. Everyone knew there were bigfoot on Old Man Miller's property, that was why the Crawleys wanted it so much. Bert thanked his lucky stars that Ele had made a full-price offer on the property sight unseen on day six and he had taken her offer without hesitation. Well, he had made the cursory effort of cautioning her about buying a property sight unseen, but when she insisted, he happily forfeit his argument. Of course, when the Crawleys found out the property had sold to someone else, they tried to offer more than the asking price, but Bert had refused, saying that his clients accepted the offer already and the closing scheduled. In record time, mind you, thanks to Bert's motivation. Because of this, Ele had walked into the Crawley's hatred completely unaware.

Bert had failed to mention all of this upfront and it seemed strange to do so later, so when the Crawleys started harassing Ele and hunting on her property without her permission, shooting guns and making threats (and likely were the ones behind her kidnapping), Bert felt tremendous guilt and responsibility.

"Man, Paul sure did get big, didn't he?" Vance asked, referring to Sam and Dorothy's son. Bert was pulled from his thoughts. Vance and Bert had caught Paul as he was slipping away from the graveside service and visited with him for a few moments and were both surprised by his sheer bulk.

"Yeah, he did. Didn't you used to coach him in baseball when you first moved back?"

"Yep. He was scrawny then, though. I wouldn't have thought he could get so big. Neither Sam nor Dorothy are very large."

"Maybe he takes steroids," interjected Nona. Her ex had gone through a weight lifting phase where he had taken steroids and really beefed up. Her ex's steroid use had been a nightmare for Nona since he already had a bad habit of knocking her around when he got drunk, and steroids only made the beatings worse.

"Huh. I didn't think of that." Vance looked at Nona like she was a genius, and Bert thought it was very nice that his friend had finally gotten the courage to ask Nona out. They made a lovely couple. The look on Vance's face made Bert think of his beloved Libby, which always made his heart ache just a bit. Libby's was the last funeral he had attended before today. The three of them stayed at the dinner and chatted until they noticed a few people telling Dorothy farewell and they followed suit. As they walked out of the church, they heard the raised voices of Abner and Jeb talking about how the murderous bigfoot must be stopped. Bert sighed and looked at Vance. "We're gonna have to do something about all of this."

Vance nodded with solemn resignation. With Sam's unusual murder, protecting bigfoot had suddenly become exponentially more difficult.

M. SPARKS CLARK

CHAPTER 3

"Oh, for the love of God!" I was simply trying to take a piss in peace in the privacy of my own home, but apparently, this was too much to ask. I listened to the whimpering and watched the little claws of doggy paws scratch and reach under the door. I flushed and opened the door for the loveable but sometimes annoying little guy.

PSA #18: Unless you desire a party to your pooping for the rest of eternity or at least until you or your pet's untimely demise, learn from my mistake and do NOT take your puppy to the potty with you.

(I know, wisdom abounds here. It's the practical things really–that make all the difference. You're welcome. I live to serve.)

Biffy sat looking up at me and smiling as I started washing my hands and face and brushing my teeth. The sweet little black and white furball I brought home only two short months ago was now a lanky teenager pup, and he followed me everywhere. The breeder was right; he was going to be really large for a border collie and I was glad about that since part of my intention in getting him was for him to help guard me and my place. I know Border Collies are not typically guard-dogs but Aunt Becky and I had one when I was a child, so I am particularly partial to the breed. After the kidnapping, I felt the need for a little extra protection (go figure), especially since they never caught people behind the kidnapping and the mystery as to why I was kidnapped in the first place had never been officially solved. (Although those of us in 5S had a pretty good suspicion as to why). While I was missing, in an odd set of circumstances, Bert and my attorney acquired on my behalf a Protective Order (or PO) against Abner and Jeb Crawley, of Crawley's Outdoor Adventures, a pair of wannabe bigfoot hunters who had threatened me and had hunted numerous times on my property against my wishes, waking me up with gunfire in the middle of the night more than once. So, the peace and quiet of late could be because the PO is still in place. That whole fiasco was one reason Sheriff Struthers hadn't been my favorite person, the Crawleys were his cousins and when I wasn't entirely forthcoming with all the information about my escape, (how the hell could I be? I had been rescued by a bigfoot, for crying out loud) Sheriff Struthers took his suspicions that I was withholding information from him as an excuse not to put too much effort into pursuing whether or not his cousins were behind the whole damn thing as we suspected they were. Anyway, my protective order was up for review in a month and I hoped that wouldn't stir up any more trouble.

I finished my night-time routine and picked up the pup, who was already too big for me to hold comfortably. It was awkward to hold him in my arms with his long, gangly legs, but I loved to snuggle him and so I ignored his size and nestled him into my neck. Biffy, of course, loved it and put his front legs around each side of my neck and laid his head on my shoulder. Bif's actual name is Bigfoot, which is what the breeders had called him because of his large puppy paws that set him apart from his siblings. When I was first holding the tiny little creature, the woman I bought him from revealed his temporary moniker to me and since I was knee-deep in my own bigfoot adventures at the time, it felt like destiny and sealed the deal for me. But Vance had been right, "Bigfoot" had proven to be an awkward name for a pet, and one that didn't quite roll off the tongue. "Bigfoot, time to eat!" "Bigfoot, time to come inside!" You get the drift. So, "Bigfoot" had morphed into "B.F.", but that was awkward too and morphed yet again into "Bif" (or "Biffy" as I most often called him) and so that was the nickname that stuck. I loved the idea, however, that if anyone ever overheard us talking about the bigfoot that our little secret society served, we could always laugh and explain to them that my dog's name was Bigfoot and it would be true. So, in some ways, my dog's name was a cover for the crazy-ass shit I was up to—that is, the preservation of bigfoot or sasquatch, just depending on what you liked to call them. I prefer the word bigfoot, although the official name of our group is 5S, standing for Society in Secret Service to Sasquatch Security. I know it's ridiculous, but to be fair, Bert and Vance came up with it when they were teenagers, which is how long they have been actively serving and protecting the creatures.

Of course, most people don't believe the creatures are real; and of those that do, many believe bigfoot to be vicious monsters. But around these parts, I've found there are more believers than not and before this serial killer mess, more believed them to be peaceable creatures, but now it seemed to be a fairly even divide whether the creatures are peaceful or vicious. From my experience, and that of Bert and Vance, at least the ones in this area, are kind, peace-loving creatures who just want to be left alone to live their lives as they have throughout history. This, of course, is getting harder and harder as people are moving into their natural forest habitat and building fancy-ass cabins like mine. It is getting harder for them to live undetected and harder for them to get the game they need to survive. These are the issues we try to help with. Bert and Vance discovered about five years ago that people all around the world had instinctively been starting their own little bigfoot protection societies. Our little group is actually part of the International Sasquatch Protection Society. We are Chapter #111, and Nona and I are looking forward to joining Vance and Bert at this year's ISPS Conference, which was to be held in Canada this year in Niagara Falls, Ontario. Vance and Bert attended last year's conference in Washington state and really wanted our whole group to go this year, but Ahmet hadn't quite come out of his hermit-dom to that degree and had flat out refused to attend.

Biffy and I were just about to climb into bed to read (me, not Bif—I haven't taught him yet) when there was a knock at my door. Biffy barked, and ran ahead of me to check things out. My instinct was to get onto him for barking, but I wanted a dog who would alert me to anything unusual, so I let him do his happy doggy barking duty. I looked at the clock; it was almost nine p.m., kinda late for anyone who would visit me. I got to the door where Bif sat wagging his tail.

"I hope to God this is someone we know." I spouted off to Bif since my "guard dog" seemed so happy about the visitor. I peeked through the little hole in the door and saw Ahmet Pamuk standing there looking self-conscious, rubbing his hand over his head in a way that made me think he was about to bolt. I opened the door and smiled. I was in my nightclothes but they were just a soft black pair of pajama bottoms that looked like they could just as easily be workout pants and a black tank top so it wasn't terribly obvious that I had been getting ready for bed aside from my freshly washed face, but since I only wore make-up about half the time these days, that too wasn't particularly out of the ordinary either.

"Ahmet!" I said cheerily as I opened the door to him. "Come in. To what do Biff and I owe this pleasure?" I said this last bit, trying to maintain a serious facade but with my cheeks quirking up into an amused smile as Bif rolled in ecstasy at his feet, so pleased was my puppy to see his friend. The 5S group had come over for dinner and a meeting on Bif's first night with me and at least once a week ever since, so Biffy and Ahmet knew each other quite well and got on great.

"Sorry to interrupt." Ahmet knelt down and was rubbing Bif's belly, his eyes flicking to the book in my hand. One of my favorite authors had just released a new book, and it had come in the mail today. I read all formats and always have at least one book going on both my phone and tablet, but with the authors I most love, I always order a print version. Honestly, my vast collection of books is what I missed most out of my belongings. All of my possessions, aside from the three suitcases and carry-on I brought with me when I moved here, were still in Evie's storage compartment in NYC. Evie had been with me the day I caught my cheating bastard ex in his affair. The two of us had promptly gone to the home I had with Doug and packed up all of my belongings, which, aside from books, were shockingly few. I left Doug all the furniture except for an antique rocker that had been my mom's and an old overstuffed velvet chair that had been Aunt Becky's. The rest of my belongings consisted mostly of the books, of course, and old typewriters that I had collected over the years and all of it was in the 4'x 6' storage closet that came as an amenity in the basement of Evie's Manhattan apartment complex. I had moved here a little over four months ago and it really was time for me to have my stuff shipped to me or to go retrieve it myself.

"Oh, no worries," I said, gesturing to the book. "I just got it in the mail today, I haven't even started," I told Ahmet as we walked into the living room with Bigfoot happily bounding along right on Ahmet's heels. I motioned for him to sit down and laughed as both Ahmet and Bif sat in unison. "Would you like a glass of wine? Or beer? Or a bottle of water?" I asked, before sitting down.

"No, no. I won't stay long. I'm sorry Ele, I should have called first. Honestly, I forget I have a phone again." When Ahmet moved here after his breakdown, he had gone into deep hermit mode and didn't even have a cell phone. Bert sold him the place, so he and Vance were just about the only people in town that knew Ahmet. Apparently, before his move here, his decline had been slow, and he continued to work for about a decade after the twin towers fell, with his capacity to handle the stress of his job slowly diminishing until he could do it no more. He had been here for almost ten years now and until two months ago, when he joined our 5S group, he still didn't have a phone.

"It's okay. But what's going on with you? You seem like something serious is on your mind." Ahmet seemed very uncomfortable. I kinda wished he would have agreed to a drink. I thought to myself that he might not need it, but I could use a glass of wine to take the edge off of things, the tension so thick in the air like static electricity buzzing around us.

"I'm having these dreams again."

"Okay..." I said, unsure what that even meant. Ahmet started again.

"After the tragedy of 9/11, I was struggling like so many people in the city—you were there then, right?" I was and even though I didn't live terribly near to the World Trade Center, living in Hoboken, I could see the towers fall from across the water. I remembered how stressful and tragic everything felt everywhere in the city during that time. We all knew someone who had died or was missing. The entire city was crippled with loss, the entire country, for that matter. I couldn't imagine what it had been like to have been so close to the trauma working ER that day. It was hard for me just as a citizen of the city.

"Yes," I said, nodding, encouraging him to continue. "It was awful," I added, lest he think I was untouched.

"Well, many of us who worked closely with the victims were struggling and, of course, there was therapy and groups for us to join to help us try and heal and I was doing okay, you know, as okay as anyone, as okay as could be expected. But then, I started having these dreams. I was in the building, running down the stairwell. I was a woman, and I was talking on the phone to my child, telling them I loved them, telling them to call and ask grandma to pick them up from school that day. And then flames would engulf me, or I would get trapped, or the floor would fall out from under me and everything would go black. Sometimes I would be a jumper and would leap from a window. I would wake up with the name of the person I had been in the dream on my lips, so I kept a little notebook next to the bed and would jot the names down and anything that felt important.

"Of course, I could never go back to sleep after the dreams. They would mess with me for several days. So randomly, one night after waking up with one of these terrible nightmares, I couldn't sleep, so I looked up the name. I don't know why. I just thought it was so bizarre that I would wake up with a name on my lips every time. As I awoke, I would nearly speak aloud. 'I am Millie Stone' or 'I am Enrique Alvarez'. I think that's why I wrote them down from the very first one, because it was simply so bizarre." Ahmet paused and I couldn't help asking.

"So what happened when you looked up the name that night?" I felt like I knew where this was going, but I just couldn't believe what I was thinking could be right.

"They were real people, Ele. That was the night I officially fell down the rabbit hole. Once I saw that the first name I looked up was a real person, of course, I had to search the rest of the names on my list, and one after another, I found them on the list of 9/11 victims. People I had never met. People who had perished in the attack. At first, I thought maybe they had been patients. There had been so many, I thought I was just having flashbacks of people, like names and faces stored in my subconscious, people who I had helped and had stuck there in the recesses of my mind, but no. They were the dead and missing. And I think, well, I can almost say that I know that I was dreaming of their last moments on this earth. Why this information would come back to me in this bizarre way in the years after their deaths, I have no idea. But I started contacting some of their loved ones and finding out that yes, their mother had called and told them she loved them. Yes, she had told them to get their grandmother to pick them up that day. And a million other details from my dreams were confirmed, time and again. Some of their loved ones seemed to take comfort. Some seemed to think I was crazy and wished I had left them alone. My therapist did not know what to do with me. She had never encountered something so strange. It was the dreams that actually ended my career and led me here, far away from the tragedy. And coming here–it worked. The dreams completely stopped when I came here. And while I had lost my life, and my career in NYC, I regained my sanity, because it was all slowly driving me crazy. I didn't want to relive these people's last moments. I didn't want to know. Every once in a while, there would be a message. The dream would end with 'tell my husband...' or 'tell my father...'. Those were always the ones that made the rest of them seem almost worth it because every time that happened and I delivered the message, the recipient of the message was transformed. They would break down sobbing and thank me over and over, and that helped me keep going. I did this once or twice a month for almost ten years following the tragedy. The hospital had moved me out of emergency to a day clinic. They were really good to all of us who had gone through the worst of it. They tried to keep us on, to help us heal, but the damn dreams kept coming until I just couldn't take it anymore. I was becoming suicidal. I wouldn't sleep for days on end because I didn't want to have another dream. It was my therapist's idea for me to file for victim aid and compensation and move far away. I think she was really afraid I was going to off myself and I was starting to be afraid as well. I googled 'luxury cabins for sale' and Bert's listing for my cabin came up and I thought there couldn't possibly be a more far off and different place from NYC than the Kiamichi Mountains of Oklahoma."

I chuckled softly and a brief flash of confusion and hurt went through Ahmet's eyes. I could tell he was trying not to be offended. "I'm sorry," I said. "I'm not laughing at your experience. God, I would never do that. I'm just a nervous laugher, and I thought it was funny because I googled the same exact phrase and ended up buying my cabin sight unseen from Bert as well. I think Bert's SEO game must be spot on." I sighed. My head was reeling from his story. "This is so crazy, Ahmet. I'm so sorry this happened to you. So, what did you mean? The dreams are back?"

"Last night I dreamed I was walking in the woods and I was attacked." I nodded, I was trying to follow Ahmet's train of thought but couldn't figure out what he meant. This had nothing to do with 9/11. Ahmet could tell I wasn't getting it. He was shaking all over, and I moved from my chair to the couch to put my arm around him. "Ele," he said dramatically. "I woke up and the words on my lips were, 'I am Sam Struthers.'"

"Oh, shit."

CHAPTER 4

Ahmet's head was in his hands now as he hunched forward on my sectional. I was gently patting his back, murmuring softly, "It's okay. It'll be okay." And Bif was nuzzling him with his snout, trying to work himself right under his hunched-over face, getting all up in his business. Bif whimpered and Ahmet laughed, wiping a stray tear away with the back of his hand that was falling from his right eye.

"It's all right, buddy," he said, patting the dog and then scratching behind his ears. Ahmet suddenly looked embarrassed and, as he turned to look at me, he said, "I'm sorry I dumped all this on you. It was all I could think of today while you all were at the funeral. And as darkness fell, anxiety gripped me and I couldn't even think about going to bed. I don't want this to start again. I don't understand why it's happening. And I don't know what to do, because Ele, I know the last moments of Sam Struthers life, but I can't go to the authorities. They will try to say it's some kind of confession. Some people around here have a hard enough time being okay with someone of my skin tone and with a name like Ahmet Pamuk being a part of their community as it is, and I've kept to myself so much that I'm sure they all think something's off with me, anyway. They probably think I spend my days locked in my cabin building bombs." I sighed at this statement, not because

I thought Ahmet was wrong, but because I knew he was probably right about what the local authorities and locals, in general, most likely thought about him.

"It'll be okay. We'll talk to Bert and Vance and see what they think we should do. Had anything like this ever happened before 9/11? Like when you were a kid?"

"Not really. That's what's so bizarre. I mean, I was always an intuitive kid and could seem to feel other people's anger or distress. I've been able to read a room for as long as I can remember. I would know when my mom and dad were not getting along just by the way the air in the room felt when I would walk through it, but that was it. That was the extent of it. I could live with that. This—" I watched as his eyes welled up with tears again. "Ele, I can't live with this." He looked up at the clock on the wall. "I'm sorry. I've already taken up too much of your time." As he got up to go, I pulled him back onto the sectional with me.

"Don't be stupid. You can't go now. This is terrible. You must have had a terrible day." He smiled a wry smile.

"The worst," he agreed.

"Well, at least have a glass of wine and a brownie with me. I've already had one brownie tonight, so you can have two to catch up with me." I smiled at him. On a whim, when I got home from the funeral this afternoon, I had baked a box of brownie mix. I try not to let myself do too much baking unless I'm having company over, even though I enjoy it. Living alone, I just eat it all myself and my aging metabolism isn't what it used to be. I never had to worry about my weight before and never did, pretty much eating whatever I damn well pleased and was never one to let the challenge of a full pan of brownies thwart me, but lately, I had noticed the needle on the scale inching upward and the waistline on my pants growing ever so slightly tighter.

I placed a glass of red and a little saucer with two hearty-sized brownies on it in front of him on the coffee table as I plopped back down in the big leather chair where I had been before he broke down. I had a glass of wine and a brownie on a saucer as well. "Who's your favorite author?" I asked, spying my new book on the end table and trying to get Ahmet's mind off of things and lighten the mood.

Ahmet took a sip of his wine and a big bite of brownie as his brow revealed he had gone into full contemplation mode. "You know I can't pick just one." I did know. I was the same way, it had been an unfair question and one I would have refused to answer as well.

"Okay, you're right. Let me rephrase that. Who are some of your favorite authors?" I asked, reworking the question into a more reasonable form. I can never pick a favorite anything either, because there are so many variables to consider and one author is my favorite in one way, but another in another way, and it is simply impossible to weigh all the things to consider and for one solitary person, or movie, or book, or anything else to come out clearly on top.

"Oh, I can answer this one," Ahmet was smiling now. I noticed he had finished the first brownie already and was tucking into the second. He was such a nice man. I felt so bad for him now that I knew the details of what had led to his early retirement. The whole thing also fascinated me, if I was being honest. He would make a great character in a book, I couldn't help thinking to myself. Ahmet started rattling off names. Some I loved. Some I hadn't ever read. Then I heard the name "Eric Willoby" and I couldn't help but interrupt because this was an author whose work I absolutely hated.

"NO!" I said ferociously. "He cannot possibly be one of your favorites. He is wretched to his characters. He tortures them and puts them through more hardship than anyone should ever have to face and then–" I was getting very passionate now, "Then—he leaves his readers just hanging. He doesn't even give you any redemption or closure. How can you possibly like that? I hate his books," I said with such a ferocity that Ahmet was clearly taken aback. But since Ahmet liked him, I didn't want him to feel personally attacked, so I added: "As an individual, however, he is a nice man. I've been on panels with him a few times at different conferences. But I hate–I hate–I HATE—his work!" Ahmet put down his brownie and glass of wine as I ranted. His eyebrows were high on his forehead in surprise and amusement.

"Wow," he said. "So I'm not quite sure I understand, are you saying you're not a big Eric Willoby fan?" I gave him the squint eye to let him know how funny (NOT) I thought he was, but we ended up smiling at each other despite my efforts. "I like the way you say 'he tortures his characters' as if they are real people." He paused for a moment, looking at me more seriously. "They are to you, in a way, aren't they?"

I laughed and felt my cheeks flush ever so slightly. "In a way, yes. It's always the hardest part of writing for me–torturing my characters. I want to coddle them. It's like they become my friends, and what kind of sadistic bastard wants to torture their friends? I want to make things easy for them. But that, my friend, turns out not to be particularly riveting reading. I can't tell you how many times I've had to rework a story that wasn't working because I was being too nice to my characters. Lately, I've started looking at it differently. I'm not the one torturing them, that is simply their story. But as the author, I am the one helping them sort it all out. That being said, I still think Eric Willoby takes it to the nth degree, his stories bloody torture his characters and then he doesn't help them sort a thing! He doesn't even give them any resolution. Or redemption. He's a monster." Ahmet burst out laughing at this, a full belly laugh, his head falling completely back, and I couldn't help noticing how handsome he was, in a subtle way—the kind of handsome that puts you completely at ease rather than on self-conscious edge. The thought startled me. I had completely signed off of men since discovering Doug's affair and was not ready to sign back on anytime soon. I would have to put that little part of my mind back in a box and be sure I kept Dr. Ahmet Pamuk in the friend box of my brain as well.

"A monster, huh? What about you, though? Your characters always have a missing loved one or find themselves in a terrible snag." This surprised me. I didn't know Ahmet had read my work. "I would hardly say you are kind to your characters."

"It's true," I said. "That's why I've had to look at things differently, so I could do my best work and not baby my characters like they were my children. My characters do always start out in a terrible fix, but I at least give them closure. Resolution. At best, they are reunited with their loved ones in the end and, at worst, with their loved one's bodies. But they have closure. I always give them closure." My mind wandered, as always, back to my own mother's disappearance and the lack of closure we had. My Grandma Goosey and Aunt Becky died without ever knowing what had happened to my mom. The way it was looking, I might die without that resolution as well.

"Closure is important to you, huh?" Ahmet mused, clearly thinking about that.

"Closure is everything." Surely he knew about my mom, but I suppose it was vain to assume he had read an article about me. I hadn't assumed he had read my work, so why would I make that assumption? It often came up in interviews. Journalists loved the angle that every book I wrote was my attempt to solve my mother's missing person's case. A truth that I had been aware of since the beginning. Writing, first and foremost, had been therapy to heal the heart of a girl who wished more than anything else that she could have known her own mother, that someone hadn't taken that away from her when she was only two years old.

"Why do you think that's so?" Ahmet pushed. He really didn't know. I shrugged, he was going to feel uncomfortable when I told him, but it wasn't a secret and if I didn't reveal it to him now and he found out later, he would remember this moment and that I had kept myself from him and right after his blatantly cracking open the most disturbing details of his life to me, it wouldn't be right.

"My mom disappeared when I was two years old, Ahmet. They never found her. Not a trace of her, not her car, nothing. And I never got closure, or even anything resembling closure. I still don't know. The least I can do for my characters is to give them that."

He was stunned. His mouth fell open and for a moment I could tell he didn't know what to say. "I'm sorry, Ele. I'm so sorry. I had no idea."

"It's okay. I know you didn't." I smiled at him. Now we had both revealed a bit of ourselves tonight. "I didn't know you had read any of my books either," I said. "Which one?"

Ahmet shrugged, and I thought I could see a little color rise in his cheeks this time. "All of them." He chuckled uncomfortably. "I'm kind of a fan. You interrupted me with your passionate opinions on Eric Willoby's work before I could say the final name, who, if I was being honest, I should have probably just answered your first question, 'Who's your favorite author?' with—in case you haven't guessed—the answer I should have given was E. Carmichael."

"Oh." I paused, unsure what to say, which was silly, but until just now, I wasn't even sure he knew what I did for a living, so the whole thing was taking me by surprise. "Thanks," I said and smiled at him. He blushed and nodded uncomfortably. "Just so you know, you played it super cool. I had no idea."

"Thanks." He said back, laughing as he got up from the sectional and gathered both his and my empty dishes. He walked into my kitchen, which was part of the same large open space, and he started washing our dishes and placing them into my drainer that was next to the sink. It was a simple act of kindness and familiarity. Of course, he had been here many times before for 5S meetings and dinner and had helped me clean up, but he had never been here by himself, it had never been just the two of us before, and the familiarity suddenly made me feel self-conscious. He looked up at me over the sink as he washed my wine glass.

"In fact, you are the only reason I said yes to 5S. If you hadn't come with Bert that day, there is no way I would have agreed to join. But I wanted to know you better. Your stories have brought me so much escape, so much entertainment, comfort, and even joy over the years. I just thought, 'Sworn hermit or not, I would be a fool to miss this opportunity.'" He dried his hands on a dishtowel that was sitting next to the sink and came back over by my chair, leaned down, and patted Bigfoot's head. "Now, I will get out of your hair. Thank you for letting me pour my story out to you. And thanks for the brownies and wine. I feel much better just having talked about it."

"Are you sure?" I asked. I was actually a little sad to see him leaving, and I couldn't help worrying about him. What if he had another dream? "Will you be okay? We can watch something on Netflix. I have a guest room if you need to not be alone." He laughed at this.

"No. I can't do that. Frank Sinatra would never forgive me. But thank you for the offer."

"Frank Sinatra?"

"My big yellow tomcat." He sleeps with me, and he keeps me on a very rigid feeding schedule. He wakes me up every morning at precisely 6:43 for his breakfast.

"Oh, my God. I think I would evict him for that behavior."

"I tried. He just sits outside my window and yowls, so I gave up. It's kind of nice though. It makes me get up and start my day. I've always been someone who loves the morning—once I'm awake. It's the waking up part that's hard for me, but he makes that simple. Pretty hard to ignore a twenty-two-pound tabby standing on your chest meowing full force in your face every morning." This mental image made me laugh aloud. Bigfoot and I were following him to the front door as we talked.

"Well, if you're sure. You're always welcome, though. I mean that."

Then Ahmet did something that surprised me. He leaned forward and gave me a soft kiss on the cheek. His scent hung in the air around me like some kind of exotic spice that I was unfamiliar with but smelled lovely. "Thank you. I didn't realize how much I needed a friend," Ahmet said simply. And with that, he opened the door and stepped out into the night.

I felt a bit swoony. What the hell was wrong with me? I was a grown-ass woman who was not interested in a relationship. He said "friend," which was the exact box I wanted to keep him in, I reminded myself as I locked the door. Then, Bif and I headed off to bed with everything I needed in life—a good book and a good dog.

CHAPTER 5

Chloe was getting the hang of things. She rang me up, and I watched as Nona coached her on my vanilla latte. Nona just recently hit her five-year anniversary of the opening of Coffee O'Clock and in celebration, she hired Chloe as her first employee, which meant before long, she will have entire weekends off instead of only Sundays and I have to admit, visions of weekend road trips dance merrily in my head. I'm completely unfamiliar with this part of the country and exploration always does a writer's soul wonders.

It was the most lovely morning; the sun was shining, Nona and Chloe baked snickerdoodles which always made me think of my Grandma Goosey, and I just turned the first book in a new series I've been working on into my publisher, which may or may not have a protagonist that bears a strong resemblance to moi and who also happens to be a part of a bigfoot preservation society. What can I say? Sometimes the facts are far stranger than fiction. When I moved here and first discovered that bigfoot actually existed and found that the creatures had taken my mind hostage, I swore to God I would never write a bigfoot novel, but those fuckers got in my head. Then, they up and got in my heart as well and that's when the trouble started.

PSA #19 Never say never.
Am I right?

But I continued to resist until I was spouting off one day about how the creatures simply needed better PR–how a lot of these cable tv shows were painting them as wild dangerous beasts and how that was feeding this new craze of people wanting to hunt them–and Nona pointed out that the best PR would be some really great novels depicting their peaceful nature and how it was such a shame that none of us were best-selling authors who could make that happen—the smart-ass!

So, I relented and agreed to explore the possibility because, quite frankly, I didn't actually think the damn idea had a snowball's chance in hell of going anywhere. I thought it would be much harder to convince my long-time agent, Sookie Evanovich, to go along with me writing a bigfoot novel than it was. I didn't think she would be willing to try and sell it. And then, I thought my stipulations: 1) that I would be allowed to release the bigfoot novels under a pseudonym (because I really have no damn desire to go down in history as 'that lady who writes bigfoot stories') and 2) that the publisher would give it a full year for the chance to make the bestseller list on its own before they revealed my true identity (which would push it to the bestsellers list by default because my name was on it and my fans would be curious). I thought all of this was an impossible thing to ask, but Sookie—miracle-worker that she is—worked her magic easy-peasy-lemon-squeezy. Then the damn novel nearly wrote itself, so here I was, well on my way to becoming a bigfoot novelist for fuck' sake. Life takes some weird-ass turns, am I right? Well, technically, I was not being revealed as a bigfoot novelist, M. Sparks Clark was. A pen name I had carefully chosen for sentimental reasons. And unless I wanted E. Carmichael's name dragged through the bigfoot trampled mud, I had better do a damn good job on this series because I needed them to be fucking bestsellers. Really, it all felt like cheating. It was nearly like writing a memoir but simply changing all the names and specific details so that characters would be unrecognizable to the public and so I couldn't be sued. I had never done memoir writing before (or even a memoir masquerading as a novel), but I was enjoying it.

I watched the men of all ages be especially nice to young Chloe. She was a looker. I wondered if they knew she was in a relationship with a woman and if they would be as nice to her if they did. The world was progressing slowly but surely, but there were little pockets where it progressed a little more slowly than other places, and from what I could tell so far, southeastern Oklahoma was slow to embrace change, at least in its open-mindedness towards same sex relationships and gender identity—human conditions that have been with us since the beginning of time but have been so suppressed, so pushed under the carpet by religion and tradition, that they were just now getting the light of day that they deserved. I hoped these people would choose kindness when they figured Chloe out. But truthfully, this little rural town in Oklahoma was often surprising me with its kindness, so why would that change now? For all I knew, everyone might already know and be supportive. Nona hired Chloe, first and foremost, because she liked her, but she also knew that she and her girlfriend, Abby, had had a hell of a time with some of their more conservative peers. Chloe had been a faithful customer for a few years now and Nona had such a kind heart and listening ear that Chloe had confided in her over that time.

So when Nona decided to hire help, she knew just who to ask. From what I could tell so far, Chloe had been a brilliant choice.

Nature called as it often does in a coffee shop and I made my way to the little girl's room. When I came out, I noticed Vance over at the side of the counter with Nona. He gave her a quick kiss, and they were chattering away with one another cheerfully, like it hadn't only been a few hours since they last spoke. Then I looked over to see that Bert was at my table.

"Good Morning, Bertrand," I said, cheerfully, and Bert winced. "No? Don't want me to call you Bertrand?"

Bert laughed. "Not really. That's what my momma called me when I was in big trouble. I can't hear it without thinking of the switch she would make me go select for my punishment when I was a kid. Since I didn't know any better, I would always get the skinniest one I could find, not realizing that would be the one that would really zing through the air and leave welts. 'Bertrand' is the kid who got those lickings and I like to forget those things."

"I'll remember that, and stick with Bert." I smiled at him and noticed there was a seriousness about him lying just under the surface. "So, what's up with you this morning?" He looked like he wanted to talk about something.

"Ahmet called me this morning and told me everything. He said that he visited you last night and talked to you as well. He's beside himself."

"I know." I felt terrible for Ahmet. "Did he have another dream last night?"

"No, thank heavens. But, Ele—" Bert hesitated at this, like he was unsure whether to continue down the mental path he was on. "If what he is saying is true, then he saw Sam's killer."

This stunned me into silence. I hadn't thought about that when he told me he experienced the final moments of Sheriff Struther's life. I don't know why it didn't occur to me that he had seen the killer. "Wait, what do you mean? 'If what he is saying is true,' you can't possibly think he's lying about this." I gasped, horrified by where I thought Bert's mind might be going. "My God, Bert, you're not suspecting him, are you?"

"No, no. Nothing like that, Ele. I think he's telling the truth, but, let's face it, the dream thing is a bit much to take in." Bert paused for a moment. "I believe him, I do. But think about how others would respond." Bert repeated firmly. No wonder Ahmet was a wreck. I'm sure he felt a moral obligation to come forward, but how could he possibly do that? Even poor Bert was having a hard time wrapping his head around it, and Bert was one of the nicest, most open-minded men I knew and was friends with Ahmet, while most people barely knew him because of his reclusive ways. People were coming a long way, but there was still a lot of prejudice influenced by the terrorism and war of the last few decades, some people were unabashedly blatant in their distaste for Muslims. Even though Ahmet's parents were from Turkey (which is just as often lumped in with Europe as it is the Middle East) and even though Ahmet was born and raised in the United States and doesn't have a trace of an accent, and even though he's not even a practicing Muslim; none of those 'even-thoughs' mattered in the eyes of people who had built strongly racist biases in their minds. Ahmet was right in assuming they would think he was the killer if he revealed that he knew things he shouldn't know. They wouldn't buy the whole dream thing. And even though records from his therapist in NYC would eventually prove he was telling the truth, all of that would take time, and due diligence, and in the meantime, Ahmet would find his ass in a jail cell if he came forward.

"You all right, Ele?" Bert pulled me from the whirlpool of thoughts spinning around in my head.

"Yes. It just hadn't occurred to me that he saw the killer. Does he know who it is?" I couldn't help lowering my voice on this last bit and looking around cautiously, even though we were at the table I liked that was a little bit set apart, Nona had music playing and no one was paying the slightest bit of attention to us.

"No, but it was a man," Bert revealed, and I heaved a sigh of relief. We had all believed that bigfoot was innocent, but it was nice to know for sure, or at least as for sure as you could be when your proof came from some sort of psychic vision dream. "I guess it could have been a woman, but that would be unlikely since breaking someone's neck takes some serious brute upper body strength. The murderer was wearing a black balaclava and goggles over a camouflage hunting outfit. They were even wearing gloves, so not an inch of skin was showing, but Ahmet said you could see that they were quite muscular even under the full body camo."

"What are we gonna do?" I asked, overwhelmed by the magnitude of what we were facing.

"We're gonna do the only thing we can. We're gonna solve these crimes the good old-fashioned way and in doing so, lift all suspicion from the bigfoot community. And then we're gonna figure out how the hell to let the law enforcement know our findings without revealing Ahmet's secret or the connection between bigfoot and Vance." I raised an eyebrow, impressed with Bert's determination. He seemed to have decided the only solution was to solve the crime. So that is what he was going to do. He damn sure wasn't going to wait around and see where this would all go without his intervention. It was one of the things I liked most about Bert. He was a man of action. No sitting around, dawdling, and deliberating for him. I could respect that.

"Well, alrighty then Poirot, how can I help?" I asked, and Bert chuckled at that.

"My Libby loved Agatha Christie and Poirot was her favorite."

"My Granny Goosey was a fan too, so I read most of them when I was ten to twelve. She died of a stroke when I was twelve and it wasn't as much fun anymore because half the fun of reading them was talking about them with her afterward. But I will still pick one up when I'm missing my granny."

"I read Libby's favorite books when I'm missing her as well. There is something about traveling where you know those you love have traveled before that feels like it brings you closer to them. Like in certain ways, you're taking the journey together. Space and time fall away in the pages of a book."

"Wow, Bert! That was just plain eloquent." I teased him and he quirked a sad, wry grin.

"What? That's not how you always see me? Eloquent... suave... debonair?"

"Yes, of course. All of those." I smiled into my cup of coffee.

Vance came over to the table and reminded Bert that they were showing some land and had to get going if they were going to make it in time. I told them goodbye as my mind swirled with thoughts. How would I approach this case if it were one of my stories?

CHAPTER 6

"Holy Mary, mother of God! What the hell happened here?" Bigfoot whimpered and hid his head under the sectional. Stuffing was everywhere. It looked like Martha Stewart took a hit of acid and decorated for Christmas, first by laying a layer of snow pulled directly from one of the cushions of my sectional over the entirety of my living room. The stuffing was literally strewn everywhere. I couldn't even wrap my head around it. How had so much stuffing come out of only one big pillow cushion on the back of the sectional? Granted, the carcass of the cushion now looked like the poor deflated body on one of those 500-pound weight loss show participants pre-loose skin surgery, but it didn't seem fathomable that one cushion worth of stuffing could cover the entire room. And yet...

"Bigfoot Carmichael!" I guess Bert was right, his momma called him Bertrand when he was in trouble and Biffy was in serious trouble and so it merited his proper name. "You are BAD! You are a bad, bad puppy. No. Noo. Nooo. NO!" I stomped my foot in emphasis of my displeasure. I was pretty sure this would be considered an incorrect form of discipline. I was "puppy-shaming" which would probably be considered wrong. I couldn't even argue. Yes, yes, I am puppy shaming because this puppy should be fucking ashamed of himself. I was livid, but then I realized—this is why people crate their animals when they are away. I always thought that crating seemed mean, even though both the breeder and vet had told me otherwise. "Why wouldn't I allow my little guy the roam of the home while I was away?" I had wondered. And now, I know. This. Apparently, this was why. I sat on the sectional next to the crime scene and Bif put his head on my lap and looked up at me with those big forlorn puppy eyes. I couldn't stay furious at that face, but I could sure-as-shit crate his furry ass the next time I went out. No more playing nice! I had learned my lesson. Crating may have seemed mean to me before, but not anymore. The vet insisted that it was actually comforting to most animals, which had then seemed absurd to me, but I was going to choose to believe it now. Aunt Becky and I never crated our dogs when I was a kid. Of course, back then in our small town in Iowa, people just let their dogs roam around the neighborhood when they weren't at home. Most of them were outdoor dogs, anyway. Did that even exist anymore? Outdoor dogs? I was halfway through bagging up all the stuffing into a trash bag when my doorbell rang. I pulled open the door and Ahmet was standing there with a shy grin on his face. Bigfoot yipped in excitement at the sight of his friend again so soon. I opened the glass screen door to let Ahmet in.

"Hello, again."

"I know. Sorry, I'm failing at this whole hermit gig lately, huh? Sorry to bug you again so soon, but I was wondering if you had time to visit a little more with me today. Holy cow, what happened here?" He had followed me in far enough to see the winter wonderland that my living room had become on this hot August afternoon. Ahmet also bore witness to Biffy rolling in ecstasy in a big pile of fluff and then flipping balls of it into the air with his nose. He had bits of fluff stuck to him all over.

"Someone is very ashamed of themselves, as you can clearly see," I answered dryly, and Ahmet laughed at the chaos. "Let's go back to the deck." I had a pitcher of tea on the counter, so I filled two glasses with ice and poured each of us a glass. This time of day, the deck was in the shade, but it was still toasty out there. "I don't know if I'll be able to focus in the winter wonderland Bif made me." Ahmet opened the back door for me. And I called Bigfoot to join us lest he decide to unburden another cushion of its stuffing. As we sat down together, Ahmet started again stiffly and with another apology for taking my time.

"Ahmet, stop. You have nothing to apologize for. You are my friend and you are dealing with some serious shit. When I was dealing with big shit, you were there despite the fact that you didn't even know me yet. And you were a confirmed hermit." Ahmet had dropped everything and come to the medical rescue of both me and Bob the Bigfoot after my kidnapping escape. "So, I think I can take a little time to talk through some things with you. Friends help each other and I want to help you if I can." I watched him visibly relax back into the chair. He took a sip of tea and started again.

"So, I don't think I communicated everything quite clearly enough last night when I told you that Sam was the one in my dream."

"You saw the killer," I said and Ahmet sighed in relief, nodding. "Bert told me this morning. Shit, no fucking wonder you are in a quandary about his. My head has been spinning with it all morning. I can't imagine how you feel."

"I don't know what to do." Ahmet put his head in his hands, his elbows on the table in front of him, head bent in total defeat. "I mean, I really hate to assume the worst about the local authorities, but I simply can't imagine that if I were to go in and tell them what I saw—in a dream of all things—that they wouldn't think I was: 1) a crackpot and 2) the moment I said something about the scene or the body that they thought I shouldn't know, assume I was the killer and arrest me. I don't want to be living in fear and distrust, but in this situation, I think I would be a fool to do otherwise."

"Me too. You can't go to them." He seemed surprised that I was so readily agreeing with him. "At least not without some kind of proof from your past life to show them that this has happened before."

"I thought of that. This morning, I emailed Dr. Walker, asking her to contact me. I gave her my new number. It looks like she is still practicing, so hopefully, I will hear from her before long. I mean, it's not like I have that much to offer them, anyway. They know where the body was found. It's not likely they think a woman did it, so they are already looking for a male suspect (at least those that haven't decided they think it's a bigfoot that did it) and it is harder than hell to break a grown man's neck with your bare hands, so if they are using their heads at all, then they've deduced that the murderer is going to be quite muscular. It seems that all I really have to offer is the balaclava and goggles which I really don't see how that information can be very helpful, but somehow it still feels like I'm withholding evidence, and then that makes me feel like I'm an accomplice and somehow guilty of something when all I did was have a dream." Ahmet slumped back in his chair and picked up his glass of tea.

"I get that. I would feel the same way, but you're not guilty of anything. You know Bert's plan, don't you?"

"No, what?" Ahmet looked concerned, wondering what Bert could be up to.

"He's decided that we will solve the crime ourselves and then tip off law enforcement. He pointed out that it's not only your abilities that will come under question, but Vance's as well. This whole mess could potentially blow the bigfoot community wide open and our connection with it. And we were going to have to solve these crimes anyway because people are becoming more and more convinced bigfoot did it and there are going to be vigilantes with guns storming the woods. It will make the Crawley's little adventures on my property seem like child's play. I don't know about you, but I don't want packs of rednecks with guns and a vengeance roaming our woods. I don't want that for JoJo and Bob and the others, and I don't want that for us!"

"Well, I guess you are going to have to call forth Detective Rainey K. Moody to help us," Ahmet said, smiling at me.

"You do realize that it is completely different to solve an actual crime than it is to make one up and help your characters solve it."

"Is it?" Ahmet raised an eyebrow in a challenge, teasing me just a little but also implying that he believed this detective I had within me was a greater asset in this whole mess than I was letting on. Maybe he was right.

"Oh, OK!" I ran in and got my notebook. I had already started working things out on paper at the coffee shop after Bert told me the whole story. I came back out and threw my notebook on the table in front of Ahmet.

"What's this?"

I sat down and opened the notebook to my notes, "Let's just say Detective Moody is already on the case." After I went over everything I had written down and Ahmet had helped me fill in some gaps, we decided we wanted to lay it out in a bigger space. A giant white board covered one wall of the laundry room that opened out into the garage. Ahmet helped me to take it off the laundry room wall and lean it against the opening of the fireplace.

At Ahmet's instigation, we had quickly worked together to bag up the rest of the stuffing into the trash bag and while I sat on the hearth and transferred my notes from the notebook to the white board, he re-stuffed my cushion and then ran out to his jeep and came back with a suture kit and sewed up my cushion, which was incredibly kind of him, and also incredibly well done.

"Are you a surgeon, as well?" I asked, looking at his perfect little stitches. You could literally not tell that the fabric had been ripped open by my beast child, Ahmet's stitches were so tiny and neat.

"No. Although I loved those rounds during my residency and seriously considered pursuing it. This, however, comes from my grandfather. He was a tailor in Turkey and I spent a few summers there with him when I was a kid, working in his shop." Ahmet tied off the knot and clipped it very close to the cushion, smoothing it with his thumb. "Tada!" He said as he held the cushion up to me. It looked brilliant, infinitely better than it would have had I tackled the task. The only difference between it and the others was that it was a bit lumpier. This, of course, couldn't be helped since the stuffing had all been pulled apart and spread about, but I was delighted that the cushion was once again in one piece and Christmas in July was over.

I had said a few more choice words to Biffy as we cleaned up and he whimpered at appropriate times, letting me know he was aware of his iniquities. Little shit.

"Thank you, Ahmet! It's lovely. It's so much better than I imagined. I was envisioning having to track down a new cushion, and if I couldn't do that, buying a new sofa. You saved the day!"

Before we started cleaning, Ahmet called Nona, Vance, and Bert and asked if they were free that evening for a meeting at my place. Everyone was eager to meet. Vance and Nona offered to pick up subs, and Bert was going to head our way as soon as he finished showing a property.

We were going to catch us a fucking serial killer! Booyah!

CHAPTER 7

The five of us sat around the living room facing the fireplace, which was blocked by the large whiteboard with names and lines and arrows. We weren't staring into a fire, but at a whiteboard with all the clues before us. Three murders had occurred, but authorities were suspecting a fourth as a middle-aged woman from southern Arkansas was missing in the Ouachita mountains. We could only hope that she would show up soon, alive and well.

In the top left corner, we had the words "WHAT WE KNOW" written in large letters. Under it was a very short list:

1) Murderer was a very muscular HUMAN—likely male.

2) All murders occurred in the woods!

3) All murders were either broken necks or blunt force trauma and all the victim's hearts looked as if they had been ripped from their bodies.

4) Sam's murder occurred at dusk–unsure about others–*check on that.

Next to number three was the note, "*Is it intentional that these resemble the kinds of wounds a bigfoot would inflict? Or just coincidence?" An additional line came out from that note, "**Is someone intentionally trying to frame bigfoot? If so, why?" Next to number four was the note, "*Why didn't Sam have his gun?" and "**Ask Dorothy?" None of us were sure if it was possible to ask Dorothy this, but we would all be watching for the opportunity.

**PSA #20: If you ever have the chance to solve a crime with your friends on a giant whiteboard in your house, listing all the suspects and clues and shit, then STD!!!
(Seize The Day! What did you think I was talking about? Weirdo.)**

On the top, in the middle of the whiteboard, was the word SUSPECTS, and the list under it was even shorter than the "WHAT WE KNOW" list. I had, of course, listed Abner and Jeb Crawley as suspects, although I seemed to be the only one who believed that could be true. Abner and Jeb ran Crawley's Outdoor Adventures and their number one adventure they were trying to market was "Bag-a-Bigfoot Hunting Adventures". I had caught them hunting on my property more than once. A bigfoot on my property (I'm assuming it was Bob) even killed three of their dogs one night a few months ago. The Crawleys had approached me about permission to hunt on my property, which I refused to give, and then they did it, anyway. When I threatened them, they threatened back, and eventually, hired thugs kidnapped me and would have killed me had it not been for the intervention of Bigfoot Bob. So, needless to say, they would probably sit at the top of any suspect list I was to make.

Bert and Vance both pointed out to me that neither Abner nor Jeb had the physique of the killer in Ahmet's dream. I left them on the list anyway but conceded by adding—*hired killer? Even I had to admit, this seemed like a long shot. Serial killers and killers for hire are two very different things. Besides, the rumor was that the Crawleys were having money problems. Of course, I had to wonder if that was due to how much they had to pay for my kidnapping, but since their involvement was never proven, I didn't really have a leg to stand on there. Regardless, serial killers are psychopaths with a taste for murder, not lunatics trying to profiteer from hunting bigfoot. But I left them as number one on the list anyway, since it was outright depressing to have no suspects. Nona was silent and reflective, but as we were all pondering potential suspects, she broke in.

"Remember how muscular Sam and Dorothy's son was?" she asked, and I heard Vance groan. Bert was shaking his head.

"You're right, Nona. I think we have to add him." Vance replied sadly, and even as the words were coming out of Vance's lips, I was already scrawling the number two under the suspects heading with the words Paul Struthers next to it. "He doesn't make sense for the other murders, but we don't know anything about him, at least not as an adult, and he could have links to the other victims that we are not aware of," added Vance. "I hate to think he's capable of such a thing, but we've got to look at all possibilities."

"Why would he come to the funeral if he was the one who killed him?" Ahmet pondered aloud. "I mean, if he was estranged, no one was expecting him to attend anyway," he added.

"True. But if you killed your father, wouldn't you think it would be less suspicious to come to the funeral than not to?" I asked. This was an interesting train of thought. "How can we find out more about him? Is there anyone local who has stayed close to him?" Sam and

Dorothy's only son, Paul, was hitting thirty and hadn't come back to the area in years as far as Bert and Vance knew.

Bert spoke. "Remember Dalton Sutherland—that little fella that won the Indian Taco eating contest the night the town voted you onto the planning committee?" He asked me.

"Sure," I smiled. "How could I forget that?"

"Well, Paul and Dalton were thick as thieves growing up. We could start there," said Bert.

"I'll talk to Dalton." Vance surprised us all by volunteering. Vance was a man of few words and a total introvert. Bert was usually the one to do the talking. "When I first moved back, I assistant coached a baseball team that the two of them were on. I had a soft spot for Dalton. He wanted it so bad, but he was such a little guy, even then, so I worked with him one on one quite a bit. We've stayed friendly all these years."

"So you knew Paul too, then?" I asked.

"Yeah, but not as well. That kid was a closed book. He had a bit of a temper and a mean streak, but he was good as gold to old Dalton and the two of them got on like bread and butter. I saw them talking at the funeral before we spoke with Paul."

"Good," I sighed, making a little star by Paul's name and drawing a line to a note that said "*Vance." "Maybe we have a real lead after all." I mused. On the far top right of the whiteboard, I listed the names of the first three victims, and on number four, I put the name of the missing woman from Arkansas with a question mark next to it. Ahmet offered to research all the information he could find on the other victims to see if there were any connections to any of our suspects, and I made a note of that on the board as well. Nona said people were always talking in the coffee shop and she would keep her ears open and also do her best to steer people away from the bigfoot trail and try to influence people that the killer had to be human. We all had our assignments, and the evening seemed to be winding down when Biffy yipped at the French doors that led out onto the deck. He was wagging his tail. Well, really, he was wagging all over.

"He always get that excited to use the bathroom?" Bert asked quizzically.

"No. I don't know what's gotten into him." I opened the door and Bif made a beeline for the woods. "Bif! Biffy! Come back. Oh my GOD, you little asshole." I muttered under my breath, pulling on my shoes as I watched Bif leap into the treeline joyously. He knew he wasn't supposed to go into the woods without me. I was about halfway through the yard when I felt their presence. I also felt a wave of peace come over me, so I assumed it must be JoJo and maybe Bob, and they didn't want me to be afraid so they were sending out peace. They seemed to be watching, always watching. It didn't even bother me anymore. Bert had warned me they would be watching when I first confronted him about the fact that he had sold me property that already had residents on it that he had failed to mention. He assured me they wouldn't hurt me, but they would most likely watch me and, from what I could tell, he was right. Usually, I would know, though. At first, I just felt like someone was watching me, and then after an encounter or two with JoJo and the big rescue with Bob, I was gradually learning to communicate with them telepathically, as Vance did. Bert did a little too, and now I was getting the hang of it. They were sending me peace, and I was doing my best to send it back to them. I stepped into the treeline. I didn't see anything but trees, then I heard Bif's happy sounds and saw his body hanging in mid-air, but quickly realized he was actually in Bob's arms and was licking his face. That is how good the creatures are at blending in. I was standing not 20 feet away and if it had not been for what appeared to be my levitating puppy, I wouldn't have even known they were there. JoJo held out her arms, and it wasn't until she made this movement that I realized she was there with Bob too. Bob passed the puppy to JoJo and while in my arms, Biffy looked awkwardly large, he looked like a teeny puppy in the arms of my bigfoot friends. I heard something behind me and turned to see Bert, Vance, Ahmet, and Nona all step into the treeline. Bob nodded at them and held up his hand in greeting.

I watched as all four of them raised their arms in response, nearly in unison. Then I realized that Vance and Bob were talking. Vance was nodding and had a furrowed brow. Ahmet and Nona stayed quiet, but looked mesmerized by what they were seeing. Vance nodded more vigorously as Bob continued to communicate telepathically with him. Bob seemed to finish up what he was saying to Vance and subtly signaled to JoJo that they should be going. Bob nodded farewell to all of them and JoJo gave the puppy one last squeeze and placed Bif on the ground and he ran over to my feet, wagging his tail, happy as a little clam. She held her hand up to us to bid us farewell and then turned to follow her mate.

"Did you see your friends?" I asked Bif, kneeling to pat his head, and then I looked up just in time to see the two of them vanish out of sight into the darkness of the forest. The oversized full moon illuminated the night sky, and the stars glowed in a field of ultramarine. The five of us headed back up through my yard and onto the deck to sit down. I offered a round of drinks, but everyone said they needed to call it a night. We each had our detective homework and Vance, Bert, Nona, and I would see each other the evening after next for a bigfoot fair planning committee meeting. It was almost September and October would be here before we knew it. There was a lot to do, and it was up in the air how much help Dorothy would be after all she'd been through. None of us, of course, would blame her if she took this year off, but she might want the distraction. Time would tell.

"You know, that is really strange, Ele," Bert said.

"What is?" Strange things seemed to abound these days, so I was clueless as to what he was talking about.

"That they came to see your dog, that they hold Bif and seem to like him. Bigfoot are notorious for hating dogs. Probably because most dogs hate them first, but still."

"It's intentional," Vance said. "Have they been coming and visiting your puppy often since you first got him?" Vance asked, already knowing what my answer would be.

"Yes. JoJo especially seems smitten with Biffy."

"They want to stay friends with you," Vance said simply. "They know the only way for your dog not to be aggressive towards them is if he knows them from the start. You're lucky you went with the puppy and not an older rescue dog. They probably couldn't have won over an old dog."

"Man, she was really getting big," Ahmet said, mostly to himself. He was referring to JoJo's pregnancy. He had confessed to me that he had been concerned about JoJo since he first discovered that she was pregnant and he felt like a silly fool for it because bigfoot had clearly done just fine on their own for however long they had existed, but he had still had the urge to provide prenatal care for the creature. "I just can't help but wonder how close she is to delivering. It seems like she is growing too quickly." We were all quiet for a moment, thinking about the excitement of the upcoming birth.

"But that wasn't the only reason they came," Vance picked back up, answering Bert's assumption that the two had just come to see the puppy.

"Oh! Do they want my help?" Ahmet asked hopefully. He really was concerned about this pregnancy.

"Not for JoJo," Vance said, almost apologetically. He could tell that Ahmet was concerned and wanted to help and both he and Bert were so grateful that the doctor had taken an interest in helping serve the bigfoot community. "But I think they are going to need you for more pressing matters. Bob wanted to let us know it was beginning."

"What is?" Nona asked.

"Signs of an upcoming war," Vance said sullenly. While this sounded ever so slightly melodramatic to me, now I understood Vance's furrowed brow and all the nodding and serious mental chatter that passed from Bob to Vance. "It seems the locals are storming the forests with pitchforks."

"What did he tell you?" Nona and Bert asked in unison.

"Hunting parties are going out in the night again and in even greater numbers. It doesn't look like it's just the Crawleys involved this time, although I'm sure they are. They are setting traps. One of Bob's family members a few miles over just almost got caught in one. They would have lost a leg if they had. The people are rising up against the bigfoot and the bigfoot aren't quite sure what to do. They are going as 'underground' as they are able, but as you all know, that's what they were already trying to do and there are fewer and fewer places for them to hide these days."

"What should we do? They are welcome to gather here on my property."

"And mine," offered Ahmet, whose property bordered mine to the north. I could see Bert and Vance's wheels turning. They owned property that bordered one another's as well.

"Between the four of our places, that's quite a bit of woods." I was encouraged by the thought. I had about 50 acres and I was pretty sure everyone else owned more land than me. "We can start a refuge."

"That would feel like a prison to them, Ele," Vance said sadly. "But we can definitely ask Bob and JoJo to let the others know that our properties will be safe if any of them need a place to go."

"We also need to talk to the people," Bert said. "Maybe we should call an Emergency Town Meeting, try to talk some sense into everyone. But this problem extends further than our community. I'll call Jim, he's the mayor of Parksville where they found the first victim. And I'll see if he's open to reason. If we can reach out to the people before the witch hunt reaches too much of a frenzy, maybe we can turn this thing around. And I definitely think we need to be sure that this year's Bigfoot Fair focuses on the friendliness of the creatures for the people around here who already believe and maybe even a little bit on the myth for those not from around here who don't. The last thing we need is more bigfoot hunting enthusiasts to come into the area." Bert sighed and rubbed his head. "This is not how I hoped things would go down this year. We have got to catch this killer."

CHAPTER 8

It was my very first Emergency Town Meeting. In fact, I had only been to one other town meeting at all since the one in which they unfairly voted me in as the newest member of the bigfoot fair planning committee. Not that I'm holding a grudge or anything. An Oklachito town meeting is a thing to behold. Since this one was an emergency meeting to discuss the growing desire to take up arms against the very creatures that had lived peacefully hidden in their woods for long before anyone in that room existed, everyone was in a high state of alarm. Ever since Sheriff Struther's funeral there had been talk about "getting rid of the no-good beasts once and for all" and no one was as vocal as Abner and Jeb Crawley or Dorothy. It seemed the three of them had made it a personal mission to rid the world of bigfoot and while I felt Abner and Jeb were clearly in it to make money, for Dorothy, it was a matter of vengeance. I suppose believing that a bigfoot killed your husband and ripped out his heart would do that to you.

Typically, at a town meeting, one of the local churches serves Indian tacos or some other local favorite as a fundraiser, but since this was an emergency meeting no dinner was being served, but one industrious local had taken full advantage of the void and whipped up a batch of something called a "peanut patty" that appeared to be quite popular. Vagina Beckler was going from person to person with a basket of these strange reddish-brownish-pinkish homemade peanut patties wrapped in cellophane. She was selling them for $2.00 each or a stack of three tied together with a ribbon for $5.00 and they were going fast. Oh, yeah. That name wasn't a typo. I had just taken a big drink of lukewarm coffee when Bert introduced her to me and I nearly sprayed coffee everywhere.

"Ele, this is Vagina." That's when the coffee nearly shot out of my nose. Thankfully, I had a napkin in my hand and quickly covered my face in a sort of cough/sneeze/nose-blowing adventure.

"Vagina, this is Ele Carmichael. I know you've been under the weather and haven't been able to come to our last few town meetings, but Ele here's the newest member of our fair planning committee." At this news, the old woman—chortled. Chortle is the only word for the sound that came out of her. I wasn't sure I had ever heard an actual chortle until this moment, and I certainly had never found a reason to use the word in my writing. But per usual, here I am, finding myself in circumstances unlike any before. Bert promptly bought a three-pack of the pinkish peanut patties and chatted briefly with Vagina, who was eager to continue her selling before the meeting got underway. I looked at him with a raised brow.

"Vagina?" I said under my breath. He chuckled.

"Now, that is a good story. You see, when Vagina was born, her momma and daddy owned two books: the family bible and a medical encyclopedia. Now, everyone liked to consult the bible in those days if they didn't already have a name they loved or a family name they were obligated to bequeath to their new baby, but Vagina's mother was a creative sort and decided she would peruse the medical encyclopedia in search of a suitable name for her new baby. It's said that Vagina's mother fell in love with two 'names' from that big book of medical wonder—that when the big day came, it was between "Vagina" and "Malaria". It's said that the traveling country doctor who attended to Vagina's mother desperately tried to talk her into going with Malaria, although he told her he wasn't a big fan of that either, but as the story goes, her mother said "No, Doc! It's Vagina, Vagina, Vagina! Huh, I think I'll use both. I'll call her Vagina Malaria Huckaby—the most beautiful name for the most beautiful baby!" Bert slapped his knee and folded into a big belly laugh when he finished the story and I couldn't help but join him. A few townspeople gave us a sharp look. The tension in the air was palpable and after Bert wiped his eyes, he noticed the glares, shook his head, and headed to the front of the room. Just then, Vance and Nona came through the back door. I caught their eyes, and they made their way towards me. I looked down and noticed that Bert had placed one of the wrapped peanut patties in my hand. Bert was hooking up the microphone into the little sound system that sat permanently on the small stage at one end of the room.

"Hey! Where'd you get that?" Vance asked with keen interest.

"Vagina is selling them," I said and burst into a small fit of giggles, which Nona joined in on. Vance smiled at the two of us and shook his head. He had known her all his life, so her name hardly seemed notable to him. She had been friends with his oldest sister and had even babysat him when he was a child. Vance had known the word vagina as a girl's name before he ever had a clue as to the anatomical definition. He left the two of them to their giggles and headed off to find Vagina.

"I wish I could have seen the look on your face when Bert introduced you," Nona joked.

"Coffee," I said. "Shot right out my nose." Nona laughed at this, and we both hushed along with the rest of the room as we heard Bert's voice fill the space.

"Alright now!" Bert's voice boomed, and he pulled the microphone a little further from his mouth. He didn't like using the thing, but a good percentage of the townspeople were half-deaf and he got tired of repeating himself and since tonight was a forum, the microphone would undoubtedly be necessary. Vance showed back up at Nona's side and handed her a peanut patty, which she looked at intently, turning it over as she studied it. I guess these were new to her as well. He had bought a three-pack and popped one into his shirt pocket and started opening the other up to dig into during the meeting. I shrugged at Nona, "If you can't beat them, join them." We unwrapped our peanut patties, and each took a bite. It was...alright. I expect if you grew up eating them, though, they would be one of those beloved treats. My eyes swept the room, and I saw a good portion of the crowd was eating a pink peanut patty. How many of those things did she make? Vagina Malaria was quite the entrepreneur.

"Let's get this party going, friends. Donny, do we still have that mic stand?" Bert asked and a young man held up a thumbs-up sign to Bert and walked to a closet in the corner and came back and sat the mic stand upright in front of the stage. Bert came down the two steps and placed the microphone on the stand. "Janice, you bring your kitchen timer?" Bert asked into the microphone and another lady sitting near the stage held up a kitchen timer for all to see. "Woman, you are a saint! Does that mean you're good with running the time tonight?" Janice must have agreed because Bert smiled, nodded, and started talking again. I couldn't help wondering at the fact that nearly everyone in the room had a smartphone on them that could easily be used as a timer. But clearly, there was something sacred about the twist dial, kitchen timer in Janice's hands, and I had to admit the first time it went off that we could hear its ring across the whole room without a problem. Maybe some things, like forty-year-old kitchen timers, actually were sacred.

"Thank you, Janice. Alright then. You all know how this works. Anyone who has something to express will be given two minutes up here on the squawk box. When Miss Janice gives you the signal, you've got thirty seconds. When the timer rings, wrap it up–and that doesn't mean another two minutes. That means shut yer pie hole and give someone else a chance. If you want to talk next, stand over here to the side," Bert gestured to a spot near him to the side where it wouldn't be terribly distracting. It was fascinating how fine-tuned they seemed to have this process. Neither of the town meetings I had been to was an open forum like this one. "You all got that?" Bert asked and there was a murmuring of agreement across the room. "Now, you all be respectful and remember, we're all friends here. I know we're gonna have some pretty opposing opinions tonight, but let me remind you that it's not gonna hurt one damn thing to hear each other out, alright? No interruptin'. No cheerin' and no jeerin'. No name callin' or being hateful to one another. When we leave here tonight, we will still be friends and neighbors. Whether I agree with you or not, I'll still help pull you out of the ditch if you get stuck, and I hope you'll do the same for me. In this town, we've got each other's backs, now let's not forget it." Bert paused here in an effort to let this sink in, and a few people shifted uncomfortably.

"As you all know, the point of this Emergency Town Meeting is to discuss the murders and the growing accusations against the alleged bigfoot in the area. I'll get us started. Janice, you got me set up for two minutes?" Again, Janice must have nodded because Bert started talking and this time he got straight to the point.

"I'd like to start by saying that most of us have lived here our entire lives. Heck, a lot of our families have been here for generations. And we have never lived here alone. You all know it as well as I do. We all have our stories. There are countless tales of how our invisible watchers in the woods have helped out—and other than a chase, or a little scare here or there—no one has ever been hurt by them. I just want to remind you that in all that time, nothing like this has ever before occurred."

"I don't talk about them much, because, in truth, I believe it is better for the bigfoot if regular people don't believe in 'em. But you all aren't regular people. You are people of the Kiamichi. These mountains are your home and I could no more convince most of you all that bigfoot aren't real than I could tell you your own mother was a myth. They've brought food to some of you in desperate times. They've brought home your babes lost in the woods. They've chased off bears and silently protected our people for longer than any of us know. Rumor has it that some of you are going out into the woods in hunting parties and laying traps. Today, I'm asking you to take a deep breath. Remember. Think of all the years we have peacefully coexisted with these guardians of our forest and give them the benefit of the doubt. This whole mess smells like something a bit more sinister to me. Whoever is behind these murders is someone who wants us to believe that the culprit is a sasquatch." Bert must have hit his last thirty seconds because Abner Crawley got up and stood in the spot Bert had pointed at.

"I want you to know that I DON'T BELIEVE BIGFOOT IS TO BLAME! I beg you. Before you go running out into the woods all half-cocked and fully loaded, think about what you are starting if you're wrong. It also doesn't hurt to remember that some of you all have kids who play in these woods. How would you feel if one of them got their leg caught in one of your blasted traps? And do you really want to kill the creatures that have done nothing but quietly keep to themselves and occasionally even look out for us? Do you really want a war with them? I know I don't." Applause rang out, including mine, but Bert quickly put his hand up to quiet us, "'No cheerin' and no jeerin', please. Thank you." Bert finished and walked into the audience and came back to sit next to Vance and Nona and me. Lots of people patted his back as he walked through and he got quite a few scowls as well.

"That's some very nice sentimental horseshit you just spoke up here, Bert." Abner's voice boomed across the room.

"Language!" I heard Janice's voice call out. She apparently was expanding her timekeeper role into mediator as well, which I admired. I debated leaving or demanding that the deputy on duty escort the Crawleys away since I held a Protective Order against them, but knew that would probably just make matters worse and for all I knew they might escort me away instead, so I kept my head down and calmly ignored the infraction. I didn't know if I had been the first of us to show up or if one of them had, so it hardly seemed worth a fuss as long as they left me alone.

"I will not lie and say that some of what Bert just shared with you all is true." Abner was saying. "Of course, we have all heard about good deeds done by bigfoot, but how many of our dogs have been killed? How many times have things gone missing from our sheds? How many times have our children felt afraid and unsafe playing in their own backyard?" Abner waxed on about what he saw were the many evils of bigfoot. After a brief promotion of Crawley's Outdoor Adventures, he wrapped things up with a heaping dose of fear-mongering. "I don't know about you folks, but I'm afraid for our wives and our daughters, our young sons and our brothers. Tell me something," his voice was growing louder. "How many of our friends, neighbors, and law enforcement officers have to have their hearts ripped out before WE FIGHT BACK?" The last bit echoed throughout the room and there was a bit of a cheer from some of the angrier-looking folks in the crowd. Abner held up his hands to show that he could honor the no cheerin' no jeerin' policy as well. I felt myself getting angrier and angrier, and Nona leaned over and asked if I needed her to step outside with me. I shook my head and took a deep breath. Abner rattled on as I closed my eyes and took deep, steady breaths. He wrapped things up and took his seat, and that is pretty much how the evening went. A back and forth between for-bigfoot and against-bigfoot filled the air. The room seemed far too evenly divided for my comfort. I hadn't realized so many people had bought into the idea that bigfoot was to blame for the killings. It made me afraid for Bob and JoJo and their unborn child. I hated to think of their baby being born into a hostile forest.

As the clock crept closer to 9:00, a small thin woman flitted nervously to the waiting spot at the front of the room and when Jeb Crawley who was at the microphone and was probably hoping to be the last voice of the night finished giving his two cents, Bert stood up in place and called out. "It's almost 9 o'clock folks, which was our agreed upon finishing time, so Ms. Finch will wrap things up for us. Let's all go home this evening in peace and think about the words of our friends and neighbors. Maybe we can find a way to meet one another somewhere in the middle. I know no one here wants anyone to be unsafe. We're just coming at it from two different angles. I know for myself, my doors are always open to any of you fine folk. Thanks for coming out. The floor's all yours, Ms. Finch." I found it ever so slightly amusing that her last name was Finch because she was incredibly birdlike. Ms. Finch nodded at Bert and very calmly began to speak. There was, however, a strength to her voice that surprised me. She made me think of a kindergarten teacher, gentle but not a pushover. She seemed kind but looked like she had both a streak of silly and stern in her when need be.

"Hello, dear friends. It's been a while since I've seen some of you." I couldn't help but notice that the room seemed to be holding its breath. There was almost a sacred silence as everyone listened and I wondered who on earth this woman was and why I hadn't met her yet. "I've listened to the back and forth this evening and you have all made interesting and thought-provoking points. Aesop said, 'Every truth has two sides; it is as well to look at both before we commit ourselves to either,' and 'A fair-minded man tries to see both sides of an argument.' I just want to say how proud I am of this community because I believe that is what we all intend to do here tonight. We have come to face this problem together. To not only listen to what one another has to say, but to hear one another. I'm proud of us because although we may be small and we may be rural, we are not backwards. And we are not rash."

"I have known many of you your whole lives. I've heard your stories, both good and bad, about our invisible neighbors, over the years. When my Theodore disappeared in the woods many years ago now, many of you came to me with your stories. Some of you with stories to convince me that perhaps he had been killed by these same beasts we debate over tonight and I will not lie and say there was not a time when I considered that may be true. But then I remembered, my Theodore loved these creatures. He called them the 'Guardians of the Woods' and they were always good to him. As most of you know, my Theodore was a naturalist and an author and would often spend weeks on end in the forest doing research for his books, and in the end, when he never returned and his body was never recovered, well, I just could not believe that the creatures were to blame. Jimmy Carter said, 'We will not learn to live together in peace by killing each other's children.' Please consider this before you rush into the woods with your guns and your traps. Let's give the law enforcement time to do their jobs, to catch whoever is wreaking this terror in our woods. And in the meantime, let's look out for one another, huh?" With that, she walked back to her seat to gather her belongings. There was a quiet murmuring as people stood and made their way to the door.

"Who the hell was that?" I asked.

"Ah," Bert smiled. "That was Matilda Finch, the town librarian and one of my Libby's closest friends. She took over when Libby had to retire." Wait, what? First of all, I wondered why the hell no one had told me about a town library. I had just assumed the town was too small for a public library. And second, that lady was pure magic. How had she just managed to hold both sides in silent reverence unless she was some kind of sorcerer? She had calmed the fire in the bellies after Jeb's attempt to rile it back up. I was unbelievably impressed, and I wanted to know her. And third, what the hell? Her husband was a writer who just disappeared into the woods, never to return? This certainly seemed like something I should have been told, but why would anyone think to tell me such things? Especially if it had been years ago. I wanted to demand the answers to all these questions, but the last remnants of magic were still hanging in the air, and I didn't want to mess that up. I bent down to reach under my seat to retrieve my bag when I heard Bert say. "Nicely done." I looked up to see Matilda walking towards us with a warm smile and a feisty little spark in her eye.

"I couldn't stand to let them get the last word," she leaned in and whispered so that only Bert and I could hear. I could see Vance and Nona across the room, deep in discussion with someone I didn't know.

"Matilda, I believe I owe you an apology." Bert turned towards me. "And you too, Ele."

"Why's that?" Matilda smiled at me. "For keeping this one to yourself? I wondered when you were going to find time to bring her into the library and introduce us. You manage to recruit a world-famous author to our little hollow and you don't even bring her into the library to meet your favorite librarian." I saw a flicker of a wince on Bert's face, I suspect that he would always think of Libby as his favorite librarian.

"That's exactly why!" said Bert. I held out my hand to Matilda.

"I'm so sorry. I had no idea Oklachito had a library or I would have been in on my own. I feel a little embarrassed now that I didn't think to ask. I just assumed—anyway, I'm Elena Carmichael. It's so nice to meet you. I think you might be a sorceress by what I saw up there."

Matilda laughed at that. "Well, I had half of them in story-time at the library when they were little and if I didn't have them I had their kids, so they were already a little bit under my spell," she winked at me when she said this. "Matilda Finch." She said and gave my hand a firm shake.

"Well, I salute you, Ms. Finch. I will forever stand by the solid truth that a good librarian can change the world," I told her warmly.

"I mean it, you two. I am so sorry I haven't introduced you before now." Bert was shaking his head at his grave oversight. "Ele, you have to go see what she's done with the place. We wouldn't have a library if Matilda and Libby hadn't taken it on as a project. Libby was the adult librarian and Matilda was the children's librarian. Now Matilda runs the whole show by herself. When they started, they had next to no budget and very little interest, but they managed to make a quite respectable little library."

"Well, I shall be in soon to see you!"

"Nothing would make me happier," Matilda said and shook both of our hands again before bidding us farewell.

"Well, I'll see you later, Bert," I said. "I'm starving." I watched as Bert pulled another one of Vagina's Peanut Patties out of his front shirt pocket and offered it to me. "Thanks anyway," I smiled, and he began unwrapping it in eager anticipation.

"I'll split it with you. You sure you don't want at least half to tide you over until you get home?"

"No, I'm good," I said, holding up my hand in protest. I walked away, smiling to myself at the strangeness of the day.

CHAPTER 9

I'm not very good at staying in my own lane. Driving or otherwise. That was what was wrong with me. The angry blare of the horn from the car I had just met on this winding mountain highway on my way into town to this evening's bigfoot fair planning committee meeting just punctuated that point in my mind. It was Ahmet's assignment to look into the other victims, but something this morning made me start poking around on my own and before I knew it, I had lost the day to my search. After I got off the phone with Sookie, I fully intended to do the rewrite, but instead I butted into Ahmet's research assignment. I knew he might find that frustrating, and that we had most likely found all the same information, but I was looking forward to calling him in the morning to compare notes. Hopefully, he would forgive me for jumping into his sleuthing territory.

I'm one of those ridiculous kinds of rebels that rebel against myself and my own plans with fair regularity. I've often praised the Gods for my success as a writer because I would suck wind at working for anyone else. I resent being told what to do, even when I'm the one telling me, so you can only imagine how I would do with an actual boss. So when we were divvying up assignments and I asked who wanted to research other victims, there was not even a flash of the thought "I should take this one," or "know thyself," oh no, I just scrawled Ahmet's name on the line when he volunteered. Of course, this morning I could think of nothing I wanted to do more than research the other victims.

There were two other victims besides Sam and there was still no word on the missing Arkansas woman, so the jury was out on whether there was now a fourth victim. I was still praying the woman would turn up, having just needed to take a little get-a-way, but the more days passed without anyone hearing from her, the less likely that became. The very first victim was Ronald Frost from Mount Bella. He was on a hike in the woods behind his own property, much like Sam had been, when he was attacked and killed. Since Robert was in the middle of a divorce from his estranged wife, no one noticed he was missing for several days and his body was starting to decompose when they found him, so some evidence was lost to time. His soon-to-be-ex was an almost-famous female wrestler, which was such an odd profession, and I thought I was wasting way too much time looking into her until I came across a fascinating bit of information about her. She had been arrested on pot charges and taken into custody on the way to what was supposed to be her big break-out fight and guess who the arresting officer had been? None other than Sheriff Sam Struthers. It seemed almost too big of a coincidence to be real, but I double and triple-checked and it was all true. She missed the fight and her career didn't end up taking off as had been expected. I was delirious with excitement. The only problem was it didn't line up with what Ahmet saw in his dream. But it was still too significant of a find to ignore. Adding Freda Frost, also known as Freda the Femme Fatale, promptly to the suspect list excited me.

I pulled into the parking lot and turned off my old lime green FJ Cruiser I had purchased from a used car dealer the next town over when I discovered that the road up to my cabin were impassable by any ordinary vehicle. I put thoughts of mystery and murder on hold to go plan a bigfoot fair. Neither Walt's car nor Dorothy's were there when I arrived and wondered whether she would show. It was our first fair planning committee meeting since Sam's death and Dorothy had not revealed whether she planned to attend, so when she walked in the door looking fine as a dog's hair (an expression of Bert's that my brain seemed to have caught like a cold); we were all surprised to see her, especially since she walked in at 6:00 on the dot instead of her usual fifteen minutes early, but before the clock struck 6:01, she was in her seat and trying to call the meeting to order. Even though Bert told her time and time again that this meeting truly did not call for such formality, Dorothy was always trying to make things more official and the tragedy had not seemed to sap that desire in the slightest.

Dorothy is what I thought of as a woman who was hard to love. She seemed to me to be on her constant high-horse looking down her nose at anyone and everyone because, in her mind, no one would ever measure up. I wondered if Sam had measured up. Was she as critical of Sam as she was of everyone else? I'd never heard a harsh word from her about him, but she also never spoke of her personal life in our meetings and, at least since I had been there, she had bolted the moment the meeting ended. Bert mentioned thinking Sam kept her on a tight leash and the reason she was such a pushy pain in everyone else's ass was that Sam controlled her so severely. But just as Vance had mentioned that their son Paul was a closed book, Sam and Dorothy were the same and one could only guess what their personal life looked like.

Dorothy spoke. "I make a motion that we allow Crawley's Outdoor Adventures to have a booth this year at the fair. I know you have your differences, but it is simply not fair that you deprive Abner and Jeb, upstanding members of our community, participation in the event year after year. They came to talk to me—" Suddenly Dorothy stopped mid-sentence. She had completely lost her voice. Her throat had constricted and the last few words came out strangled. We all looked at her and her eyes were now brimming with tears. Nona put her hand over Dorothy's. I was none too fucking pleased about this motion of hers—upstanding members of the community, my ass—but it was hard to get too mad and lash out at a woman in obvious distress and mourning.

Dorothy began again. "I was visiting with them the night Sam was taken from me. He had gone out to look for wild mushrooms. With all the rain, it's been a good year for them and Sam loves—" Her voice cracked at the error and she corrected herself. "—loved mushrooms." I had to control my imagination as this line brought up images of the fine sheriff "tripping on 'shrooms" which I knew was ludicrous and while it amused me, it would not stand for me to look amused while Dorothy was speaking of her husband's last moments on this earth. I made a concerted effort to control my face. Dorothy didn't need any new reasons to hate me.

PSA #21: If inappropriate laughter ever threatens to escape your unwilling lips, think of dead puppies; because in the infamous words of a certain demented radio "Doctor", the dead ones—puppies, that is—are not very fun.

(Well, scratch that! If you're a real sicko like me, that might make you laugh even more.)

Tripping sheriffs, dead puppies, and demented radio personalities had me on a roller coaster of emotions until Bert took the opportunity to work his all-important question in. "Did Sam often go into the woods unarmed?" Bert asked. It surprised me to hear Bert take advantage of the moment for our research, and I was really curious what Dorothy's answer would be. Dorothy paused. It was as if the thought had not occurred to her before.

"No, not terribly often. But he'd just changed out of his uniform and was probably just wanting to relax. It wasn't dark yet when he left and he knew he wouldn't be going far." Still, it seemed like Dorothy was wondering why Sam had gone unarmed now as well.

"You were saying you were with Jeb and Abner when Sam was killed?" Nona asked quietly and kindly.

"Yes." Dorothy's voice cracked again. "They came over to petition for my help on being allowed to have a booth in this year's bigfoot fair. They said every year you deny them." Dorothy looked pointedly and angrily at Bert.

"Alright, Dorothy," Bert was now addressing her request. "Why do you think we should include them? You know our mission has always been to maintain the magic and wonder surrounding the legend of bigfoot, not to vilify the creatures. Abner and Jeb clearly want to present them to the world as monsters to be afraid of."

"Yeah, so people will pay them to hunt the creatures," I thought, but had the good sense not to say aloud.

"Well," Dorothy made a little harrumphing sound and was wearing a very sour expression. I rolled my eyes. I couldn't help it. This ought to be rich. "Maybe they are monsters. Have you ever thought of that? Hmm? You and Vance are always so darn sure of yourselves." She looked like she was just getting going and was building up steam. "And who decided what our mission would be? Hmm? I don't remember ever getting to vote on that." She raised an eyebrow at the other three men at the table, Bart, Walt, and Vance, and even flashed a quick glance at Nona. I was largely ignored, which was fine by me, as I was not likely to hold my tongue.

"Dorothy, what's going on?" Vance asked softly. Vance had a pretty good suspicion he knew what was going on, but he hoped he was wrong.

"It's just...I mean...YOU DIDN'T SEE HIS BODY! His chest..." Dorothy choked a sob now. "It wasn't human—what it did to my Sam."

"So, you believe what people are saying, then?" Vance continued with his soft, steady voice. "—That bigfoot are to blame for Sam's death?"

"Well, maybe I do. I mean, before this, I liked to think sasquatch was the stuff of legends, that they were simply mythical beasts. But now I wonder. And Abner and Jeb say–" Oh shit. Abner and Jeb were in her head. Since they were who she was with when Sam died, it is likely they were the first ones she called. They had probably been filling her head with stories. This was not good, not good at all. And what a strange coincidence that the two of them were with her when Sam went missing. It was frustrating in the sense that it provided them with an alibi, but curious that they were there at all that night. To my prejudiced mind, it only served to compound my certainty that they were somehow involved, but I doubted that the others would see things my way.

"Dorothy," Bert's somber tone interrupted my thoughts. "Did you know that Abner and Jeb threatened Elena's life?" Dorothy hesitated and then Bert added, "More than once?" She hadn't known this. It was obvious from the look on her face. "In fact, they were Sam's number one suspects behind Elena's kidnapping." Dorothy's mouth opened in surprise. "Ele even has a protective order against them in place, so you see, even if I wanted to allow them to be a part of the festival, it wouldn't work because they cannot be within 100 feet of Ele and you know how busy all of us are during the fair. Elena will be all over that place. It just won't work." His voice sounded apologetic, but we all knew that my protective order simply provided a convenient excuse to exclude Crawley's Outdoor Adventures from the fair for yet another year. If I didn't have the PO, the answer would still be no. Dorothy's mouth was set in a grim line. Her eyes flared fire in my direction. "Right back atcha, bitch!" I thought, but I held my tongue and did my best to keep a neutral expression on my face. See how mature I am?

When Dorothy finally spoke, both the venom behind her words and the words themselves shocked everyone. "I see now where I stand on this committee. If that's your answer, then I quit!" She pushed her chair back from the table slowly and deliberately and with a rigid back and her head held high, she got up, walked to the door, and just before exiting turned to us and with absolute venom in her eyes and words said. "You. Will. Regret this." We were all stunned into silence. After a long moment, Bart Longfeather, an old Choctaw man in his eighties who had been on the planning committee since the fair's conception, and who usually remained silent but was instrumental in pulling together all the native storytelling, native events, and booths run by natives and who always had an ornery glint in his eye that had made me instantly like him, heaved a big sigh of relief.

"Finally," he said. "Good riddance!" None of us could help but laugh, even though I could tell the others found it ever so slightly mean, but Dorothy had been a pain in everyone's backside from the beginning. Bert shook his head sadly.

"Well, alrighty then. Next order of business." The formality of Bert's language almost made me laugh aloud again. Too bad Dorothy wasn't here to hear him.

The rest of the evening was a scramble to divide up Dorothy's tasks, which turned out to be easier than expected. Thankfully, she was nothing if not thorough and since she liked everyone to know how hard she was always working; she had turned in detailed notes at the last meeting (before Sam's death) on where she was on all of her organizational projects, including the phone numbers of vendors, food trucks, porta-potties and such that she had been working with. She made it incredibly easy for us to each take a portion of the list to work on ourselves. In fact, it was so easy that we simply cut the three pages of notes in half with a pair of scissors and gave each of the six of us a half-page of projects to add to our own. It was a little sad that a woman who had clearly thrown everything she had into the fair for the past decade or more could leave her post so easily at the relief of all involved, but no one could deny that the mood was much lighter without Dorothy and there was much more laughter. Turned out the ornery glint in Bart Longfeather's eyes was legit. Bart was a card. He was throwing out one-liners the rest of the evening. His previous silence in meetings was simply evidence of his solid distaste for one Ms. Dorothy Struthers.

CHAPTER 10

I had already called Ahmet twice this morning and texted once and was getting so impatient to talk to him I was about to drive up to his cabin when Bif started barking and wagging his tail. Moments later, I heard a motor coming up my road and Bif ran to the front door. It really was quite impressive how much more keen a dog's senses are than a human's. Bif and I went out on the front porch to greet our visitor and, sure enough, Ahmet pulled up in his Jeep.

"Sorry to bother you," he immediately said upon getting out of his vehicle.

"Bother me? I'm the one who has been calling and texting you all morning."

"You have? Hmm...I wonder where I left my phone." I couldn't help laughing.

"You've lived so long without that thing now that you're really having a hard time adjusting, aren't you?" I asked with a smile.

"Yeah," Ahmet readily admitted. I noticed he had his laptop under his arm. "You're not going to believe what I found!" he said excitedly.

"Yeah, about that—"

We made our way into the house and I explained my little dip into his waters; I apologized and told him I knew it wasn't my place and that I totally trusted his ability to research. I'd simply had an itch to dive in myself, but he didn't seem to be upset—not upset at all, actually. "So, what did you find?" He asked excitedly.

We were setting our laptops up on my dining room table and I plugged mine in. "You need to plug in?" I asked, reaching my hand out in an offer to plug his in as well.

"No, I'm good. So, spill the beans," he ordered. He was excited. "Whatcha got?" I knew he wanted to share what he had learned. He was eager for me to share first, so he could, too.

"You first," I said. It seemed the least I could do after stealing his assignment was to let him announce the find first.

"Okay," he said excitedly. "Maxwell Barnes, the second victim," he clarified in case I didn't remember, "went to university with Paul and it looks like they had two classes together during their time on campus. I couldn't find any other connections between them, but that seems significant, doesn't it? It connects Paul to not only his father, but to a second victim!"

"It does!" My excitement was growing as well, because not only was that new information to me, but I had found something entirely different. "I didn't catch that! But, did you look into the soon-to-be ex-wife of Ronald Frost, the first victim?"

"The wrestler?" Ahmet said, but not as if he had found anything else interesting about her.

"Yes! Freda the Femme Fatale was arrested for possession of marijuana on her way to what was supposed to be her break out fight, her big break."

"Okay," Ahmet was listening, but wasn't making any connections yet.

"Guess who was her arresting officer?" Ahmet's eyes suddenly got as big as saucers.

"You're kidding?"

"Nope. They listed Sheriff Sam Struthers as the one who took her into custody and caused her to miss her big break. So, she was divorcing one victim and likely had a gargantuan grudge against another."

"Wow! Connections to two victims and motive. I'm impressed." I could tell Ahmet was getting excited and could see exactly the moment he realized she didn't line up with what he had seen in his dream of a muscular man, so I pulled up a full-body picture of Freda. She wasn't one of those voluptuous wrestlers. She looked more like a bodybuilder. Her bikini top was stretched across pure pectoral muscle; there was not an ounce of fatty flesh on her chest. And no implants as many of the wrestling women had.

"But look." I showed him the picture. "You said every ounce of skin, including the hands, was covered. Imagine this body covered in hunting gear. I think it is possible she could be confused with a male. She's a tall, muscular woman with cropped hair." I watched as Ahmet tipped his head sideways, looking closely at the picture, then squinting at it, like he was imagining her in a balaclava, goggles, and full camo.

"Hmm...maybe." He agreed slowly. He studied the picture more closely. "Actually, yes. I can see how this could be who I saw. Holy cow! We just went from having no strong leads to having two!" Ahmet held up his hand in a high five and I obliged him with one, although it felt silly to me and he must have been able to tell. "Not a high-fiver?" He asked, smiling.

"Not until now. But that was kind of fun. I've never done anything athletic in my life to make someone want to high-five me. But now I can see why it's a thing." I held up my hand now for another high-five and he obliged me with a slap on the palm. Bif yipped in excitement at our unexpected merriment, afraid he was missing out on something, and we both laughed at him as Ahmet rubbed the top of his head.

PSA #22: If you, like me, have spent a lifetime deprived of the primal joy of the high-five, it is never too late to start. Get to slapping—STAT!

"Okay, let's see what else we got?" We researched together and compared notes until about 2:30 in the afternoon, when I suddenly realized that I was famished. I was out of everything. "You want to go into town for a bite?" I asked. Ahmet hesitated, and I remembered his hermit ways as I watched a mental war going on in his head right before my eyes. "No worries." I quickly said, "I've got..." I opened my fridge and then my cabinets. "Eggs, peanut butter, and oatmeal."

"Mmm. My favorite." Ahmet smiled at me. "I need to get going anyway, though." He said, gathering his things. We each decided which research trails we were going to follow. It turned out that it was good to have both of us researching because, although we both came up with a lot of the same things, we came up with a lot of different information as well.

"I promise to stay in my lane this time," I said.

Ahmet smiled as he stood from the table and slipped his laptop under his arm. "Hey, no problem! You probably shouldn't make promises we both know you can't keep. Besides, you found some good stuff that I didn't!"

"And you found good stuff that I didn't." I countered.

"We're a good team." He nodded and flashed me one more big grin and so help me if my goddamn heart didn't flutter just a little bit when he did.

"Yeah, thanks for dropping by," I replied, determined to ignore my heart, which clearly had a mind of its own. Ahmet headed to the door with Biffy on his heels, then stopped before opening the door and rubbed the pup's head again, scratching behind his ears before taking his leave. I heard his motor start and slowly fade as he drove away. Ah, man. I forgot to tell him about what happened with Dorothy. Oh well, I shrugged. I'm sure I'll see him soon. The thought made me smile, and I reassured myself that it was simply because it was nice to deepen our friendship.

I scooped a spoonful of peanut butter out of the jar, took a bite of it, and called Nona. I didn't know if she would pick up or not. It was usually slow this time in the afternoon at her shop. Her end-of-day rush shouldn't be starting for another thirty minutes or so. I was happy when she picked up on the second ring.

"Hey, you!" Nona answered happily. "Where've you been? You didn't come to get coffee yesterday or today."

"I got busy researching our case." My voice sounded a little gummy from the peanut butter. I swallowed and continued. "Ahmet and I just met and talked over what we found. You wanna get dinner at Cookie's when you close?" Cookie's Kitchen was a hometown diner across the street from Nona's coffee shop. It was just diner food, but everything I had eaten there so far was delicious.

"That sounds amazing!" Nona said. "Meet you at 5:15? For some reason, I'm starving."

"Must be all that good sex you're having." I mused just to mess with her. I could practically hear her blushing.

"Ele!" Nona exclaimed, but then she giggled and said, "Maybe."

I laughed at her. Nona and Vance were so freaking adorable together, but they were both a little old-fashioned, so while it was none of my damned business, my wisecrack was also just me letting all this sleuthing seep into my private life. I thought surely they were sleeping together by now, but I honestly didn't know. Not that it was any of my business. And good grief, the thought of baring my naked ass to someone new at this age, well, let's just say it was not high on my list of priorities. I'd been with Doug for a decade and a half and didn't have much experience before that. The whole introverted writer thing seemed to get in the way of sexual prowess, which, just for the record, was perfectly okay by me. Well, good for them, I thought. They had waited long enough to finally find each other. I was happy for them.

"I'll be there at closing!" I said, hanging up as I grabbed another big spoonful of peanut butter and screwed the lid back on the jar. That would tide me over for the next couple of hours, when I would meet Nona and would likely get something delicious and fried and not very good for me for dinner.

On a whim, I turned on the TV. A local news channel interrupted programming with a special report. "Official reports say that hikers in the Ouachita Mountain Federal Reserve Area discovered the body of Clarice Thompkins today. Details surrounding the death appear to match what locals are now calling the Sasquatch Serial Killer." My heart sank. They found her like the others and they had actually dubbed the murderer the "Sasquatch Serial Killer". This was not good. This was SO. Not. Good. And the moniker was not going to help our cause one damn bit.

The first thing out of Nona's mouth as I met her on the sidewalk outside her place while she was locking up was, "Have you heard?"

"Isn't it awful? They found her body, and they killed her in the same way as the others." The whole thing made me feel sick. "And to make matters worse, they're calling them—"

"Sasquatch Serial Killer." We said miserably in unison.

"How are we going to turn this tide? This is like a tsunami."

"When does your book come out?" Nona asked anxiously.

"Not soon enough." It was sweet that she was putting so much hope that my friendly neighborhood bigfoot novel, Bigfoot Watching Woman Watching Bigfoot, would make a difference. (Okay, so maybe it was more memoir than a novel, but we were going to call this pure fiction since no one would believe otherwise.) I wasn't as sure as Nona seemed to be that the people who believed the creatures were man-eating beasts were going to be affected by my tales of a kinder, gentler sasquatch, but I agreed that it couldn't hurt. "Unfortunately, it will still be about nine months, so definitely not soon enough. We need to clear bigfoot's name and we need to do it fast. Nona opened the door of the diner and held it open for me, and we walked in and headed for our favorite booth in the corner. Darla, the old woman who had waited tables there for over fifty years, waved at us, grabbed a few menus, and headed our way."

"You wanna share a basket of fried pickles?" Nona asked suddenly, before we even sat down. "Like, for an appetizer?"

"Okay." I've never had fried pickles before and they sounded rather disgusting, but Nona explained how they were dill pickle chips like you put on hamburgers, but are battered and fried and shockingly delicious with ranch dressing. I have two substantial food weaknesses, three, if you count coffee. Sweets & salty fried carbs. Essentially, what that means is that everything that is bad for you and makes you fat is what I really want to overeat when I'm stressed, and even though this bigfoot serial killer thing wasn't technically *my* stress, somehow it was starting to feel like it was. I don't want to see anything happen to Bob and JoJo and all the other creatures that live in our forest. I also don't want anyone else to get hurt by this vicious killer, and now that we are "on the case", it feels like we bear a certain responsibility for any death here on out, I know it doesn't make sense but my heart has taken responsibility to fix this. It's an interesting aspect I think I need to explore more in my next Rainey K. Moody book, I don't think I've ever delved into the emotions of feeling somehow connected and responsible for murders that occur after you are "on a case". So I guess all this real-life experience and perspective I am gaining is opening my mind to things like—fried pickles, what can I say?

We slid into the booth across from one another, and Darla took our drink orders. Darla still wore the old diner waitress dress with the white apron, she did not wear the hat, but she had perfectly round basketball old lady hair and it was an utter mystery to me why this continued to be an old lady thing. Some old women today were still wearing the same old lady hairstyle I remembered Grandma Goosey wearing. It's like some people must wake up on their 70th birthday and suddenly think a white permed and set basketball-shaped hairdo is the shiz—utterly baffling. I gazed at the menu intently and decided on a compromise, one that sounded delicious. Since I was already having fried pickles for an appetizer, I decided to go with a salad—the compromise; you ask? It was a Fried Chicken Salad–a bed of lettuce covered with tomatoes, cucumbers, red onions, shredded cheddar, croutons and, you guessed it–Fried Chicken, topped off with honey mustard and ranch–on the side, of course. Perhaps it might be a tad bit misleading to present my dinner choice as if it were a healthy balance to the fried pickles, but it was a salad after all. Just let me have my fantasies. Darla set down our iced teas and the basket of fried pickles, took the rest of our order, and then headed over to tell some teenage boy who was burping the alphabet loudly at the urging of his friends to cool it. Nona and I were getting a kick out of watching Darla get on to the teens. They clearly liked her, and she liked them, but she wasn't taking any crap off of them and told them if they didn't "cool their jets, they could just mosey on out of the cafe." She must have kicked them out before too, because everyone did exactly what she asked when she made the threat.

"Did you hear what Dorothy is up to?" Nona asked tiredly.

"Up to? Since last night?" What could she possibly be up to? I wondered.

"Yep, and you're not going to believe it."

"What?"

"Well, during a lull today, I called all the food trucks on my list that we were still waiting for confirmation on, and after about the third confusing call to an unconfirmed truck, I realized what was happening. Dorothy is starting her own festival, and she is siphoning off our vendors for her event."

"What?" I couldn't even force the words to compute in my mind. "She's *what*? How?"

"Well, on the third call, yet another person answered in utter confusion, 'but we already are doing a bigfoot festival in Oklachito, Oklahoma on that day,' things became more clear when she added, 'I just talked to the woman this morning.' Of course, when I heard that, my heart just sank down to my toes, and I asked her if she remembered the name of the woman she talked to. 'Well, it was the same lady I talk to every year, kinda bossy—Delores?' She said unsurely and so I countered, 'Dorothy?' and she got all excited. 'Dorothy, that's it!' I don't know what else she could be up to. She must be organizing some kind of fringe festival." The moment she stopped talking, Nona started chain eating fried pickles with the commitment and focus of an Olympic gymnast.

"Maybe she just went back to her regular job without telling us. Maybe she's just pretending like she didn't quit." I suggested.

"I wondered about that too," said Nona. "So I called Bert, but he hasn't heard a peep out of Dorothy today, so if that's what she's doing, she hasn't let anyone know. Bert said he will go talk to her, so I guess we will find out soon enough." Nona went back to inhaling the crusty fried pickles, and I took a second one. It wasn't my favorite thing in the world, but I could see how it could grow on you, and Cookie's had the best homemade ranch I had ever tasted (seriously, I could happily just sit and eat it by the spoonful like soup). I did a deep dip covering my pickle in ranch dressing and popped it in my mouth.

"So what did you and Ahmet find out today?" Nona asked curiously. I got so into telling her everything that I only ate about half of my salad. Darla boxed the rest up for my lunch the next day.

CHAPTER 11

On about the third ring, I realized that this was not a dream and opened my eyes. The room glowed from the lit screen of my phone and I saw through blurry slumber the name AHMET glowing in the darkness. I grabbed the phone and answered.

"Ahmet, are you okay?"

A strangled "Ele" came out of the speaker, and then all I could hear was erratic breathing on the other end. It almost sounded like he was hyperventilating. Shit! He must have had another dream.

"Ahmet. It's okay. You're okay. It's over," I said soothingly. "For whatever reason, the universe is letting you see these things. It must be for good. It must be to help us catch the killer." I could hear that his breathing was calming down. He must have dreamed of the latest murder, what was her name again? Clarice Thompkins. She was the missing woman that they had finally found today. I bet anything that is what it was. I didn't want to ask, so I kept just saying reassuring words to Ahmet. The last thing he needed right now was to be grilled.

"Thanks, Ele." His breathing normalized further. "I'm so sorry I woke you."

"It's okay," I reassured him. "Are you okay?"

"Ele, I really, really don't want this."

"I know you don't. I'm sorry it is happening to you again. I guess it was Clarice this time."

"Clarice?" He was confused.

"The missing woman. I guess you might not have heard, but they found her body today. She was murdered in the same manner as the others, but this time, just over the Arkansas border. The police are now calling the murderer the 'Sasquatch Serial Killer'."

"What?" Ahmet said, now fully alert and utterly alarmed. "When did you find this out?" he asked and I realized that even though I had only last seen him at 2:30 that afternoon when he left my house, a lot had happened.

"Right after you left today I switched on the TV and saw the news report. I'm sorry. I should have called and let you know." Guilt enveloped me, as if a warning from me that they had found Clarice may have prevented Ahmet's dream. Or at least it may have given him a heads up. "I should have warned you in case a dream about her might be coming."

"But, Ele, that's the thing." Ahmet sighed deeply, sadly, took a long pause, and then said, "It wasn't Clarice. Ele, I think there's already been a number five–and his name is Barnett Weathers. He was just a kid—" His voice cracked and a little sob came out. "Like a seventeen or eighteen-year-old kid. What should I do? I feel like I almost have to go to the police on this one, don't I?"

"God." It was all I could say. "God DAMN." I said, when I could finally utter two syllables. I felt so angry and so helpless.

"You really cuss a lot, don't you?" He mused calmly.

"I suppose I do. Does it bother you?"

"Not really."

"You don't cuss at all, do you?" I suddenly realized I had never heard as much as a hell or a damn escape from Ahmet's lips.

"No." He answered simply and then, with just the slightest hint of amusement, he asked, "Does it bother you?"

I smiled in spite of myself and the situation. "No." I sighed. We sat in silence for a while. I could feel his anxiety decreasing. It was almost like I could feel his heart rate normalizing.

"I don't want you to go to the police," I said plainly.

"I don't want me to go to the police, either." He said agreeably.

In moments like these, simple truth talk is all that will do. "Have you heard from your therapist in NYC?"

"No, I just got another auto-generated 'Out-of-the-office' message."

"Shit."

"Yeah."

I put Ahmet on speaker as I googled Barnett Weathers. Barnette was an unusual name and only one option came up that looked to be in the age range of the victim Ahmet had dreamed of. One of the social media accounts hadn't been updated for several years and he looked like a child in those pics. He had an account on another platform, though, which he obviously used a lot. His most recent post was from three days ago. It had to do with taking an orientation class and how he was looking forward to his upcoming freshman year as a Boomer Sooner. A small sob escaped my lips. His voice came quickly, urgently, softly, "What's wrong, Ele? Are you okay?"

"I just googled Barnett Weathers and saw that his most recent post was from a freshman orientation class he took three days ago. He was about to be a Freshman at OU."

SASQUATCH SERIAL KILLER

"Çüş!, Yuh!" I heard him exclaim under his breath in despair and I had either misheard him or he was speaking in another language. I had never heard Ahmet speak a word of anything but excellent, accent-free English, so it surprised me to realize he even knew his family's native tongue. Although I don't know why it surprised me, he told me he spent several summers in Turkey working with his grandfather at his tailor shop.

"What does that mean?" I asked, intuitively already knowing the jest of it.

"It's what my dad always says when something is unbearable, terrible, and too much to handle. I don't actually know the exact translation." Ahmet said softly.

"Do you think anyone even knows yet?" I asked suddenly. It truly was almost too much to bear to realize that the two of us, whispering on our phones in the middle of the night in our separate cabins in the woods, may be the only two, other than the killer, of course, that knew that Barnett Weathers was no longer breathing on this planet, that his body was lying somewhere, lifeless and cold and waiting to be discovered. It wasn't right. And yet, still, I couldn't help really not wanting Ahmet to go to the police. I didn't want to ask Ahmet to recount his dream or even think of it at all for that matter, but of course, he couldn't help it, so I asked anyway. "Did you see anything that would be helpful to the police?"

Ahmet stayed silent, thinking. I knew he was reliving the dream in his mind, sifting through images to see if anything he could bring to the table would make a difference. "I'm not sure," he finally said. "It happened by the bank of a river. Near the overhang of a cliff. He was fishing."

"Did you notice anything different about the killer? Anything showing this time that differed from your dream of Sam's murder? Any identifying features?"

"Not features, but the goggles were different this time. There was still not even an inch of skin or hair showing," Ahmet was silent for a little while. "This kid put up much more of a fight than Sam did, however." His breathing became quick and labored again and I could hear him trying to maintain control, the anxiety practically oozing through the phone.

"It's okay." I began again, softly. "You're okay."

"I may be," he choked. "But that poor young man—is not."

The two of us lay there for I don't know how long, just breathing. Bif must have been able to hear Ahmet's voice through the phone line because at some point he had joined us and he was now up, leaning his head on my shoulder near the phone and would occasionally let out a small whimper. Commiseration was all my pup and I could offer Ahmet. Bif and I would stand with him. He was not alone. Eventually, we must have all fallen back asleep, because a loud meowing suddenly jolted me awake. It sounded like I imagine a mountain lion cub to sound, a starving mountain lion cub. I looked at the time—6:43. Ahmet wasn't kidding, Frank Sinatra takes breakfast seriously. I heard Ahmet stir and mutter something indiscernible to the cat. "Good morning," I said and could practically hear Ahmet jump.

"Ele! Oh my God, Ele. You're still there. I'm so sorry."

"It's okay. Frank woke me up. How are you feeling?"

"I don't know. Better, I guess."

"Want to come over for breakfast?" I asked without thinking, surprising even myself. Clearly, I wasn't thinking because I hadn't shopped since yesterday when I was down to eggs, oatmeal, and peanut butter. But what the hell? It was just breakfast and I could make that work.

"Sure," Ahmet said, and I was surprised but pleased at his acceptance of my invitation. "Do you have grapefruit spoons?" he asked, which, for some reason, made me laugh.

"No, but I don't have grapefruit either, so I think we are safe."

"I'll bring both grapefruit and the spoons." He said gallantly.

"Alright, well, I guess I'll make the coffee and would you prefer oatmeal, eggs, or both with your grapefruit?"

"Surprise me." He said just as Frank let out a yowl that practically shook my walls, I can't imagine how loud it was at his place. This, of course, woke Bif up and he barked. I heard Ahmet laughing at the whole chaotic mess.

"See you in a little bit," I said, hanging up the phone and pulling myself out of bed. I stumbled to the kitchen to start the coffee.

I had never been a big fan of grapefruit, but I know from experience that enough sugar can make anything palatable. Ahmet, who didn't use any sugar at all on his half, raised his eyebrows in surprise as I ladled spoonful after spoonful of sugar across the top of mine. His grapefruit spoons with their little sharp, toothy tips made me smile. "My Aunt Becky had grapefruit spoons just like these," I said, studying the bamboo handles.

"These belonged to my parents," Ahmet answered as he dug into his half of the grapefruit he had brought over to share with me. "I have been using them for as long as I can remember."

"Do you eat grapefruit every day for breakfast?" I asked.

"Most days, unless I run out." Next to our grapefruits were steaming bowls of oatmeal. I actually had bananas, frozen blueberries, almond milk, and almond slivers, so this was a more respectable-looking breakfast than I initially thought I would be able to serve him. His grapefruit offering rounded the whole thing out nicely.

Ahmet took a long sip of his coffee. "I guess after breakfast, we should see if there are any missing person reports yet."

"Yeah. I was thinking the same thing." I said, taking a big bite of sugar and grapefruit. "Not bad," I said smiling. "If you add enough sugar." Ahmet kind of chuckled. The atmosphere was so strange. We were sitting with the heaviness of the knowledge that a young man was dead and that, most likely, his family didn't even know it yet. And yet, there was also the warmth of camaraderie that comes from going through something together. It was a stretch, but I felt like this must be how soldiers felt when they were pinned down in the trenches of war—the heaviness of war combined with close friendship forged by a common experience. "I was thinking, Ahmet. I wonder if your dreams have to do with the proximity of the murder. You had dreams of 9/11 when you lived near to the fall of the towers. How far away were you from ground zero?" I asked, suddenly realizing this could actually be significant.

"I lived about 6 miles from ground zero..." I could tell Ahmet's wheels were turning. "I think my doctor may have had a similar theory to what I think you are thinking."

"And you probably live within seven or eight miles of the Struthers' place? We'll have to ask Bert for sure, but I think that seems about right. You certainly live within ten miles. Maybe the reason you've only had dreams about Sam and this new kid and not the others is that their murders were in a closer vicinity to your home. It sounds bizarre, but it's all bizarre, isn't it?"

"You may be right. I never thought about it, but I have had several nightmares growing up of people being murdered. The whole, 'I am—' thing didn't start until the twin towers fell though, so I just thought they were dreams. What if they were all real?" This realization seemed to shake Ahmet to his core—the idea that people had been murdered in his vicinity and he had somehow known about it like the other side was reaching out to him in some way. "Ele, I don't know how I can keep this from the police."

"I know. I was thinking the same thing. We have got to try and get ahold of your old psychiatrist again first, though. Because all of this sounds so bizarre, you need proof of your abilities before you go in." We finished up our oatmeal and coffee, and I took the dishes to the sink.

"Are you ready to see if there's a missing persons report yet?" I asked him and Ahmet made a sharp nod and started googling Barnett Weathers on his phone. I heard him let out a long sigh.

"What does that mean?" I asked, placing the washed dishes into the rack to air dry. "What did you find?"

"Only the social media accounts that you found last night. At this point, no one knows. The question is: should we be the ones to alert the authorities or should we wait? I hate the idea of his body just laying there and knowing this while his family waits and worries."

"I think we should call Bert," I said. Somehow Bert had become the wise old sage of the group, even though I knew he wasn't that much older than the rest of us.

"I do too," agreed Ahmet, already dialing Bert.

"Mornin', Ahmet! How's it going?"

"Well, not so good, actually. Ele and I were wondering if you could come and talk to us about something. I'm at her house."

"I'll be right over." Bert hung up the phone, and I knew from experience that Bert would be here within ten or fifteen minutes. He had come to my rescue more than once during my short residency in Oklachito. Ahmet and Bif went outside, and I went to finish getting ready for the day and to put on some shoes. I looked at my face in the mirror. I didn't hate what I saw. The lines were subtly announcing that middle age had caught me in its snares. But overall, I thought I looked okay. I put on some moisturizer, mascara, and tinted lip balm and thought about how odd this new friendship with Ahmet was. How strange it was to feel so at peace in his presence and yet not particularly motivated to see if there was anything more than friendship there. I hadn't had breakfast with very many men in my life and even though this breakfast was completely innocent and not after a night spent together unless you counted sleeping on the phone together, which, of course, I didn't. I just decided not to let myself get too hung up on it. He was quickly becoming a good friend, and it's such a golden thing when friendship comes easily with a person. I didn't want to "look a gift horse in the mouth" like my grandma used to say. As I was tying up the laces on my second shoe, I heard Bert's Land Rover coming around the bend in my driveway and heard Bif yip. By the time I was heading to the front door, I could hear Bert, Vance, and Ahmet talking. I opened the door and the three of them were already making their way up the steps.

"Come in! Hey Vance, I'm glad you could come too. You all want some coffee?" They were already making themselves comfortable around my dining room table and I didn't have anything to offer them to go with their coffee, but they both declined anyway, so Ahmet dove right into telling them about last night's dream.

CHAPTER 12

The four of us had been talking for almost two hours, weighing out all the pros and cons of reaching out to the police. Bert thought if Ahmet was to go to the police, he should bring the local attorney Rob Abbot with him. Robert Abbot was the attorney who had assisted me in getting the PO against the Crawleys and from what I could tell was the decent sort of attorney, which also from what I could tell, was not always the case with attorneys. Bert was going to go discuss the whole thing with Rob when he left here, as they had been good friends for years. We all agreed that before Ahmet went to the police, he had to get ahold of his old therapist in NYC and get her to send a digital copy of his file or a letter or something that would back the validity of the story of the psychic dreams, in order to prevent the police from jumping to wrong conclusions.

Ahmet was keeping a pretty good eye on information on Barnett, checking Google every little bit to see if any missing person report appeared. Nothing formal had appeared, but Barnett's mother had logged onto his account and asked if anyone knew where Barnett was. When Ahmet read the plea from Barnett's mother out loud to us, we all nearly broke down under the sadness of it and the weight that her message implied. This was now undeniably real. What Ahmet had dreamed was not just a creation of his sleeping mind, but he had somehow witnessed the young man's murder. We had already known and believed this, but the mother's outcry brought the weighty truth of it down on us like an anvil falling from the sky. I always wondered why anvils fell from the sky in those old cartoons I watched as a child. I remember spending a solid year of my young childhood, eyes keenly tuned to the heavens just in case this was a legitimate thing to watch out for. At some point, I realized that this must almost never happen in real life and relaxed my ever-vigilant watch for falling anvils.

"Hey," I suddenly remembered Dorothy's rogue festival and wondered what Bert had found out. "I know it's off-topic, but is Dorothy really planning a rogue bigfoot festival of her own?" Bert sighed. This, of course, wasn't nearly as heavy of a topic as a dead teen, but it wasn't much of a mood lightener either.

"She is," Bert said, shaking his head. "She's channelling all of her anger over the loss of Sam into the belief that bigfoot killed him." He sighed a large frustrated sigh. "I did my best to convince her otherwise, but she isn't budging on the matter. She also isn't budging on her festival. The Crawleys have her organizing their own festival designed to 'educate the public on the dangers of bigfoot'. She is also going to try and pick off any of our vendors that she can, she made that clear. She actually ended our conversation with the words 'All's fair in love and war,' so I told her she had been a friend and an important ally over the years and that I loved her and refused to be at war with her."

"What did she have to say to that?" Vance asked. Ahmet was just listening, trying to catch up, as this was all news to him.

"Nothing. She literally turned her back to me and refused to acknowledge me again. So I left." Bert had taken off his hat and was shaking his head and rubbing the top of it. He seemed legitimately sad to be at odds with Dorothy. Since I had always been at odds with Dorothy, that part didn't bother me. What bothered me was the idea of a festival spreading lies about bigfoot and trying to incite fear among the people. It was such bullshit, I looked down and realized I was clenching my fists. It all made me so angry I could burst.

"She's lost the one most dear to her," Ahmet said softly. "She is desperately looking for justice, for someone to blame. I know how that feels, but she is taking a dangerous path. Hatred and fear never, ever, make things better. Even if Sam's killer had been a sasquatch, which we know it wasn't, but even if it was, this would be the wrong path."

"Nona says we just have to pray for her." Vance agreed, and I let out an audible sound of disgust. Some kind of quasi-laugh that was riddled with cynicism and anger.

"Careful there," Bert said kindly, putting his hand on my arm. "You don't want to take the same path as Dorothy, Ele." I knew they were right, but it was all just an unnecessary pain in our ass right now and it pissed me off.

Suddenly, I felt an intense sense of alarm and then Vance, who was the most adept at communicating with Bob and JoJo, said aloud, "JoJo's in trouble. It's the baby, and it's too soon." We all leapt from the table and headed out the door. Ahmet ran and grabbed a bag from his vehicle and by the time we made it to the treeline Bob was there waiting for us. We could barely keep up with him as he led us through the woods to JoJo. Finally, Bob slowed down by a very thick stand of trees and brush. He kind of sidled in sideways and we followed and there in the woods where young saplings had been woven together into walls and pulled together at the top. We slipped into the dwelling and immediately heard JoJo's moans. She was on the floor on a pile of pine needles and long, dried grasses. She was lying flat on her back and looked miserable. Geesh, Ahmet was right. She was huge.

"Vance, get her permission for me to help her. Let her know I will need to feel around her stomach and will have to check to see if she is dilated as well."

"God." Vance was completely unprepared for this conversation, but started transmitting this message to both Bob and JoJo simultaneously. I could tell when he got to the part about checking to see if she was dilated by the straightening of Bob's back and the anger on his face. To Ahmet's credit, he looked Bob straight in the eye when he saw Bob's discomfort and said in a soothing tone.

"I only want to help her."

Bob made a low guttural sound that seemed to communicate a sad relinquishment and a blessing to move forward. Ahmet then looked to JoJo and knelt down beside her to see if she was giving her permission. She must have had a contraction or some kind of pain because she grabbed Ahmet's arm and nodded furiously. Then the magic happened. I had watched Ahmet tend to Bob's gunshot wounds after he had rescued me a few months ago, but this was different. There was such a kind gentleness to his approach with JoJo. He immediately gave all of us instructions.

"She needs hydration. Vance, you, Bert, and Bob get water. We need to keep her hydrated." Vance communicated this to Bob, who seemed to pull out of nowhere a bladder-type container that looked like it might actually be the dried bladder of some kind of creature that was about half full of water. He handed that one to me and Ahmet motioned for me to give JoJo a drink from it. Bob then pulled three empty ones, again seemingly out of thin air, kept one and then handed one each to Bert and Vance and indicated for them to follow him. I thought it was a little bit funny that Ahmet had sent all three of them on this task, but quickly realized it was to give JoJo privacy while he examined her.

"OK, Ele. I'm gonna need you to help me as much as possible in communicating with JoJo. I need to see if the baby is alive." Just then there was a visible movement on JoJo's stomach and Ahmet laughed. "Alright then. It seems the little one is helping us out." He began feeling around on JoJo's stomach. He seemed very intent as he did this, and his brows furrowed a few times, like he was trying to decide something. "Can you try to let her know I need to check her?" He asked me quietly, and I delicately approached the subject with JoJo. First, I sent calming thoughts and energy and then I imagined Ahmet checking her. JoJo's eyes widened, and I knew she understood me, so I again sent thoughts and energy of love and help. JoJo then brought her knees up as one might naturally do in labor and again nodded. I held her hand, which made mine seem like that of a small child, but she seemed to appreciate it and responded with a gentle squeeze. Ahmet had been listening to her heartbeat and then to her bulbous abdomen with his stethoscope. He pulled on a pair of gloves and moved down between her legs and whispered. "It's okay. I don't want to hurt you. Do your best to relax." I did my best to translate this into a thought that JoJo might understand. She tensed up as he began to check her and then seemed to relax. Her eyes were closed, and I suddenly got such a strong wave of the feeling of the words 'save my baby', and by 'feeling of the words', I mean, they weren't the actual words per se, but I knew without a doubt her intention. She would endure anything, even the hands of a strange human man on her, if it would save her baby.

After Ahmet finished checking her, he indicated for her to move onto her left side and then asked me if I would help him communicate this to her. "She needs to tilt her body to her left side. She is trying to go into premature labor. However, she is not very dilated, so she is not in any serious danger as long as we can get the contractions to stop. We may be able to stop the premature labor, but she will need to stay off of her feet while making an effort to not lie directly on her back. She should lay as much as possible on her left side and she needs to stay fully hydrated." He handed JoJo the bladder of water and smiled at her, motioning to her she needed to take another drink and JoJo took the odd container and drew deep swallows of the cool liquid. Her breathing relaxed as well as she handed me the container of water. I wasn't sure what to do with it, so I just held it. It was then that I noticed the dried flowers woven into the wall above the bed. A few months back, when I was first getting acquainted with the bigfoot couple, I had, on a whim, purchased JoJo a beautiful bouquet of flowers. I could now see that JoJo had dried the flowers I gave her and worked them into decoration on the wall above her sleeping palate. I smiled at the flowers and JoJo smiled at me.

"Ele, can I talk to you for a minute?" Ahmet asked softly.

"Sure." I smiled at JoJo and removed my hand from hers and patted her arm gently. "I'll be right back," I said, sending her thoughts of love. We moved to the other side of the room if you wanted to call it that, as we were only ten feet away at most, also since she couldn't probably understand what Ahmet was saying, this seemed silly but I understood Ahmet's desire to keep JoJo calm.

"It's twins," Ahmet said. "I believe they are both alive. I'm quite certain I caught two separate heartbeats. I don't know if this is common in bigfoot but it explains why she seems to be growing more quickly than I had expected. Can you ask her how soon she expects the babies to be born? Or I guess, just start with the singular, baby, if you are able. We have to let her know that there is more than one, but I think we should wait and do that when her mate is here. I don't know if she will have any concept of the timing, but then again, when Bob came, he told Vance it was too soon, so she must have some kind of idea. Gorillas gestate a month shorter than humans, so I'm wondering where these creatures fall into the mix. I'm guessing closer to human gestation, but since I don't know for sure and it would be helpful to know what JoJo knows."

"I'll try," I said, I moved back to JoJo's side and although the news of a multiple-birth was surprising, it didn't feel tragic and so I was able to exude thoughts of peace and safety. I did my best to send the intention of Ahmet's question, 'when?' 'When will the baby come?' And shockingly, I saw the image of three full moons. I laughed in delight as the image popped into my mind and JoJo smiled at me. She seemed to be feeling much better now that she was hydrated and lying on her left side. With my help, Ahmet told her that often premature labor can be stopped if the mother will stay off her feet and that lying on the left side and hydration are both the natural ways to stop labor. It wasn't much, but it was something. Since we didn't have access to any of the drugs that humans used to stop premature labor, it would have to work. We were determined to see JoJo healthily through this pregnancy.

"She says in three full moons."

"OK," said Ahmet. "If the baby is due in three full moons, then we need to keep these little ones in for a minimum of another month, but honestly with no way to incubate them, it would be better if we could manage at least, two. Of course, the full three would be even better. Just then Bob, Vance, and Bert came through the door. I watched as Bob placed the bladders of water carefully between three large stones that I had not even noticed. He took the bladder from my hand and walked toward JoJo, who was resting peacefully. He knelt next to her and gave her another drink of water and then placed it with the others.

"We have news!" I said to Vance and Bert excitedly and I watched as relief covered their faces. They could tell by my excitement that I at least believed everything was going to be okay. Ahmet, of course, having a much better understanding of the seriousness of the situation, was more somber. We all looked to Ahmet to explain further.

"She is having a multiple-birth," Ahmet told them. Bert and Vance looked confused for a moment and I exclaimed, "Twins!"

"I believe the babies are both alive and well. I believe I caught two different heartbeats. Twin deliveries are often successful with a natural delivery and that is what we are going to believe for since a c-section is a bit out of the question," Ahmet said, looking around warily. "And somehow I don't see a way to get JoJo into a sanitary, safe place for a c-section to occur. Not to mention, I haven't ever done one on my own and even the few I assisted on were years ago during my residency." He stopped for a moment. "So, Vance, you think you can help us tell the lucky parents the good news?"

Vance looked happy and a little afraid for his friends. "Of course I can."

"Can you also please tell them that JoJo is going to need to be confined to bed rest as much as possible until the babies come? And I will need to be checking on JoJo regularly."

"We can set her up at my place!" I said excitedly.

"NO." The three men said in unison and Bob and JoJo were now curious about what we were saying so we moved over to them and Vance began to tell them the exciting news that it would be more than one baby coming and that she would have to stay down in order to keep them inside for hopefully at least two more full moons.

It was the first time I saw Bob smile. He put his head to JoJo's and held her and I wondered at how similar these beings were to us. JoJo revealed that she had been suspicious that this was the case. JoJo and Bob both knew stories of twins, although they had never met any personally. It was a joyous time and Bob, at one point, even put his hand on Ahmet's back in friendship. Since we knew there was no way any of us would ever find this place again on our own, we agreed that once a week, Bob would come to my house and Ahmet would meet him there and the three of us, and when possible, Vance as well, would go to check on JoJo. When Bob was about to lead us home, I leaned down to hug JoJo. It surprised her, but also pleased her. I imagined two happy, healthy, bigfoot babies and although I had no idea exactly what that might look like, I could tell that JoJo caught my sentiment.

CHAPTER 13

How could we be bummed after that? I floated back to my cabin completely giddy about the news of not one baby, but two!

PSA #23: When you discover that the bigfoot couple living in your backyard are having TWINS and, in your overactive imagination, you are already calling yourself Auntie Ele, it's time to PARTY!

I never had children of my own, but unlike most people who choose not to procreate, I really do like kids. It just wasn't in the stars for me. Doug was adamant that he did not want to have kids and I was busy with my career anyway and thought that if he was the one for me and he didn't want kids, then it simply wasn't meant to be. Sometimes, I wondered at how much I had given up for a man who, in the end, wasn't even able to stay faithful, but que será, será. I tried not to let things that were out of my control get me down. And besides, I was going to get to be an auntie to twin bigfoot babies. Who the hell can say that? Okay, Auntie might be a stretch, but a girl can dream.

Just as Bob left us at the edge of my yard, a phone rang and we all looked at one another to see who was ringing. Ahmet startled, with a total look of surprise, felt his chest pocket and pulled out the ringing device. Since nearly everyone who even had his number was standing before him, a phone call was the last thing he was expecting. I took one look at his face and landed back on the ground with a thump. The lovely floating sensation the news of twins brought on ceased as I looked at Ahmet's face. Something was clearly wrong. Ahmet mumbled several affirmatives and then a "No," then finally, after listening for a long time, said, "Well, thank you so much. Please call me if you are able to locate it." He ended his call and looked at us forlornly.

"Dr. Walters has had a stroke." It took me a moment to realize that Dr. Walters was the psychiatrist who had helped him through his healing after 9/11 and was quite likely the only official on the planet who could verify the validity of Ahmet's psychic dreams.

"Surely her office still has your file," I said hopefully.

"That's the thing, that was Dr. Walter's office manager. Apparently, Emily had the stroke three months ago and is still a long way from coming back to work, if ever, so the office manager is just coming in once a week to answer messages, pay bills, stuff like that. She said that they are only required to keep records for six years from the last date of consultation, so I may be out of luck. But—Dr. Walters does keep some more specialized cases longer than that. The problem is that those files are kept off-site. She is going to talk to the doctor's husband to see if they still have my file, but she doesn't know how long that will take." Ahmet sighed. "I don't think Mr. Weathers can wait that long. I may just have to take my chances and go talk to the authorities without the file." This felt like a very bad idea to me, but who am I to tell Ahmet what he should or should not do? But then again, when has something like that ever stopped me from giving my opinion?

"I don't think you should do that!" I said bluntly.

"Well, I can't leave the poor kid lying there." Ahmet's voice was ever so slightly raised. Not so much that anyone would notice, but since Bert, Vance, and I knew how soft-spoken he was, it was obvious to the three of us that Ahmet was asserting himself. I was just about to assert myself when Bert spoke.

"You're right, Ahmet." What? I was thinking I was just gonna have to give the two of them a piece of my mind when Bert continued. "It would not be right for you to withhold any vital information, but right now, you don't have any of that. I'm afraid that if you go in now, certainly if you go in now before a report has been filed and announced to the public, you will be putting a bullseye on your own head. When the authorities announce Barnett Weathers is missing, you, me, and Attorney Abbot will go in and talk to them, but I really don't think we should until then. The only thing you really have to offer at this point is a description of the clothing and the body build of a completely covered assailant and the slight possibility that the victim's body is somewhere in a ten-mile radius of your home, which we don't even know for sure, and again might be met with suspicion."

Ahmet seemed to take this all in. He nodded and immediately checked his phone again with a quick google search of Barnett Weathers. No new news. At this point, even though I knew that poor young man's body was out there waiting to be found, no news felt like good news. I did not want to see an innocent man, who was becoming a good friend, arrested for this. Just then Vance's phone rang, and it was Nona, so Vance walked off across my yard, filling Nona in with all the news of Ahmet's latest vision and then also of Bob and JoJo's close call and exciting news.

"I need to get home," Ahmet said. The familiarity we had shared that morning seemed to have faded and I could feel the polite wall was building back up between us. "I need to do some research on multiple births and order some supplies. Ele," he softened a bit as he said my name. "Would you be willing to go into town and get some prenatal vitamins? I'll text you the better over-the-counter brands. What is going to be good for humans will most likely work for them as well, and she needs all the help she can get right now."

"Of course," I said, happy to have an assignment, to be able to do something to help JoJo and Bob. Suddenly, I heard Bif scratching from inside the house. Oh, God! I had forgotten to crate him when we left in such a hurry. The shiny new crate was largely unused. Hopefully, I didn't have another winter wonderland scene to deal with. I opened the door and let Bif out. He greeted me enthusiastically but quickly so that he could move on to the others. Bert and Ahmet both happily bent down to give my puppy a good back-rub and then Bif wiggled off excitedly to get some love from Vance as well.

"Well, I better head out too," said Bert. "I'll go over to Rob's office and explain everything. Are you comfortable with that, Ahmet?" Ahmet looked anything but comfortable with that, but what could he do? If he was going to talk to the police, he definitely needed an attorney present.

"Are you sure you trust him?" Ahmet asked seriously.

"With my life," Bert said resolutely.

"Well, I trust you, and I'm gonna need all the help I can get, especially if I can't get hold of that file. I hope Dr. Walters is going to be okay. She's a really special person. She saved my life." Ahmet seemed like the weight of the world was on his shoulders, and in many ways, it was. He was the sole witness to a series of serial killings, but he couldn't even come forward without becoming a suspect and risking his freedom. He was single-handedly now responsible for being the attending physician at a high-risk bigfoot birth. Right now he knew there was a young man lying dead waiting to be found and he might be the only one who could help facilitate finding the body quickly and he had the added joy of knowing that when he went to bed tonight, he may very well be subjected to witness the next killing. I felt so bad for him, I wanted to hug him. Instead, I said, "Rob's a good guy. He was a lifesaver for me when all my shit was going down." Ahmet nodded, getting ready to head for his jeep. "Hey, let me know if you need anything else. I'll run into town this afternoon for the vitamins." He gave me one last smile and nod and climbed into his vehicle and drove away. Bert and I stood in companionable silence for a few moments, watching Ahmet drive away.

"He's a good guy," Bert said softly, and I looked over at him to see him eyeballing me. Like he was thinking there might be a little bit more between the two of us than we were saying. There was not.

"He is." I agreed. "But don't get any ideas in that head of yours," I said in a threatening voice. Bert laughed out loud and held his hands up in a kind of 'don't shoot' stance. Just then, Vance came walking back toward us.

"How's Nona?" I asked with a smile.

"Frustrated to have missed out on so much. Kinda feeling like the rest of us, though—sad about Ahmet's vision and excited about twin bigfoot babies."

"I think I'll go in and see her and see if I can get any work done there this afternoon."

"I'm sure she would love that," said Vance sincerely. "She misses you when you don't come in everyday. You got her used to the company," he smiled at me as he said it, he had that look in his eye of someone who is so ridiculously smitten that even the mention of their love gives them googly eyes.

"You ready to head out, Vance?" Bert asked, since Vance had ridden with him. "I've gotta stop by and see Rob Abbot, but I can drop you back at the office before I go."

"Sounds good to me," said Vance agreeably. From what I knew of Vance, agreeable was his natural state. Sometimes I wish I had more agreeability in me. I seemed to always have my fists up, but oh well. You do you, boo. I reminded myself. I waved as Bert and Vance backed up to turn around and head back down the cow trail of a road that led up to my place. I still needed to call someone about that. Bif and I headed into the house to see what kind of destruction he had wreaked on the place while I was in the woods. I opened the door and was pleasantly surprised to see everything in perfect order.

"Well, aren't you a good boy?" I said, rubbing his head and congratulating him. I pulled a doggie treat from the cabinet and gave it to him, then I made my way to my bedroom for a shower and change before I headed into town. Geez, Louise! It had been a hell of a night and morning. It didn't seem like only ten or so hours had passed since Ahmet had called me, gripped in a panic attack after waking up with the vision of Barnett Weather's murder. I almost felt like I could crawl back into bed for another few hours of slumber, but decided against it. A shower would do me good, it would wake me back up, and hopefully, Nona would still have some pastries left when I got there. A vanilla latte and one of her delicious treats were just what I needed. Well, maybe not needed, but it was certainly what I wanted.

CHAPTER 14

I was freshly showered, dressed, and ready to work. As I drove into town to try and locate some prenatal vitamins and head to see Nona, my phone rang. Sookie! I had not talked to my agent and friend for far too long.

"Hey, Sookie!"

"They're not buying the whole kidnapping-and-escape bit, Ele. They're asking for another rewrite."

"But that's exactly how it happened!" I said stubbornly. Sookie sighed. The fact that she had agreed to sell my memoir-pretending-to-be-a-novel, *Bigfoot Watching Woman Watching Bigfoot,* was still a bit surprising to me, really. I knew this was a lot for Sookie to believe, to take in. At least, I thought she believed me. "Don't you believe me?" Sookie Evanovich had become one of my best friends over the years. I know that doesn't sound very professional, but we couldn't help it. We had spent a lot of time hashing over storylines and marketing strategies, and we just always ended up laughing when we were together. I missed her. Sookie was silent for a moment.

"It's not about whether I believe you, Ele. It's about telling the best story. Stop writing a memoir in your mind and let novelist Ele take charge. They think you can tell that bit better."

"Okay, I'll rewrite it," I sighed. "Was it the masks? Because even I thought that was too much, but, like I said. It's what happened."

"No. They actually like the Tortoise and the Hare masks." Sookie started laughing, and I ended up joining her.

"I miss you," I said sadly, suddenly overwhelmed by a feeling of homesickness. It was like I had been on this alien planet for just a smidge too long and my systems were breaking down. My chest hurt. I missed the occasional air quality alert, walking or taking public transit everywhere, and bagels. I had not had a bagel that truly satisfied my soul since my arrival in Oklahoma. But most of all, I missed my friends, especially Sookie, who was currently in full agent role and for whom I was making that difficult.

"I miss you, too. How soon can you get it to me?"

"Geesh! Pushy!" I thought about the insanity of my life right now and how we were trying to track down the Sasquatch Serial Killer. "A week?"

"A week? I know you can do better than that."

"We're trying to catch the 'Sasquatch Serial Killer' here! I'm a bit distracted."

"Ooh yeah, I heard about that. Wait, that's happening where you are?" I sucked Sookie in despite her efforts to keep us on track. "I thought that was in Arkansas."

"The killings are happening along the Arkansas/Oklahoma border."

"Shit Ele, I didn't realize. Be careful!" Now Sookie sounded concerned for me again. She'd done everything she could think of to try and get me to move back after the kidnapping, and while it was tempting, for some reason, I couldn't seem to leave yet. She was silent for a few seconds. "Okay, a week. Just write it like you write the action scenes in your thrillers and you will be fine."

I knew this was a big deal. Sookie had my back, but she usually pushed me to give the publisher what they wanted. But that's why she was so good, she knew when to push me and when to push back at them. The fact that she was pushing back for me meant a lot.

"Thanks, Sookie. If I can get the rewrite done faster, I will. I promise."

"Thank you, Ele. Ope! I gotta go, have a conference call in a few minutes. Talk soon!" And with that, my long-time agent and friend, was gone.

PSA #24: Never underestimate the power of good friends and good coffee to set the world right.

I was right. Coffee 'O Clock and, more specifically, Nona, was just what I needed. I missed this friend too. Things had been weird lately, and I wasn't seeing her on the daily like I had been ever since moving to the small Oklahoma town. I needed to get back to working every day at her shop, that was how the two of us had become such fast friends and I missed my old routine. And obviously, Sookie would appreciate me getting back to a regular writing schedule.

PSA #25: Oh, and libraries! Good books and libraries are also exceptionally beneficial for making everything right in the world.

It took longer than I was expecting to track down the prenatal vitamins for JoJo and I had decided to fulfill my promise and run into town to the Oklachito Public Library. No wonder I had never seen it; it was tucked away in an old house that someone who had no heirs had left to the city. It was a lovely place, but situated in an older neighborhood on the side of town, on a street I had never traveled down before. Matilda was delighted to see me and she showed me every nook and cranny and by the time I left, my head was buzzing with things I could order for the place to make it function even better. I couldn't help noticing they didn't have any of my books and when I mentioned it, Matilda laughed and said they had all of my books, they were just always checked out, so I made a mental note to take them an extra copy or two of each of my titles. She also ordered me to check my calendar so she could nail me down on a time to come and do a reading for them. I hated doing those but didn't have the heart to refuse, so I promised I would check my schedule.

So now that I had finally made it to Coffee O'Clock, I was ready for an afternoon cuppa and some kind of baked goodness. I walked into the empty shop and saw Nona busy behind the counter by the ovens with her back turned to me. Instantly I was hit with the most lovely lemony smell that seemed just right for an afternoon treat, but when I looked in the pastry cabinet, it was bare.

"Oh, no!" I said, and Nona turned with a smile.

"Hey, you! Oh no, what?"

"Oh no, I'm too late for a pastry." I smiled back, gesturing to her empty case. "It's okay, I didn't need one anyway, but damn—whatever you made today still smells delicious." She turned away from me, picked up a muffin pan full of lemon blueberry muffins, and turned around to hold the pan out to me.

"You're in luck! After a crazy busy morning, things got slow, so I was testing out a new recipe. You can be my first taste tester."

I tried to hide my enthusiasm and instead look skeptical. "How much does it pay?" Nona sighed a mock exasperated sigh and turned back away from me, taking her lovely muffins with her.

"Never mind, then. I'll just put an ad on Craigslist–'taste-testers wanted,'"

"Cut it out! And give me one of those–STAT!"

"Stat?" Nona laughed again and turned back around, holding out a beautiful treat.

"Yeah, didn't I sound official, saying 'stat'? I work it in as much as possible. I find it makes people take me more seriously."

"You're such a goofball," Nona said, laughing as she went to work on my vanilla latte without even asking if that was what I wanted. She didn't have to. I was a creature of habit with my coffee and rarely ventured off of my established path, even though I continually vowed to myself that I was going to drink tea in the afternoons instead of coffee. I pulled a twenty from my wallet and placed it on the counter just as she was finishing up my drink. She rang me up and started to give me my change, to which she received "the look" from me and promptly distributed the change into the tip jar just as a timer went off behind her.

"You have time to join me?" I asked before carrying my computer bag and goodies to my favorite table in the corner that caught the afternoon sunlight just perfectly.

"I'd love to. Let me pull out this last pan of muffins and I'll be right over." I got myself all situated at the table by placing my laptop bag (with my laptop in it) against the leg of my chair by my feet. A lot had happened since our dinner at Cookie's last night. Nona sat down across from me with a muffin of her own and a steaming cup of tea. That is what I was supposed to be drinking. I had promised myself, "coffee in the morning, tea in the afternoon", but, truth be told, I was thrilled shitless when Nona started my vanilla latte on autopilot. After all, I didn't want to be rude. She was enabling me without even knowing it. We bit into our muffins almost simultaneously.

"Oh my GAWD," I said with just a smidge too much pleasure. It is quite possible I was replacing orgasmic pleasure with food pleasure and let me tell you, these muffins delivered. "Please tell me you will be adding these to the menu," I said, taking another bite and closing my eyes as I let the sweet lemony goodness melt in my mouth. Nona was a tougher critic than me. She took another contemplative bite, chewed reflectively, and finally said, "Yep, I think these are keepers."

"So what did you think about JoJo and Bob's news?" I asked, smiling. Nona's face broke out in a fierce grin as well.

"Can you imagine how cute twin baby bigfoots will be?"

"I know. I was excited about just one, but two! Hopefully, they will want help from us. I can't tell if they have much of a support network with the other bigfoot or not. They seem to be pretty solitary creatures, like they partner up and that's it. Not a lot of gatherings, from what I can tell." I knew I was personifying them more than I should, hoping they might want me to help out, to babysit even. It was ridiculous, but I simply could not control my imagination.

"Yeah, I think you're right, for the most part. Vance says they do occasionally gather in small groups. JoJo and Bob have offspring that have grown up and left home. I wonder if they will come back to visit when the babies are born. I wonder what they will think of twin siblings." Even the idea made me giggle.

"What?" asked Nona, knowing I had something going on in my head.

"I was just imagining having this conversation with Evie or Sookie back in New York City. Do you realize that we are discussing our excitement regarding the possibility of babysitting bigfoot twins who are expected to arrive soon? Do you ever marvel at how different your life is here?" A sprinkle of giggles spilled from Nona as well.

"Yes. Sometimes I wonder what my younger self would have thought if I would have told her I would be running a coffee shop in a small Oklahoma town, working in secret to protect the bigfoot civilization, while publicly helping to plan and run a Bigfoot Festival that tries to promote the magic, wonder, and mythical status of the creatures. It's crazy, right?"

I nodded. "Yes, it's crazy," and we both laughed, thinking about it.

Suddenly Nona went pale as a ghost. "What's wrong?" I asked.

"I don't know. I don't think the muffin is settling with me. Suddenly, I feel sick." She got up from the table and rushed to the restroom. I listened at the door and heard her throwing up, so I went behind the counter and got a clean dishcloth and got it wet with slightly cooler than room temperature water. I also made her some ice water and headed to the door. "Nona, are you okay?"

"Yes," came her weak voice through the door.

"I have ice water for you and a cool cloth for your face. Can I come in?"

"Sure." I opened the door and saw her now sitting on the stool fully clothed. She was still white as a ghost. I passed her the water, and she took a drink and handed it back to me. I handed her the cloth, and she slowly stood up, moved to the sink, and wiped her face while looking in the mirror. "This is the third time this week this has happened." Nona confided in me, looking concerned.

"Have you gone to the doctor?" I asked, and then I had a shocking thought. "Oh, God!" I accidentally said aloud. Could Nona be pregnant? She must have read the expression on my face or my mind, because she answered.

"I don't know. I don't think so. I started menopause last year. I haven't had a period in six months, but I was googling last night, and while my chances are slim of getting pregnant. It is possible."

"Are you on birth control?"

"No. I haven't had any need for birth control for years." I understood this as I had let my prescription run out when I left Doug, moved here, and swore off of men for eternity.

"And you guys haven't, you know, used protection?" My line of questioning was far more personal than usual. Nona blushed and shook her head no. We both heard the bell ring and came out of the bathroom together and were relieved to see it was Chloe and her girlfriend. They looked at us and then at each other in confusion.

"Nona just got a little sick, so I was helping her. How are you guys today?" Nona started making her way behind the counter, but she still looked like hell, all pale and shaky, and both Chloe and I immediately stopped her. Nona sat back down at the table where we had been sitting together.

"We just came in to get a drink and hang out." Chloe and Abby smiled at Nona and me. They were so cute and young. Some days, I struggled to recall what it felt like to be that age, while on other days, I woke up bewildered by how fast time had flown by. "I'll make our drinks and if anyone comes in, I'll take care of them. You and Elena just sit and visit."

Nona looked relieved. "Thank you, Chloe. I just tested that new lemon blueberry muffin recipe we were talking about the other day. You guys help yourself and let me know what you think. Ele says I'd better add them to the menu, and I was on board until I threw mine up." She smiled at Chloe, who was already behind the counter making drinks for her and Abby. She handed a muffin to Abby, who wasted no time in taking a bite.

"Oh my God!" Abby said enthusiastically, taking another bite. I liked this girl.

"They're delicious, right?" I said to her, as she nodded happily.

"You want another one?" Chloe asked me, and I looked at Nona.

"Will you feel sick watching me eat another one?" I asked her.

"Go for it," Nona smiled. "Live your best life." I laughed and accepted the muffin from Chloe. Nona was starting to get her color back, and I sat at the table with her and we went back to visiting while Abby and Chloe chattered away at the counter, teasing each other and laughing.

"Let's go get some tests when you close and see if we can find out for sure," I said quietly, and Nona nodded with a slightly panic-stricken expression. I tried to imagine how I would feel in Nona's shoes and thought "panic-stricken" about covered it.

We talked about Barnett Weathers quietly and I googled to see if anything new came up on a search. There was no new news and according to the answers to Barnett's mother's question she had asked on one of his profiles, no one had seen Barnett for a few days. My heart hurt for Barnett's mother. Vance called to see if Nona wanted to have dinner with him, but she told him she had already made plans with me.

"Have you said anything to him?" I asked Nona, and she looked alarmed.

"NO! I didn't really start worrying until today when I got sick. Three times seemed like too many times to be a fluke. I'm either sick or you know what," she said, glancing toward the girls, not even wanting to say the word aloud, "but something is definitely going on."

She looked really shaken up. I reached over and placed my hand over hers. "It's going to be alright," I reassured her. "Whatever it is, it will be alright and we will face it together."

"But Vance—" Nona didn't finish what she was saying, but her face said it all. She was terrified as to what Vance would think if she were pregnant.

"Vance is a wonderful man. It will be fine." Nona nodded, her eyes thanking me for the reassurance. Nona looked at her watch and got up from the table.

"Almost quitting time. I better clean up." Chloe, Abby, and I helped Nona with closing duties, and we finished in record time. Not another soul came through the door while we were doing it so unlike usual, Nona turned the sign to 'closed' five minutes early and we all headed out. Nona hopped in my car with me and we decided to go to Dollar General in the next town over and thought we would get some dinner there. All traces of nausea had left and Nona declared that she was now 'starving', so we headed to Hootsville for pregnancy tests and pizza.

CHAPTER 15

The Hideout, a small Oklahoma-based pizza chain, was officially my favorite pizza in Oklahoma, not that I had tried that many, I didn't have to. It was that good. There was still one little mom-and-pop Italian joint in NYC called Giuseppi's that beat it, but The Hideout was a close second. The Hideout's crust was perfect. Crunchy on the outside, chewy on the inside, and simply delicious. I believe a good crust sets a pizza apart. I know all of it is important, the sauce and toppings of course matter, but the thing that differentiates a pizza is a good crust. Take the one thing that usually gets ignored and make it noteworthy and you've officially done something special.

Nona called the pizza in just as we were heading into town. The Hideout was on the other side of town from the Dollar General but the whole town didn't take more than ten minutes to get across so we would have the perfect amount of time to retrieve the pregnancy tests before picking up our pizza and heading back to Nona's. As we pulled up to Dollar General, I watched as Nona pulled a newsboy cap from her bag. She was already wearing sunglasses. "Man, I didn't bring a disguise. No fair!" I protested, and when she pulled a baseball cap out of her bag and handed it to me, I started laughing. I hadn't worn a ball cap since a brief tomboy phase I went through when I was ten. I put it on and looked in the mirror. It was an oddly effective disguise. I thought I looked very different in the cap.

PSA #26: Whenever life provides even the subtlest of opportunities to wear a disguise, by all means, WEAR A DISGUISE! Life is short and playing like you're a spy is fucking fun.

"No one will ever recognize us," I announced, and we hopped out of my FJ Cruiser and headed into the store. When we reached the aisle with the pregnancy tests, I watched as Nona looked all around before pulling two from the shelf. I pulled off three more. "If two is good, five is better." We were heading toward the register when I noticed Paul Struthers looking at the clearance stocking caps. I nudged Nona, and she followed me as I casually passed by where he was digging through the stocking and ski caps. He had three ski masks in his hand, the kind with the cut-out eyes and mouth. He never noticed us and we made a beeline with our pregnancy tests to the register.

I watched as the girl behind the register kept looking back and forth between us and the tests and then back at us again. She had that dull look that some people get when it seems maybe they gave up on life before they ever started giving it a good try. She saw me looking at her and said in a disinterested monotone voice, "Aren't y'all a little old?"

"Shut up," I said and handed her my card before Nona could. The sad thing was, the girl didn't even look offended. She just ran my card and handed it back to me without taking much notice of my rudeness and—well, that made me *feel* rude. "I'm sorry," I said. "Stressful day."

The girl nodded. "I get it," was all she said and, by the defeated look on her face, I realized that she probably did. We left the store with the bag of pregnancy tests and as we got into my vehicle, Nona commented.

"Nice of you to apologize."

I sighed. "It was rude of me in the first place."

Nona nodded in agreement. "But, in fairness," she said with a slow smile spreading across her face, "it was rude of her to comment on our age." We started giggling for no good reason.

"Let's go get the pizza. Now I'm starving too. Don't ask me why, though. I kept down both of my muffins." Nona started giggling again and before we knew it, we were headed back to Oklachito with a large Gangster Special which consisted of a medium specialty pizza and an order of seriously delicious breadsticks. We had polished off the breadsticks by the time we were pulling into Nona's driveway.

Nona unlocked her door. I carried in the pizza and asked, "Ok, what's it gonna be? You want to eat or pee on a stick first?"

"I think we better eat first. Depending on what the stick says, I may not feel like eating later and I've been noticing that if I don't eat, I get sicker." I nodded in agreement and set the box on the little table as Nona got down two plates and pulled two flavored bubbly-waters out of her fridge? "Do you want lemon or grapefruit?" She asked, and I took the grapefruit.

"So that was weird seeing Paul Struthers digging through clearance ski masks during an Oklahoma heatwave. I mean, why would he need ski masks?" I gave her a look, a look to suggest that just maybe, Mr. Paul Struthers was the suspect we were looking for.

"That was weird. But the murderer wears a balaclava according to Ahmet's vision, so the ski masks really don't mean that much."

"Unless he was digging, looking for balaclavas." I raised my eyebrows and Nona laughed at me. "OR Ahmet is using the words interchangeably. I'm gonna have to ask him if the killer is wearing a balaclava or a ski mask."

"Well, I guess. But that seems like a bit of a stretch, Ele. Still, we should let everyone know what we saw. I thought it was weird that he was even in Hootsville. Is that where he lives?"

"I don't think so. I thought Bert and Vance said he lived in Arkansas." We each reached for a second piece of pizza and talked and laughed like everything was normal and Nona was not about to find out if her life would soon be turned upside down.

The two of us paced back and forth, stopping occasionally to look at the third stick in a row that was lying on paper towels on Nona's kitchen island. One line on a test signified a negative result, two lines were positive. She had one test with two very vivid lines and one test with one very vivid line and one faint line. We were waiting to see what number three would say. Nona was really pacing while reading her phone. "It says here: 'If two lines show up, even if the test line (T) is very faint, that's a positive—or pregnant result.'" Nona flopped down on her sofa and put her head in her hands. "Oh my god, a baby. How can I be having a baby? That girl was right. I'm OLD!" Nona had tears streaming down her cheeks.

"It says here though that: 'Sometimes, women who are going through menopause have high levels of HCG, which could cause a pregnancy test to show as positive even though you wouldn't truly be pregnant.'" I tried to offer hope, even though I found myself getting a little excited about the idea of Nona having a baby.

"But that would mean there was no baby." Nona said suddenly, and I realized she too was riding this roller coaster of maybe-it-wouldn't-be-so-bad-no-it-would-be-the-worst-thing-in-the-world that I was riding on her behalf. I've never been pregnant. I haven't even had a pregnancy scare, so I could only imagine the trip Nona was on right now. I walked over to look at the third test, where once again two very vivid lines had formed on the test. Nona looked at me expectantly.

"Two lines." She stood up from the couch and carried the last two pregnancy tests to the bathroom with her. I sat down and waited for her to emerge with two more sticks of plastic with pee on them. Later that evening, after a monsoon of tears between the two of us, Nona called Vance and asked if he could come over. The two of us stood at the counter looking down at four very positive tests and one, maybe. After much deliberation, Nona had decided that telling Vance sooner was better than later and she might as well get this over with. I gave her a big hug.

"Vance is a good guy. He will understand. Of course, they might be false positives," I said gently, knowing that even though this was a hopeful, positive thought, she and I were both already getting used to the idea of a new human growing inside her and that news would be difficult to hear as well. But Nona honorably believed that Vance had the right to ride this roller coaster with her. I gave her one last squeeze and headed out. Vance was pulling around the corner, coming to Nona's house just as I was pulling around the corner, leaving. His brow was furrowed with worry. I smiled at him and gave a small wave and he smiled and waved back, a small rush of relief showing on his face. If I was smiling, surely it couldn't be that bad, could it? I could almost see the thoughts flit across his face in the brief moment we exchanged greetings.

PSA #27: Expected or not, there are way, *way* worse things in the world than a positive pregnancy test.

I was about out of town when I heard the sirens and saw the police cars coming toward me. It looked like three police cars were headed my way at full speed, blaring their sirens all the way. I wondered what the heck was going on, if my memory was correct, Oklachito only had three police cars. Suddenly, I wondered if they had found Barnett Weathers. I pulled over to the side of the road to wait for them to pass and watched as they flew by me. In the middle car, my eyes locked with Ahmet's. He was sitting in the back seat of the middle car, looking about as lost and scared as a fellow could. Shit. Shit! Shit! SHIT!

As soon as the last car passed, I pulled a u-turn and followed the cars to the station.

CHAPTER 16

I pulled up to the front of the station as the police cars pulled around to the side entrance that led to what I could only guess was the holding cell area. I watched as the officers removed Ahmet from the vehicle and walked him to the side door. He looked over and saw me as he was walking down the sidewalk. I leaped from my vehicle and yelled, "What the hell is going on?" just as the police took Ahmet through the door. I rushed into the front entrance to find out what was going on.

"WHAT—the HELL—IS GOING ON?" I repeated myself to the confused-looking woman at the desk.

"Excuse me?" She asked, unsure how to respond.

"Your *police officers*," I emphasized these words with a disdain implying it was absurd to even consider them as such, all the while hearing my grandmother's voice in the back of my head saying, "Ele, you'll catch more flies with honey than vinegar," and also knowing I should heed the voice but being somehow unable to do so. "Your police officers have arrested an innocent man." I finished. The woman rose from her desk, saying "Just one moment," to me as she left the small front lobby room. I stood there at the desk, I was trembling with rage and fear and adrenaline. I wasn't sure which was coursing through my veins more, but the combination of the three things seemed to relieve me of my good sense, along with any small amount of politeness I may normally possess. A tall young man in uniform came out the door with the woman following closely behind him.

"Can I help you, ma'am?" He asked politely.

"I hope the fuck so!" I answered impolitely. "Why did you arrest Ahmet Pamuk?" I demanded.

"I'm sorry, ma'am, but I'm afraid I can't answer that."

"I want to see him."

"I'm afraid I cannot help you with that either, ma'am. I suggest you go home, get some rest, and come back tomorrow. It is possible the prisoner will be allowed a visitor at that time."

"I WILL ABSOLUTELY NOT GO HOME and you had better figure the fuck out a way to let me talk to him RIGHT NOW!" The man's jaw had gone rigid the moment I dropped the first f-bomb and had not relaxed since. I knew I needed to cool down, but I couldn't. This was not fair. And arresting him in the evening when no lawyers were available was even more infuriating.

"GO HOME." The officer said forcefully and walked toward the door he had come in through.

"Are you kidding me?" I yelled at him. "You've got the wrong guy, you fucking morons." Suddenly, before I knew what had happened, I had been thrown in the holding cell next to Ahmet, but I hadn't made it easy on them. I kicked and screamed and fought tooth and nail. The officer whom I had spoken with had picked me up in a bear hug hold from behind and deposited me into the cell and, without taking another look my way, left the room.

Ahmet's eyes were as wide as saucers. At least I was getting to see him. This wasn't quite the way I had been planning to do it, but it was better than nothing.

"Hi," I said.

"Hi."

"What happened? Did you call them?"

"No. I was going to do as Bert suggested and wait, but the next thing I knew there were three police cars surrounding my cabin and they were yelling at me through a megaphone, guns drawn, to come out with my hands up. So I did. And they arrested me. That's all I know."

"They didn't tell you why they were arresting you?" I asked.

"No." They simply said the whole spiel you always hear on tv. "You have the right to remain silent...yada, yada, yada."

"So they haven't given you your phone call or told you anything?" I asked incredulously.

"Well, in fairness, Ele. You pretty much stirred up trouble the moment we got here. They haven't had time to do much of anything with me. They just deposited me in the cell and then went to see what all the fuss was about." I stood up and went to the door of the cell. I wanted to rake a metal cup against the bars like they do in old prison movies just to make a racket, but I didn't have one. In fact, I had nothing. I must have dropped my purse and phone during the struggle. I might not have a cup, I thought, but I've got a hell of a set of lungs on me.

"Fuck you, FUCKERS! Fuck you, FUCKERS!" I chanted repeatedly at the top of my lungs and then the door between the holding cells and the office where the policemen had their desks in the small Oklahoma town of Oklachito slammed shut.

"Ele, calm down." Ahmet was sitting peaceably and I don't know why, but the combination of him telling me to calm down and the genuine peaceful look on his face just made me madder.

"Don't you tell me to calm down!" I said with such an intensity that Ahmet's eyes widened. He had obviously witnessed my wrath, but it had never been aimed at him before. Oh yeah! There was something in there that could fight. I could see the slightest spark of it, and I wanted it to come out. I was sick of his calmness, his kindness, his turn-the-other-cheek-ness, his goddamn Gandhi-like presence. He looked shocked, completely abashed at my intensity. Well, I took that as a challenge. "That's right. You heard me. I will NOT calm down. This is wrongful imprisonment—of both of us now." Ahmet gave me a look that would suggest my imprisonment might not be entirely wrongful and that only served to make my blood boil hotter. "Why don't you fucking stand up for yourself? Why don't you fucking fight? They didn't even give you your one call and they sure as shit didn't give me mine!" I started shouting at my jailers again while Ahmet scowled at me. I had pissed him off. Well, good. It was about time he got pissed off.

"I WANT MY PHONE CALL! I DEMAND MY RIGHTS! I WANT MY PHONE CALL! I DEMAND MY RIGHTS!" I shouted this about twenty times in a row while Ahmet's face slowly transitioned from wincing to glaring at me until finally another guy whose badge said Officer Wainwright came in and handed me my phone through the bars. I plucked it from his hands haughtily and then moved back into the cell, out of his reach. I hit Bert's name, it rang and then I heard Bert's voice, "Mountainside Realty. We're not able to take your call but we sure do want to talk to you, so please leave yer name and number and we'll get back to you just as soon as we are able. You have yourself a nice day."

"Bert! They are holding Ahmet and me in the Oklachito city jail against our will! Help!" I hung up and Officer Wainwright reached in for the phone but I hit Nona's number, it went straight to voicemail as well, so I left the same message. I knew she and Vance were likely deep in conversation at the moment, so I wasn't surprised that she hadn't answered.

"Give me the phone," Officer Wainwright demanded.

"Not until I talk to a human and not a machine!"

"That's not your call, lady. Give me the phone." He enunciated each word slowly and carefully. He was clearly pissed and using every bit of self-restraint he had in dealing with me. I didn't fucking care. I dialed Vance. Maybe if I called him as well, they would realize something was wrong.

"Give me the phone!" I got another goddamn voicemail. I shouted the same message to Vance. Officer Wainwright was losing his cool. He reached to the back of his belt for his keys and then he swore under his breath because they weren't there. "GIVE ME THE PHONE!" He shouted. I gave him a defiant smirk instead and pushed one more name in my contacts. "Doug Eubank". Doug was my cheating-bastard ex and, quite frankly, the last person I wanted to talk to, but I was running out of people to speed dial and I knew if he saw it was me, he would pick up. I hadn't talked to him other than through a few cordial emails since he came to woo me back to the east coast with him a few months ago. I was kidnapped shortly after that and a lot of shit had gone down since.

"Ele?" Doug's voice came out loud and clear and Officer Wainwright cursed under his breath and headed into the office.

"Doug! Listen, I am being held against my will at the Oklachito police station. These fuckers have arrested me for no goddamn reason and I can't get a hold of anyone else."

"Ele! Okay. I'll call our attorney."

"No! Well, maybe, but call Rob Abbot first. He's the attorney who went with us to the police station, remember? I don't know his number, but find it, and keep calling him until you get through to him. And I might need our NYC attorney as well, I don't know. Just get me the fuck out of here!" Just then, Officer Wainwright entered the cell and forcibly yanked my phone from my hand.

"You sorry S.O.B.!" I shouted and out of the corner of my eye, I saw Ahmet just shake his head. He crossed his arms over his chest and physically turned his body away from me so he couldn't see me and I couldn't see his face. Asshole.

"Ele!... Ele!" I could hear Doug's faint voice as I watched the officer click the little red circle hanging up on Doug. If looks could kill, Officer Wainwright was guilty of my homicide. He locked my cell without a word and as he headed back to the offices I yelled, "Aren't you even going to give Ahmet his call, you sorry son-of-a-bitch?" I crumpled onto the bench in my cell and scowled at Ahmet. I hated using the word son-of-a-bitch. I had tried to delete it from my cursing vocabulary, but old habits die hard and it was such a beauty of a choice word that in times of real trouble, it would raise its ugly head again. I had never really understood it. I'm insulting you, but it's actually more of an insult for your mother. I guess it made sense. There was a whole slew of "your momma" insults, so I guess to insult one's mother was the greatest insult of all, but I still didn't like using that one. The finer semantics of popular curse words were a silly thing to think about at a time like this, but what else was there to do? It wasn't any fun to ponder my fate. I had just made Officer Wainwright pretty angry. I knew that whatever books could be thrown at me, they would throw. I had already fought—physically resisting arrest, so that one was a given. Is there something else they can charge you with for cursing at them from your cell? Probably—the fuckers.

CHAPTER 17

"Want a piece of gum?" Ahmet held a stick of Big Red gum out to me like a peace pipe. I hesitated, then took the offering.

"Thanks." Truth was, my mouth was dry, I was as sad as I could be, and Ahmet and I had been sitting in silence for far too long. There were no clocks in the room and neither of us was wearing a watch, but I guessed it had been at the very least an hour since the officer had taken my phone from me and slammed the door behind him. It felt more like three. "I'm sorry," I said softly. "I don't know what came over me. I was just so pissed."

"I know," Ahmet said, simply. I noted he had not said it was okay, but I got the sense that he at least understood. It was strange. I've always heard from my girlfriends how anger is the default emotion of men. If they're feeling confused, it comes out as anger. If they are sad, it comes out as anger. This hadn't been the case with the men in my life. Of course, there really hadn't been many men in my life once my Aunt Becky had settled down with Barney when I was about fifteen. I dated a little bit in college, but not a lot. I never knew my own father and my grandfather passed before I was born. So mostly, there was Barney and there was Doug Eubank, and unfortunately, they were both cheating bastards. Nice enough fellas if you could ignore the cheating bastard part, but I could not.

I don't know if it was the lack of male influence in my life that had created this default-to-anger emotion in myself or what. Maybe I was trying to balance out my feminine energy, but when my friends would discuss men and their anger issues, I would always find it fascinating because though the men in my life did not default to anger, I sure-as-shit did. And here I was, with another man who apparently was unique in this area as well. Ahmet's default emotion clearly wasn't anger. I'm not sure what it was. It was like every emotion Ahmet experienced revealed itself as quiet reflection. It was annoying as hell. I knew most women would give their eyeteeth to have men in their life that did not default to anger, and here I was just trying to instigate some kind of spark.

"I don't understand what possibly could have happened. Why would they come to your house? How could they even know anything? It just doesn't make any sense."

"I've been wondering the same thing," said Ahmet. "My only guess is that maybe they have either found Barnett's body or have officially declared him a missing person and they put traces on the search of his name. It's the only thing that tracks. I've probably searched his name a couple of hundred times since the dream. You've probably searched it quite a few times as well, so who knows? Maybe you were about to be picked up next. Maybe you just made their job easy for them by following me here."

"That actually sounds plausible, doesn't it? If I were trying to find someone's killer and had access to run traces on internet searches, that's what I would do. It stands to reason that the murderer would want to know when the body had been found or when the person reported missing. Maybe if that's the case, the real killer is sitting in a cell somewhere, too." I said, hopefully. "I can't believe I didn't think of that. We should have just kept my TV on instead of searching for his name online."

"Don't blame yourself. Why should you think of this? It's not like you have extensive experience as a killer." Ahmet smiled at me and then a light of realization dawned on him.

"No, but I do have extensive experience thinking like one. It's how I unfold my stories." Ahmet nodded, realizing it was true.

"Well then, good one—way to blow it!" Ahmet teased, good-naturedly.

"Ah!" My mouth opened in surprise and a shocked little burst of air came out of me. Ahmet had just zinged me pretty good. I was typically the smart-ass of the two of us, so the surprise of it made me laugh. He was now trying to hide a smile under a stern demeanor, but I could see a little dimple keep twitching on his left cheek, giving him away. "I KNOW! Can you please allow me to chastise myself now, just a little? I could have prevented all of this if I had just had my head a little more in the game."

"I think your head has been plenty 'in the game'," said Ahmet, smiling at me kindly. Gone was the smart-ass. The sweet, thoughtful guy was back. I could hardly be disappointed. It's unbelievably nice to have sweet, thoughtful men in one's life.

"Hey!" I suddenly remembered seeing Paul Struthers digging through the ski masks. "You said the killer was wearing a balaclava with goggles. Was it knit? Like those stocking cap/ski mask kind?" Ahmet was already shaking his head.

"No, it was like an under armor stretchy kind of fabric."

"Are you sure?" I asked, uncertainly. I was feeling pretty stoked at the potential of Paul being the killer. Especially since Ahmet had found the link between one of the other victims being Paul's classmate in college. Ahmet's eyes narrowed like he was really trying to see it again in his mind's eye.

"I'm positive it was fabric and not knit," he said with finality after reviewing the visions in his mind. I was just trying to sort out what Paul Struthers was doing buying stocking caps in the heat of the summer and also accept the disappointment that I hadn't solved the case as I had hoped when the door opened and a detective-looking fellow in a black vest came into the room with us. He began unlocking the door and when he turned a little to wrestle with the lock, I caught just a glimpse of the letters F-B-I on the back of his vest. He opened the door to the cell and extended a hand to each of us. "Ahmet Pamuk. Elena Carmichael." He said as he shook each of our hands consecutively. "I'm Special Agent Tucker McGee." He introduced himself. "I'm afraid there has been a bit of a misunderstanding."

"There sure as hell—has." My last word came out more gently and slowly as Ahmet put his hand on my arm. He did not want the angry lady to come back, and I couldn't blame him. Thus far, Agent McGee hadn't done one thing to merit my raised voice.

"Sorry about that, ma'am." Special Agent Tucker McGee was nothing like the FBI agents I usually wrote about. He seemed like a nice, older, gentleman—hitting retirement age, but not quite there yet. He had that same easy amiability that Bert had about him, the one difference being you could almost feel the hard edge just under the surface that he could bring out when need be. It was Ahmet's desire that need NOT be, and so I yielded my ferocity and instead asked a simple question.

"What the heck is going on?"

"Well, that's the deal. There was a bit of a miscommunication between our offices and the local police. We intended for them to bring Ahmet in peacefully for questioning, perhaps even simply arrange a time for him to meet us here to discuss matters. Unfortunately, their interpretation of this was to arrest him at gunpoint."

"Why did you want to talk to him, anyway?" I asked before Ahmet could get a word in edgewise.

Detective McGee raised one eyebrow at my line of questioning. "Interesting you should ask that, since you were on our list to question as well. I would think you, ma'am, would know exactly why we wanted to talk to Ahmet." I had the good sense to look a little sheepish.

"You've been on our watchlist," the FBI agent told Ahmet and Ahmet went wide-eyed once again, thinking he was on some sort of terrorist watchlist which would have been absurd. "Well, not *that* watchlist," Agent McGee clarified, "but we are made aware when there are psychic reports of crimes, and we had so many extra heads on the 9/11 case that they alerted us to the dreams you were having years ago. And so when you searched online for Mr. Barnett Weathers multiple times, it pinged in the system. Of course, the FBI came in on the case when it became apparent that there was a third victim. Your searches indicated to us you must be having your dreams again." Ahmet and I both looked surprised at this knowledge and I watched as Ahmet's stiffness lifted and he showed visible physical signs of relief. He was fine with talking to the FBI about his dreams. Ahmet was so relieved that they were not making the assumption he was the killer that he was almost light-hearted. He wasn't, of course, but that is what that kind of relief can do to you. You can appear light-hearted in the face of murder and mayhem.

"You two come with me." Agent McGee led us out of the cell and through another door that I hadn't even noticed before, as no one had come in or out of it since we had been there. Inside the room, there was another FBI agent who was female, Deputy Sheriff Burroughs, who had been acting sheriff since Sam's murder, and Police Chief Winters. I had met Deputy Sheriff Burroughs after my kidnapping, but had never met Police Chief Winters. They each reached out to shake our hands. The Police Chief apologized to Ahmet for the misunderstanding and my blood started to boil as Ahmet graciously offered immediate forgiveness. Ahmet must have felt my anger as he placed his hand on my arm again in a steadying way.

Chief Winters gave a little snort as he shook my hand and said, "I hear you made quite a stink! Agent McGee said you were a little spitfire." I couldn't decide whether to sass off at this or just nod, but Ahmet's steady hand on my arm must have been working because "Yeah...sorry about that, Chief. I get pretty steamed when I think things are not fair," came flowing out of my mouth. He laughed and said, "You and me both, kid." I found his use of "kid" amusing because he couldn't have been more than five or ten years older than me, but I was relieved he was taking it all in good humor, maybe they wouldn't file charges against me. Special Agent Melanie Brothers introduced herself and shook each of our hands as well and gave me what I interpreted as a quick nod of solidarity as the only other woman in the room. Just then, the door opened again and Attorney Rob Abbot joined us. It was standing room only. Not really, but it was quite packed. They had placed chairs for all of us around the table in the room and as we sat down, Rob shook Ahmet's hand and introduced himself. "Bert and, uh...Doug–" Rob looked at me on this one, "sent me. Bert filled me in on everything earlier this afternoon before you were arrested, I hope that's okay."

"It's fine. I'm happy to finally meet you, Rob," said Ahmet. I realized for a self-proclaimed hermit, Ahmet was sure getting a whole load of people in his life these days, but he seemed to be handling it fine.

"Alright then," Special Agent McGee took command of the room. "I want to begin by re-establishing that our desire to meet with Dr. Pamuk and Ms. Carmichael in no way indicates that we believe them to be suspects in this case. We believe Dr. Pamuk—and Ms. Carmichael, by association—might have some information that could be helpful in our investigation." Everyone in the room gave small nods of acknowledgement to this. The amount of gratitude I felt at this clarification surprised me. "Since I'm not sure if everyone in the room is aware of this, I will give a little backstory on Dr. Pamuk, if that is alright with you?" He looked at Ahmet and Ahmet nodded.

"Of course. Of course." Ahmet said. I could see that he would rather not share all of this with the room full of people, but knew that he must and was probably glad that the FBI agent was at least breaking the ice for him.

"Dr. Pamuk has psychic visions that come to him in dreams. In the past, they have been remarkably accurate. He had hundreds of them in the years following 9/11." Ahmet had not known that his psychiatrist, Dr. Walker, had shared this information with the authorities. I wondered how he was feeling about her now, although knowing Ahmet, he was not holding a grudge against the woman who was currently fighting for her life after a stroke. I think I would probably be a little pissed if I were him, but what else is new? "In fact, if we understand correctly, Dr. Pamuk moved here under the counsel of his doctor in an effort to stop the dreams. Is that true?" Again he turned to Ahmet, who nodded an affirmative. "Why don't you pick up from there Ahmet and fill us in on your dreams relating to what they are calling the Sasquatch Serial Killings?"

"Okay," Ahmet cleared his throat. "Well, I've lived here almost seven years now and until Sheriff Struthers' death, moving here has worked—I had not had another dream of that—nature, that is until Sheriff Struthers' passing," Ahmet paused.

"After doing some research, Dr. Walker, the psychiatrist Dr. Pamuk had been seeing after the trauma he experienced during 9/11, thought that perhaps it was a proximity issue. She suspected that if Dr. Pamuk distanced himself from the location of traumatic deaths, he may no longer experience the echoes of the tragedy." Agent McGee interjected. "Or at least that's what your file says."

"She never told me that," said Ahmet. "But it makes sense. That's what Ele and I started wondering when I had the dream about Sam. If that's the case, though, then Barnett is close." I saw people in the room all make slight shifts in position. I could tell everyone was as affected by this news as I was. We had to find this kid quickly.

"So I started looking for remote areas to move to and after searching for cabins for sale, I came across Oklachito and found the cabin I am living in now." Ahmet continued. Everyone was silent but clearly listening intently, hanging onto his every word. "A few weeks ago, actually the day of Sheriff Sam Struthers' funeral, I had my first dream here and in it I was Sam." Ahmet stopped to clarify. "This is how the dreams happen. I am always in the body of the victim and usually, I relive those last few minutes of their life as seen through their eyes." There was a slight murmur in the room as someone imagined the pain of that, but I wasn't sure who had made the sound. Ahmet recounted every detail of Sam's death to the room as he had dreamed them. When he had finished with the account, the room fell silent for a moment until Police Chief Winters said, "Well, I guess that blows the Sasquatch theory out of the water."

"Yep," agreed Deputy Sheriff Burroughs.

Both of the Special Agents knew Ahmet had more to share, so after a brief pause, Special Agent Melanie Brothers gently urged Ahmet to continue. "But there's more, isn't there?" she asked pointedly.

"Yes." Ahmet sighed and continued. "Last night—wait, what time is it even?" He knew they arrested him at around 9 pm. It must be at least three in the morning. Agent Brothers looked at her watch and said it was a little after 2:00 AM. No wonder everyone looks like hell, I thought. I smiled at Rob Abbot and thought how nice it was of him to be here with us in the middle of the night. Thus far, he hadn't said a word, but it was nice that he was here to intervene on our behalf if it became necessary. "Yes, then. You understand, by last night, I mean the one before this monstrosity of an evening." Ahmet clarified good-naturedly and there were a few soft chuckles. "Last night I was awoken in the middle of the night with another dream. Elena and I have recently become friends, and she was the first one to which I confided my dream about Sam. I was so shaken up by the dream about Barnett that, gripped by a panic attack, I called her. I woke her up and I assume she must have been able to hear my erratic breathing and realized what was happening because she started talking me down." He looked at me and I nodded in reassurance.

"I assumed he had a dream about Clarice Thompkins as they had just found her body that day. When I asked him if it was about Clarice, he didn't know what I was talking about."

"This time I was in the body of a young black man. I was fishing. My heart was light, and I was having a great time until I was attacked from behind. I dropped my fishing pole and fought. I was hit repeatedly, but I kept fighting. Finally, I fought into a position where I could see my attacker—a muscle-bound figure stood before me, completely covered in camouflage, a black balaclava, and goggles again, but they were different goggles this time. I almost overtook him, but my foot slipped on a rock and I fell down. I wrestled his leg for a bit, but lost my grip. That was when he pounced on me and got his hands on each side of my head and just twisted. Then everything went black. And as usual, I woke up with the victim's identity on my lips. Every dream ends this way. I woke up and said, 'I am Barnett Weathers.'" Ahmet was shaking and silent. The trauma weighed so heavily on him, my heart hurt for him and for the poor young man. I could hear the voices softly discussing this, but I wasn't listening to their words. My hand was on Ahmet's back, consoling him again. He wiped his eyes with the back of his hands, sat up straight, and apologized.

"No need to apologize, son," said Special Agent McGee. His voice was low and compassionate, again not how I usually wrote my FBI agents. "As you all may have guessed by now. This is why we wanted to bring Dr. Pamuk in for questioning. About eight hours ago, Barnett Weathers hit the twenty-four-hour mark and officially became a missing person. His mother had been hounding the police before this.

The moment he hit the list, our tech team automatically does a scan to see if anyone has searched the victim's name in the last twenty-four hours. Only two names came up and those two people are here with us."

"Damn it! So no one else searched? I was hoping the actual killer may be sitting at a police station somewhere like us." I spoke aloud without thinking.

"I'm afraid not. Either they knew better or they didn't know the identity of their victim. If the killings are random, this is a possibility." Agent McGee replied. "I think we've got all we need for now." He looked around the room to verify this and everyone nodded except for Rob, Ahmet, and me. "We should all go get some rest. I truly am sorry for the manner in which you were arrested, Ahmet." Agent McGee apologized and Chief Winters' grim expression implied he would be talking to his subordinates in the morning about all of this. "Dr. Pamuk, Ms. Carmichael. We would like to discuss things further with you tomorrow if that will work for you." Agent McGee said.

"Of course," said Ahmet.

"Chief Winters, would you like to give Dr. Pamuk a ride or shall we?" Agent McGee asked the chief of police.

"I can." I offered and then looked to Ahmet to be sure that would be alright with him. He nodded. We all stood and several people shook hands with one another while Ahmet and I looked for how to exit.

"Come out here with me," said the chief and we will get your belongings back to you and you can be on your way.

"You're not filing charges against me?" I asked, a little surprised. I had really pitched quite a fit. I focused on looking contrite and meek and gave serious consideration to begging for mercy.

PSA #28: When you've made a complete ass of yourself and have been thrown into jail because of your bad behavior and then, a glimmer of hope appears that you might, *just might*, not be formally charged—by all means, show contrition and remember, you are not above begging for mercy.

"Officers Roberts and Wainwright won't be too pleased about it, but no," the Chief chuckled again in a low rumble. "If Dr. Pamuk here has the decency to forgive us our transgressions, I guess we can turn the cheek a little about a fired-up woman coming to the defense of her—" he stopped short, unsure as to what our relationship was.

"Friend." Ahmet and I said in unison.

"—friend." Chief Winters echoed us, finishing what he was saying, and handing us both our belongings. As we walked out of the door, I suddenly felt every bit of that fact that it was, by this time, 3 AM and I had been held in a police cell for over half the night. All the adrenaline that had been rushing through my body keeping me alert was gone.

"You okay?" Ahmet asked. I could only imagine how lovely I looked. He was looking pretty rough himself.

"I'm fine. You?" I asked. He nodded and yawned. "Hey, do you mind just sleeping in my guest room tonight? I am suddenly so tired, I don't know if I can safely get you to yours and then back to mine."

"Not at all. Frank Sinatra will be miffed to miss out on his wet food at first sign of light, but he has a bowl of dried food there if he gets hungry. And I'm afraid I might kill him if he were to wake me up so soon anyway," Ahmet smiled good-naturedly, "so you might be saving a life."

Ahmet and I climbed into my Cruiser and headed to my cabin. The sky was still dark, but the full moon was shining brightly above and the stars sparkled in their places as if nothing at all unusual was going on. We made our way inside and I sleepily pointed Ahmet to the guest room and told him to make himself at home and I immediately headed to my room and collapsed.

CHAPTER 18

Bigfoot was licking my cheek, and my phone was buzzing. I picked it up and saw that it was 9:45. Late for me, but not considering last night's "adventures". Nona was texting again. I could see the little floating dots moving. I had several texts from her and Vance and Bert, even Doug. They must have texted shortly after I left them messages. It looked like Rob Abbot had filled Bert in after we left last night, and Bert must have passed the information onto Vance and Nona because they knew we were out. I gasped, suddenly remembering Nona's news.

> We're fine! We're fine! But what about you?

I texted Nona.

> How did he take it?

I still could not believe my middle-aged friend was going to have a baby. It was surreal. Of course, there was the chance that it was a false result caused by menopause. The smell of coffee hit my nose, and I pulled myself from the bed, phone in hand, Bigfoot happy at my heels.

As I walked into my living room, I discovered Ahmet sitting in a chair with a cup of coffee and his phone in hand.

"Good morning," he smiled at me. He looked a bit disheveled in yesterday's crumpled clothes, stubble on his chin, and a serious case of bedhead. I must be quite the sight to behold as well, I had forgotten to even look in the mirror, my nose following the blessed scent of coffee. "I hope it's okay, I made coffee and ate one of your bananas. I poured myself a cup of coffee and smiled and said, "Of course, it's fine. I told you to make yourself at home." Just then, my phone buzzed.

> He was really REALLY shocked
> —but happy.

Nona's text came through and just as I was "hearting" it, she sent another.

> I called Dr. Randolph, the Obstetrician in Hootsville and she had a cancellation this afternoon. Vance and I are going to find out if it's real or just a false positive. Oddly enough, I don't even think we know what we are hoping for.

I was dying to tell Ahmet, who was watching me frantically text Nona with an amused look on his face.

> Can I tell Ahmet? He's here.

An immediate set of two exclamation marks appeared on my text and I clarified.

> NOT LIKE THAT! He slept in the guest room. We didn't get out of the police station until well after three and I was too tired to take him home.

> Yes. You can tell him.

Ahmet was drinking his coffee, I looked up at his amused expression and he said, "You look like a teenager texting your girlfriend. What's up?"

I laughed. "I feel like a teenager texting my girlfriend. It's Nona, and I just got her permission to tell you something that you are never going to believe." I sat down on the corner of the couch closest to the leather chair where Ahmet was having his morning coffee.

"Permission, huh? Now I'm intrigued." He smiled. He set down his phone entirely now and was eagerly awaiting what I would reveal.

"So. Last night, Nona and I went over to Hootsville to pick up some pizza from The Hideout."

"I love that stuff." Ahmet nodded, waiting for more.

"And...a pregnancy test." Ahmet looked shocked. "Well, actually five pregnancy tests."

"For...?"

"NONA, of course! I'm not seeing anyone!"

"That's what I thought. Well?"

"They were all positive." Ahmet set his cup down at this news. "How old is she?" Ahmet asked.

"Forty-six."

"A year younger than me..." Ahmet said softly, reflecting on the whole thing and I couldn't help note that made Ahmet a year younger than me. I thought we were about the same age, but it's hard to tell sometimes. "And Vance?" Ahmet asked.

"Fifty-three." Ahmet nodded. I knew he was now calculating likelihood and risks. "It could be a false positive." He said cautiously, not sure how I would take this.

"Oh, we know. We did all sorts of googling last night. Do you think it's likely there would be five false positives?"

"Possibly. High HCG levels can cause false positives, and so there really could be five false positives. Getting pregnant naturally after 45 is next to impossible. And with Vance being older as well."

"Well, Dr. Randolph, the OBGYN in Hootsville had a cancellation this afternoon, so Nona and Vance are going to go find out today."

"Wow." Ahmet leaned back in his chair, kind of dazed and shaking his head. He picked back up his cup of coffee and took another sip. I could see that he was getting low, so I got up and topped up both of our cups without asking.

"I know," I said, responding to his reflective demeanor. "Can you imagine?" I asked. "At our age?"

"Not really." He said softly. "But what a blessing." I was a little surprised by this, but oddly, it was how I had felt as well.

"Do you regret not marrying and having kids?" I asked and saw Ahmet stiffen. He was silent, and I realized that I had accidentally trodden onto bad terrain. "I'm sorry. You don't have to answer that. It's just that sometimes, well, sometimes, I wonder how it would have been if things had turned out differently. Doug didn't want to have kids and since I thought he was the one for me and I was so busy with my career anyway, it didn't seem like that big of an issue. But sometimes, I wish..." We sat in silence and finally, after a long while, Ahmet spoke in a near whisper.

"My wife died in 9/11. She was one of ten women who perished in the attack that was known to be pregnant." I gasped. I had no idea. Ahmet had never mentioned having been married before.

"I'm so sorry...I didn't know." I put my hand on his arm, and he laid his hand over mine.

"I wonder all the time what it would have been like. Maybe it was my great sense of loss that sparked the whole dream thing, but it was also what made the dreams so difficult to bear. Every time I watched the death of another 9/11 victim in my dreams, I imagined the deaths of my wife—" Ahmet was clearly overcome with emotion. "—and child."

"Did you ever—" Ahmet must have known I was going to ask if he had dreamed about his wife's death.

"No. I never did. And even though part of me longed to, I think I'm glad I never did. I don't know if I could have handled living her death over in my dreams."

"You mean, you lost your wife and unborn child and continued to work through the nightmare?" I could not even imagine how Ahmet had done that. How could you care for the wounded and dying while your wife was missing?

"I kept thinking she would show up in the wounded I was caring for. She rarely worked in the towers, so my supervisors were completely unaware that I was working while not knowing if my wife was safe. They would have likely excused me otherwise, but everything was so insane, there were so many injured, it was all hands on deck. So I just worked and prayed and prayed and worked." The two of us just sat there for the longest time, sipping our coffee.

"I'm so, so sorry." I finally said again. There was nothing else to say. Ahmet just nodded to me again, acknowledging my words as he sipped his coffee. I watched him shake off the sadness and then he spoke.

"You know, if Nona and Vance actually are expecting, the child will grow up potentially as friends to a couple of baby bigfoot." Ahmet had a full-on grin now at the thought of this and I burst out laughing.

"Oh my God, you're right!" I hadn't thought of that. I giggled like a schoolgirl at the thought and Ahmet watched me, smiling with soft eyes.

"I like giggling Ele much better than angry Ele."

I shrugged. "Me too. Too bad there are so many ass-hats around who bring out angry Ele." Ahmet smiled and shook his head at this.

"OH MY GOD!" I said again excitedly. "Now I can't stop thinking about a little Vance-and-Nona baby growing up with bigfoot babies. It's the cutest thing ever." Just then, Ahmet's cell phone dinged with a text and again he looked surprised. He picked it up and said, "It looks like the FBI would like to talk to me again at 2:30 pm. I guess I should get home and shower and change." He looked a little sad to have to leave.

"Was there anything online about Barnett?" I asked, knowing that Ahmet would have looked immediately. I would have too if my day hadn't started with a barrage of texts from Nona.

"Yes. They are asking for any information to be called in. They haven't found a body yet and I'm sure his family is still hoping this is just a crazy pre-college trip that Barnett didn't tell anyone about and that they will find him safe and sound." We both looked miserable.

Wow, life was a roller coaster with all the good news then bad news floating about.

"Let me go get on my shoes and I can run you home. Do you want me to come with you this afternoon?" I asked.

"No. It's okay."

CHAPTER 19

"Dorothy Struthers is the world's biggest pain in the ass! I don't care if she is a grieving widow." I slammed my belongings down on the counter at Nona's. It was just the two of us except for Mr. Huckaby sitting in the corner, and we both knew he kept his hearing aids turned off most of the time and seemed to be lost in one of those western novels he liked so much. When he first found out I was a writer, he kept pitching western novel ideas to me. He hasn't given me any lately so I suppose he's given up on the likelihood that I would switch genres and become the latest and greatest in the western arena, little does he know I'm now writing bigfoot novels under a pen name, a fact that even I find hard to believe at times.

"What did she do now?" Nona groaned. She was already working on my vanilla latte. Nona's tolerance of Dorothy was waning as well as she kept discovering wrenches the woman was throwing at us as well.

"Well, with all the craziness of late, I am behind on my Bigfoot Fair duties. So this morning after I ran Ahmet home—STOP IT!" I said, laughing at Nona's arched eyebrow. "He slept over in the guest room because, by the time we got out of the police station this morning, I was so tired I could hardly see straight. I just wanted to get home to my bed, so he agreed to stay over. That is it. Nothing more. Anyway, after he left, I tried to make calls and catch up on all of my responsibilities. The fair is less than two months away! We have got so much to do!"

"I hate to break it to you, but it is only one month and six days away."

"Shite!" I said.

"What did she do this time?"

"Well, I started emailing and calling on the remaining booth vendors that we have not received the deposits from and every one of them has jumped ship. One even said they were told that this was a new and improved festival and they were expecting much larger crowds than our festival draws." Nona cursed under her breath, which, oddly enough, lightened my mood.

"We have to call an emergency planning meeting. We need a plan." Nona said angrily. I texted Bert and asked when they might be willing to meet for an emergency planning meeting. I told him that there were some things we needed to deal with. Not two minutes later, I received a text back from him.

IF YOU AND NONA ARE BOTH AVAILABLE, WE CAN DO IT TONIGHT AT 6. I'VE TALKED TO EVERYONE ELSE AND THEY ARE GOOD WITH THAT.

"Can you come tonight at six?" I asked Nona. "You and Vance will just be getting back from the doctors, won't you?"

"If Vance said yes, then I'm okay with it," Nona told me. I texted Bert a quick 'we'll see you then' and turned to Nona.

"Are you nervous?"

"Oh my God, Ele! What am I going to do if I actually am pregnant? I haven't been pregnant since I was 22!"

"Well, it's not like I'm one to talk, since I don't have a clue about what it's like. But, my solid guess is that you are going to love that child like nobody's business and you are going to be the best mom the world has ever seen—again." Tears escaped from the corners of Nona's eyes and she grabbed my hand and squeezed it. "And you have a whole band of us excited to help you."

"Thank you, Ele."

"I'm probably not even pregnant. It's probably a false positive."

"Maybe. Let's just believe together that whatever is best will be. I don't know much else we can do other than that." I said, giving her arm a gentle pat. Nona agreed and wouldn't let me pay for my pastry and coffee. I didn't argue with her for once and just said, "Thank you."

After a solid three hours of working on my rewrite, I thought I had created a scene true to my story, but that Sookie and the publisher would be happy with. I smiled in satisfaction and hit "send". I noticed it was almost 2:30. Nona was giving Chloe last-minute instructions, and she made her way out the door to meet Vance for her doctor's appointment, just as I was heading out.

"Good luck!"

"Thanks!" I watched as Nona climbed into Vance's truck with him and gave him a peck on the cheek before buckling herself in the center seat. So cute. Like teenagers. "Pregnant, unwed teenagers," I thought, cracking myself up.

Although Ahmet had told me he didn't want my company, I was itching to know what the FBI wanted, so I drove over to the station. Ahmet was getting out of his vehicle just as I drove up and looked over at me with a questioning expression mixed with what I hoped was relief. I parked, got out of my vehicle, and walked towards him.

"I know you said you didn't want company, but I had an itch to join you. Do you mind?"

Ahmet sighed, "Actually—" He paused, for a second I thought I had annoyed him by overstepping my boundaries. I'm not always good with boundaries, being a bit of a stubborn-typed human. "That would be really nice," he admitted.

It was my turn to sigh in relief and I fell into step with him as we walked up the same sidewalk I had angrily marched up the night before. Ahmet opened the door for me and I noticed as I walked through that these were all new faces. I followed Ahmet up to the counter.

"I have a 2:30 appointment with Agent McGee and Agent Brothers," the eyes of the woman behind the counter widened as she told us to wait just a moment. I guess it isn't every day that the FBI uses the station for interviews. Before we could count to ten, Agent Brothers came through the door following the receptionist and met us both warmly, shaking our hands and asking us to follow her. We went back to the same room we had been in last night, but there was a lot less tension in the air today, probably because Ahmet and I both knew now that Ahmet was for sure not a suspect. Agent Brothers motioned for us to sit down and offered us both bottles of water, which we accepted. She came back with four ice-cold bottles of water and Agent McGee on her tail. They joined us at the table, sitting across from the two of us.

"Ms. Carmichael, I didn't expect to see you here," Agent McGee said with a neutral expression on his face. I couldn't tell if he was okay with my presence or not.

"I know. I'm just nosy and couldn't help myself. Do you mind?" I asked openly.

Agent McGee chuckled.

"Not at all. You've got a mind for these things and we can use all the help we can get on this one." This confused me until I realized he must know I write thriller/mystery novels. It was the only explanation for him to say I have a mind for murder. "As I'm sure you two are aware, Barnett Weathers is now officially a missing person. We wanted to talk to you more in-depth about your dream and what you saw when Barnett was being attacked. You said he was fishing? What details can you remember about where he was?" Ahmet closed his eyes and took a deep breath.

"He was on the river and there was a pretty decent-sized cliff wall on the other side of the stream from him and near to where he was fishing there was a bit of a cliff side with an overhang but where he stood there were woods behind him." Ahmet began quietly. "About twenty feet upstream from him, there was a bend in the river sharp enough that I could not see well around it." I watched as Agent McGee scratched down notes hastily on a pad of paper, while Agent Brothers typed frantically into her laptop. "The sound of the water is pretty prevalent, so he must have been in a real rushing part of the river, maybe with some rapids nearby. Yes...come to think of it, I noticed when the fishing pole was knocked out of his hands that the current swept away it. Also, the bank where he was attacked was very rocky rather than sandy. And the trees came up nearly to the water's edge where Barnett was standing. That must be how the attacker was able to sneak up on him without him noticing." I thought it was interesting how Ahmet would go in and out of using the first and third person when speaking of Barnett. I guess, since Ahmet was actually the victim in the dreams, he struggled to separate himself from the victim. Ahmet opened his eyes, and we watched as Agent Brothers showed something on her screen to Agent McGee. "I think we start here." She pointed to the screen and then, noticing our eyes were on her, turned the screen so we could see. It was an aerial map of the river and she had zoomed in on a bend in the river that seemed to be a rock cliff on one side and a forest on the other. "What is your address?" Agent McGee suddenly asked Ahmet and as Ahmet recited it to him, Agent Brothers typed it in and made a little hmm sound, nodding in affirmation to Agent McGee. "This bend is within a ten-mile radius of your home," she said excitedly. Agent McGee was already talking to someone on his phone and the two stood. "Thank you so much for your help today. We will let you know what we find." He said kindly, in answer to the unspoken question on Ahmet's face.

The two of us walked out, and I looked at my watch. "Well, Vance and Nona should be meeting with Dr. Rudolph right now." I mused, wondering what they would find out.

"Ele, it really is incredibly unlikely that there's a pregnancy," Ahmet said gently.

"I know...I know...and it would probably be best if there's not. I just can't help being excited." Ahmet put his hand on my arm as we stopped by my car. I smiled at him.

"I'm excited by the idea too," Ahmet confessed, smiling back at me.

"Well, we shall see."

"You want to grab a bite to eat?" Ahmet asked cautiously. "I was too nervous to eat earlier and haven't had anything since your banana this morning." All I'd eaten was the pastry Nona fed me. Ahmet surprised me, however. I was usually the one to suggest a meal together.

"Sure. I'm starving too! Ever gone to Cookie's?" I asked, curiously.

"Only take out," he smiled.

"Then it's time you get to know Darla. You're gonna love her." I wasn't exactly sure that was true, but the old school diner waitress was a hoot and I would enjoy watching her interact with Ahmet, so whether it was true or not, I was certain our late lunch/early dinner would be enjoyable either way. Ahmet followed me in his car to Cookie's and as we walked up the sidewalk to the diner, the door flew open and I was standing face to face with Abner and Jeb Crawley, and Dorothy. I felt myself go boiling mad in 0.2 seconds flat. I was about to share my displeasure when Jeb started mock gagging.

"I smell camels! Damn nasty creatures. You smell camels?" Jeb fake gagged again, nudging Abner in the ribs and laughing a vile laugh. Both of them with their eyes plastered on Ahmet.

"Ah…good one," I said, dripping in mock sincerity, "you racist cock-suckers!" I yelled out and Dorothy gasped. I saw both Abner and Jeb's faces go red.

PSA #29: Fuck maturity. Never—ever—miss the opportunity to call a racist a cocksucker.

(I mean it, it's good for your mental health, not to mention delightfully satisfying.)

"I believe you are not supposed to be near me." I stomped past them with Ahmet on my heels and we went into the diner. Unfortunately, the diner door did not close quickly enough for Ahmet and me to miss Abner's last attack.

"You uppity bitch, don't think you've escaped for good. You will get what's coming to you."

Darla, the waitress who looked to be at least in her seventies with her round little old lady helmet hair, was spry and youthful in her movements. She was wearing her pretty pink old-school diner's waitress dress, and she met us with menus at the booth as we each slid into our side. Ahmet was looking out the window at the two men and Dorothy, who were glaring at us, still standing where we had left them on the sidewalk.

"It's about time you came in and sat for a spell—always 'to-go' with this one," Darla said, pointing a thumb at Ahmet with a smile and then looking him up and down real good. After a moment, she gave him an ornery grin and barked out a laugh. "What can I get y'all to drink this afternoon?" Darla asked as she placed the menus in front of us.

"I'll have iced tea," I said to her, forcing myself to smile after our encounter outside.

"Me too." Ahmet gave Darla a truly genuine smile, and I marveled at him and his easy way of letting things roll off of him.

"I'm sorry about that mess outside," I said quietly as Darla left to make our drinks, I glanced back out the window and the three of them were getting into their vehicles with scowls on their faces.

"Why? You didn't do anything. Well—except antagonize them further by calling them names." He had the slightest hint of a smile in his eyes as he said this.

"Does that happen often?"

"Not too often," Ahmet said, opening his menu. "Of course, I also never leave my house, so there is that." He shrugged, and I laughed and we both seemed to make an unspoken agreement to put it behind us, but not before Ahmet made one last comment. "You know, Ele. They still seem to have a pretty big beef with you, and if they are the ones who hired your kidnappers in the first place–well, I'm concerned for your safety. You should probably stop intentionally antagonizing them." He added this last bit softly.

"Noted." I replied smiling as I opened my menu and looked at him over the plastic covered folder. "How do you feel about fried pickles?"

CHAPTER 20

There were grim expressions all around the little folding table in the Quonset hut community center where the Bigfoot Fair planning committee all sat. Vance and Nona had come in a few minutes late, both looking happy and at peace, whether this meant they were happy about having a baby or happy about not having a baby, I hadn't figured out yet. But for the moment, all our minds focused on more pressing matters–that is, what the hell we were going to do about Dorothy and the Crawleys siphoning off all our vendors for their fringe festival that was sure to be full of bigfoot hunts and bullshit propaganda about the evils of bigfoot.

"What if we looked at this as an opportunity?" Bart Longfeather, the older indigenous gentleman, who since Dorothy's departure had almost become a chatty Cathy, suggested.

"What do you mean?" Bert asked, clearly keen on finding a different way to look at things.

"Well, you know how we've always kind of wanted this festival to be a celebration honoring them and promoting them as the peace-loving creatures we believe they are?"

"Go on." Bert nodded.

"Well, if Dorothy and the Crawleys are hell-bent on their hate fest, what if we just came all out and made our festival a Bigfoot Love Fest? I mean, why not? If–what is it my grandkids like to say?" He paused and thought for a moment. "If haters gonna hate, then lovers gonna love!"

We all sat in silence for a moment until Nona and I burst out laughing in unison and everyone immediately joined in. There was something so funny about an 80-something-year-old Choctaw man saying "haters gonna hate".

"It's brilliant, Bart!" I said, slapping him on the back.

"You may be onto something," pondered Bert. "What if we were openly intentional about hosting a 'We Love Bigfoot Festival'? My guess is that is going to settle better with most of the guests who are just coming to this thing for lighthearted entertainment than what Dorothy and her gang are up to. Most people are simply fascinated with the legend, hopeful that bigfoot might be real, and eager to hear stories. I think most people want to love bigfoot, not be afraid of them."

"You know—" Mr. Longfeather was clearly coming up with his next brilliant idea right before our eyes. "There are loads of stories about bigfoot helping folks over the years. My grandpa got deathly ill one winter when my father was a child. He and his siblings were trying to do enough hunting to keep the family alive, but they were still pretty little and the game was hard to come by that year, when a deer with a broken neck, still warm, showed up in front of their house right by the porch. My granny swore she saw the bigfoot who left it for them walking back into the tree line. So she taught her young-uns to skin and dress a deer that day and the meat was enough to get them through the rest of the winter. My grandpa healed up by springtime, but my daddy always told me he might not be here if the bigfoot hadn't taken mercy on them." Bart shared this and then his idea seemed to fully gel in his mind. "What if we gathered up a bunch of people with these kinds of stories and hosted a 'WHY I Love Bigfoot' storytelling event? Maybe by the campfire? And we could serve free Indian tacos!" He added excitedly. These people sure loved their Indian tacos.

Bert, Vance, Nona, and I looked at one another. Bart and Walt didn't know about how Bob had saved me from my kidnappers and likely never would. I could almost read Bert and Vance's minds. They liked keeping bigfoot in "legend" territory. They preferred that the public not actually believe and spreading these kinds of stories would only grow the believers club, but at least it would grow it for the better. All these news reports of the "Sasquatch Serial Killer" were tainting people's views. People were becoming believers anyway. It would be far better for people to believe them to be helpful peace-loving creatures rather than killers. Nona laughed out loud. "I've found our new mascot. We could put him by the entrance where all the cars come onto the grounds." She turned her phone around and showed us a picture of one of those giant blow-up characters you see at car lots, it was a bigfoot hugging a big red heart.

"Send me that link, Nona. I'm going to order that right now." I could see that Walt Riley, the accountant and treasurer of the event, was getting antsy. He'd stayed pretty quiet during the meeting and I realized he was probably thinking of the cost of rebranding the event. "Don't worry, Walt. This one's on me. In fact, I would like to make a donation to cover the cost of all the rebranding." Walt was now smiling and nodding.

"That's right nice of you, Ele," Walt said.

"Well," said Bert, "I think the only thing left to do is vote on our new name. Should it be the 'Bigfoot Love Fest' or the 'I Love Bigfoot Festival'?"

The 'I Love Bigfoot Festival' won hands down. I think the words 'Love Fest' together made a few people nervous that we would have our own creepy Woodstock bigfoot-loving orgy thing happen, the thought of which made me laugh out loud. Walt and Bert looked at the books and decided that offering free Indian tacos was well within the budget and we once again divided up the list of vendors and exhibitors so we could call them and share the new theme with them. We decided simply to be honest. If Dorothy was drawing lines in the sand, then we would openly share that we were in the bigfoot lovers camp, not the haters, and that our festival's message would be wholesome and family-friendly and well, friendly in general. We would not be spreading more fear surrounding the creatures. Maybe a few of those who had gone to the dark side would come back after hearing from us. Regardless, we'd come up with about six new easy-to-pull-off events we could host around the 'I Love Bigfoot' theme, so we were all feeling pretty happy by the time the meeting ended.

"Thanks, Bart!" Bert acknowledged the older gentleman. "You got us back on track. Thank you for coming to the problem from a different angle. I think you're right. As much as I hate that Dorothy and the Crawleys are doing this, I think it is an opportunity to make our fair even bigger and better than before."

"Well, everyone's gone off the deep end." Bart's old gravely voice rumbled thoughtfully. "I hate to see Dorothy going down this path of believing one of 'em killed Sam. I feel like if they wanted to kill us, most of us would be dead by now. Nope. I think this is the work of something far more evil than bigfoot." We all nodded in agreement and started cleaning up to go home. When we were putting away tables and chairs, I saw Vance squeeze Nona's hand and give her a quick peck on the cheek before she headed to the restroom and I suddenly could not wait a moment longer to know. I followed her into the restroom.

"SPILL IT!" I demanded as I heard Nona tinkling behind the door of her stall and she laughed out loud.

"Well, give me a minute. I don't want to tell you like this." My heart leapt. Why would she care about how she told me, unless...?

"Well, then hurry up!" I said, excitedly. I heard Nona flush, and she came out beaming. She walked to the sink and washed her hands, smiling the whole time, and I was nearly bouncing up and down on my spot in anticipation. She dried her hands under the blower and I watched as the skin on her hands did the same thing mine did under those dryers these days. It pooled out under the force of the air, like liquid skin. It is as if after forty-five or so, skin starts slowly letting loose of the body. When her hands were dry, she turned to me and put a hand on each of my shoulders and smiled at me fiercely.

"It's a baby." She said, and I squealed and threw my arms around her. Nona kept talking in my embrace. "We got to hear its little heart beating and Dr. Rudolph even has an ultrasound machine, so she did an ultrasound and so far, everything looks healthy. I am EIGHT weeks along, Ele. We must have gotten pregnant the first weekend we were together."

I pulled back and raised an eyebrow at her, "You guys got busy pretty quickly then, and here I was just a week ago, wondering if you were sleeping with him yet." I joked with her merrily.

"Quickly? I don't know what you're talking about! I waited over two decades to sleep with that man, thank you very much." Nona joked, and she looked so happy my heart was about to burst for her.

"Oh Nona, a baby!" I hugged her again tightly, doing that rocking back-and-forth thing people do when they are so happy and don't want to let go of the moment. We pulled away from one another and I could see tears running down Nona's cheeks; then I realized my face was wet with tears too.

"Oh, Nona! You're good with it, then?" Nona nodded.

"The doctor said at our ages it's like a one in a million chance and you know what Vance said when she said that? He said, 'Well, then if it's a girl, I think we should call her Millie for being our one in a million.'" Nona was absolutely glowing. I know it's cliche, but she really was glowing. She looked so happy, so radiant, so—shiny! I hugged her again.

"Well, I guess that answers my next question of how Vance is taking it."

"Oh, Ele. When we heard the heart beating, he started crying–just balling like a kid. He was so embarrassed he kept wiping away the tears and apologizing and I told him that those tears were about the sexiest thing I had ever seen," she blushed and her hand flitted to her belly in that universal sign language of those "with child." We came out of the restroom together smiling and Bert, Walt, and Bart were all hugging Vance and slapping him on the back.

"I guess the secret's out, then!" I said, smiling at them all. Bert came toward Nona with open arms and embraced her, and I gave Vance a hug as well.

"Congratulations, Nona! Congratulations." Bert patted her back and unless I was seeing things, his eyes were a little watery too. Walt and Bart came in for congratulatory hugs as well. Well, one thing was for certain. This child would not be lacking the love of a whole bunch of old people. We all made our way out to our cars and headed off, bubbling with the excitement of the news. I glanced quickly at my phone as I took it out of my pocket to put it in the little nook in the dashboard and saw that I had missed two calls from Ahmet. I hit the button to call him back and started the engine.

"Hey!" I said happily. "What's up?"

"Ele!" Ahmet sounded happy too. "They found him." My heart suddenly sunk into my belly like a bad batch of biscuits.

"Oh! I didn't think it would be so fast."

"There's something else," Ahmet said excitedly.

"What?" I couldn't imagine what in this horrible scenario Ahmet could be excited about.

"He's still alive."

"WHAT?!"

"I don't know all the details, but Agent McGee said that Barnett woke up after passing out from the trauma of his neck breaking and he saw his attacker looming over him with a knife pressed on the center of his chest. Just as the attacker was about to force the blade into Barnett's chest cavity, something grabbed the attacker from behind and pulled them off of him. For just a flash, Barnett thought he saw a giant hairy man, but then he couldn't see what was happening anymore. He said that whatever it was, it sounded like a wild animal and that the attacker was screaming in terror. He also said that even though the whole thing was terrifying, he felt an unusual sense of peace. Barnette couldn't move because of his neck, but he thought he heard something hit a tree and fall, and then he heard running. He passed out again from the pain and when he woke up again, FBI agents were surrounding him. Barnette was laying very near where the agents thought he would be based on what I saw in my dream. He has a broken neck, and a surface wound on his chest from where the attacker was making the initial cut with the knife. That bled out a bit, but not so much as to kill him." Ahmet was sobbing. "Can you believe it, Ele? He's alive!"

I couldn't. I was in shock. And once again, as has been the case over and over since moving to my cabin in the backwoods of Oklahoma, I could hardly believe what was happening. None of it seemed real.

I swung into the Choctaw Nation Travel Center and bought all four of the packages of bacon they had in their grocery fridge. When I got home, I called yet another emergency meeting, this time of the 5S group. It was truly the era of emergency meetings. I texted everyone and asked if they could come to my house for breakfast the next morning, and before I knew it, I had confirmation from the whole group, including Nona, which surprised me.

> Chloe said she can come in and cover for me, so I'll be there. What's up?

> You'll find out in the morning.

> Oh, OKAY!

> :)Good night!

> Good night! Oh yeah, I'll bring muffins!

<3

I loved that woman. I had been so excited about Ahmet's news; I hadn't shared Vance and Nona's news with him. I just told him I thought we should have a 5S meeting at my house the next morning to tell everyone and he agreed to come and give everyone an update. I was on complete and total emotional overload. When I got home, I snuggled down with Biffy and fell into a deep, deep sleep.

CHAPTER 21

Everything was good, of course, with the exception that they had found no murderer. We all sat around my table on the deck enjoying the fellowship, the bacon I had made a big stack of this morning before everyone got here, and more of those heavenly blueberry lemon muffins Nona started serving at her shop. We were living like gods, so of course, coffee also flowed freely, although I noticed Nona limited herself to one cup.

"First things first. Ahmet, I believe you are the only one yet to hear the news–drum roll, please." Bert obliged me by beating his hands rapidly on the tabletop as I held my hands out to Nona and Vance, encouraging them to spill the beans. They looked at one another, and then Vance nodded at Nona. He wanted her to tell the news.

"It's official!" Nona announced happily. "I may currently be the oldest pregnant lady in the state, possibly in the tri-state area!" I thought everyone's cheeks might burst from the size of the smiles in the room. I caught the slightest flicker of concern on Ahmet's face for just a flashing moment, and then it was gone and replaced with happiness and congratulations. Ahmet asked them a million questions, and we all drank our coffee and ate the bacon and muffins. Then it was Ahmet's turn to share. I cleared my throat.

"Ahmet! When are you going to tell everybody? After all, it is why we called this little get-together." At this, all heads turned to look at Ahmet and he smiled. Apparently, everyone was so happy to gather for breakfast that they had forgotten there was a reason for our gathering.

"Well, I didn't want to horn in on Nona and Vance's news, but I have a bit of good news as well. It hasn't been released to the public yet, so I'm swearing you all to secrecy," Ahmet paused for effect, "–the FBI found Barnett." Everyone sobered a bit at the news as I had. Another body, no matter how badly everyone wanted it to be found, was never good news. Unless... "The good news is that Barnett was still alive!"

"But your dream?" asked Nona.

"I know," said Ahmet. "When everything went black, I just assumed. In the past, that seems to have been the case with my dreams. But, I guess he just blacked out from the broken neck. Here's the kicker, though, guys–and Vance, I'm gonna need your help to ask Bob and JoJo about it when we go out to see JoJo later today, but it seems a bigfoot may have saved Barnett from having his heart removed like the others. Barnett told Agents McGee and Brothers that he woke up just as his attacker had the knife to his chest, but something grabbed the guy,"

"Or gal," I interjected. No one but me put much stock in the professional woman wrestler assailant theory, but I wasn't dropping it as a possibility.

"Or gal," Ahmet added. "ANYWAY!" He threw a mock glare in my direction at the interruption. "Someone or something pulled the attacker off of Barnett, and by the sound of it, threw the attacker into a tree. Barnett said that for a flash, he thought he had seen a large hairy man, but he knew that couldn't be right." Everyone at the table was agog—their mouths were hanging open in shock. Everyone except for me and Ahmet, who both wore ridiculously large smiles. "And get this," Ahmet said excitedly, "a compress of leaves was plastered on Barnett's chest to slow down the bleeding although Barnett had passed back out and didn't know how the leaves got there."

"You didn't tell me that!" I exclaimed.

"So how did they find him so quickly?" Bert asked perceptively. He knew there must be more to the story. Ahmet blushed, and I interjected.

"Ahmet's dream!" I exclaimed. "Yesterday, the FBI asked to meet with Ahmet again to get more details from the dream. I went with him even though I wasn't invited." Vance shrugged and looked conspiratorially around the table.

"Never stopped her before," he said wryly, with a smile in his eyes.

"Ah!" I gasped in shock. "I think I like you better when you're quiet." I gave Vance a shove with my shoulder and laughed.

"They asked for details about the terrain that I hadn't thought of before, but when I closed my eyes and thought about the dream, I could remember what I saw. There was a cliff on one side of the river where Barnett was fishing and it was heavily wooded nearly up to the river's edge on the side where Barnett was. And there was a bend in the river that I couldn't quite see around. When they started poking around on the map, they had a good idea about where he might be. And since it turned out to be within a ten-mile radius of my place, that sealed the deal for them and gave them a place to start looking. Turns out he was near where they thought he would be based on these details."

"And they got to him in time?" Bert asked in awe. Ahmet nodded. "Well, I'll be."

"AND it looks like a bigfoot is not only *not* to blame, but maybe came to the rescue. So the press really needs to drop this 'Sasquatch Serial Killer' nonsense." I said, indignantly.

"You know they will not go public with that information, don't you? The information linking bigfoot to saving his life," Vance said seriously.

"Why not?"

"Because they never go public with anything like this. And whether you like it or not, it's probably for the best. Mythical beasts, aliens, anything woo-woo will forevermore stay in the woo-woo category. You might as well accept it now, girl." Nona said with finality.

"Hey! Guess what else we decided last night?" I turned to Ahmet, since he was the only one of us not on the fair planning committee.

"What?"

"Since Dorothy and the Crawleys are insisting on an event that vilifies bigfoot, we renamed our fair the 'I Love Bigfoot Festival'. We're shamelessly going public with our mission to spread a positive message about the big, hairy folk in the forest." I smiled triumphantly. Bert shrugged at Ahmet, who was looking at me like I was a little bit crazy.

"Can't hurt," Bert said, looking at his watch. "I hate to leave, as I'm having a helluva nice time, but I have an appointment at 10:30 to show some property, so I've got to skedaddle."

"I should probably get going too," said Nona. "I don't want to hold Chloe up all day." Chloe and Abby had a fairly successful resale business. They were professional thrifters and garage-salers who used their stellar fashion and design sense to find treasures and resale them online, and Nona knew Chloe had a big day ahead of her. The two of them got up from the table. Nona bent down and gave Vance a peck on the cheek and he smiled at her like she was the sun, the moon, and all the planets wrapped up into one. My heart lurched a little. Oh, to be looked at like that again. Well, don't get your hopes up, kid. I chastised myself.

After they left, Vance, Ahmet, and I had another cup of coffee and petted Bif, who was making the rounds, begging for the leftover bacon. "Can you still go with us to see JoJo and Bob?" Ahmet asked me, just to be sure.

"I wouldn't miss it. I hope she's doing okay."

"You know, Vance. This time next year, you'll be introducing your own child to a couple of toddling bigfoot babies, God willing." Ahmet and I grinned at the stunned look on Vance's face at the thought of it.

"I hadn't thought of that!" Vance rubbed his head with an incredulous look in his eyes. I put my hand on his shoulder.

"It'll be okay. You got this." He smiled at me.

"It's pretty hard to believe, isn't it? I'm so glad I was there for the ultrasound. It made it so real."

"Did everything look okay?" The doctor part of Ahmet couldn't help but ask. Vance nodded.

"Yeah. The doctor said so far, so good. I guess they will do a blood test that will let us know the likelihood of whether the baby has Down's Syndrome, which apparently is the largest risk at our age." Vance kinda shrugged as he said this. A what-will-be-will-be kind of resignation rested on him. "My cousin Tommy has Down's Syndrome, and he is one of the kindest humans I know. So, I think there are far worse things that could happen than that."

"Fatherhood already looks good on you," Ahmet told him, and Vance seemed really pleased at the comment.

"You don't have any other children, do you, Vance?" I asked. I thought I knew the answer, as no one had ever mentioned any.

"No. I just didn't find the right gal to settle down with. At least not until I found Nona again." Just then Bif barked happily and started heading back to the treeline where Bob and JoJo usually met us, but I grabbed him. We all stood up, and I ran Biffy into the house to his crate, much to his dismay. I took the last few slices of bacon as a consolatory treat for his suffering and put them in his crate with him. I'd worry about the dishes when we got back. Ahmet picked up his doctor's case that he had brought with him and I grabbed the prenatal vitamins Ahmet had asked me to pick up in town for JoJo. I wondered if she would take them.

My eyes popped out of my head when I saw JoJo. She was enormous. Like freakishly huge, even for what you would imagine a bigfoot carrying twins to look like, but she seemed happy. And Ahmet said her heart rate and blood pressure seemed stable. He was working with a lot of guesswork here as to what was normal, but he compared her rates to Bob's. I wasn't sure at first Bob was going to let him, but after Vance and he had a few moments of telepathic communication while Ahmet and I stood in silence. Bob moved forward and nodded for Ahmet to listen to his heart and take his blood pressure. Ahmet seemed impressed by Bob's rate. I guess the bigger the heart, the lower the rate. In humans, the female's heart rate tends to be 8 to 10 beats faster per minute than her male counterpart and JoJo's was only 12 beats faster than Bob's which considering the sheer size of the babies in utero, Ahmet thought was pretty good.

I could tell Vance and Bob were talking about something else now and JoJo seemed to notice as well. Suddenly, I wondered if bigfoot could eavesdrop since the communication was telepathic. Could one intentionally dip into the other's thoughts? I tried but got nothing. If I had to guess by the serious looks on their faces, I would guess that Vance was asking Bob if he knew anything about Barnett. But it was possible I was just projecting because that is what I would be asking about, and I knew Ahmet had implied a desire for Vance to do this. Ahmet was moving his hands around JoJo's stomach with his stethoscope, stopping every so often and leaving his stethoscope resting in one place while he wore an intense expression on his face. Bob seemed to be distracted by Ahmet's actions.

"Well," Ahmet spoke aloud now, letting Vance know he wanted his help. I was pretty much just along for the ride today, although JoJo had reached out and taken my hand and held it when Ahmet was feeling around on her stomach. "I wish I had an ultrasound, but again, I think I can pretty confidently say that there are two babies. And I believe I felt movement from both of them. All of JoJo's numbers seem good and her color seems good. Can you try and communicate with her to take these vitamins?" Ahmet looked at Vance hopefully.

"I think I better demonstrate." I opened the bottle and pulled out one of the giant pills. Thankfully, I had a bottle of water with me. I popped a vitamin in my mouth and took a drink of water while Bob and JoJo watched. Then Vance started communicating with them and JoJo nodded. I handed her the bottle, and she looked at it closely. I took it back from her and showed her how to press down and turn. I gave it back and after just a few attempts, she got it. Bob was on top of things now because he passed her that dried deer bladder canteen full of water. JoJo cautiously put the pill in her mouth, made a face, and then took a big drink of water and swallowed it. I cheered, and that seemed to alarm them both until I sent them happy feelings and I could tell Vance was explaining it to them. They smiled at me.

"Be sure they understand only one per sunrise," Ahmet said. She could probably do with two since she is so large, but it's safer just to go with one. "Tell them everything looks great and to just keep doing what she's doing. I guess I'm finished unless they want to ask me anything." He looked at Vance, who looked at JoJo and Bob, and then smiled at each of them and nodded.

"They say 'thank you,'" said Vance.

"Did you tell them your news?" I asked Vance. He blushed.

"No. You think I should?"

"Of course!" Ahmet and I said in unison. We were way more into this idea of baby bigfoot and Vance-Nona baby growing up together than we had any business to be. It was just going to be so ridiculously cute I could hardly stand it. Then we heard the gunfire. Three shots and they couldn't have been more than a half-mile away. We all looked alarmed, and Vance forgot all about his news. Bob motioned for us to get low to the ground and he laid on the ground curled around JoJo, embracing her. We heard voices in the distance and although I've never been much of a praying woman, I began to pray that they would move away from us rather than closer. This was my damn property, although it could have been Ahmet's since the voices and gunfire sounded north of us. I felt a sense of relief at not having let Bif come with us. The last thing we needed was to hush a dog or keep it from running off toward the voices. Who the hell was shooting guns on our property this time? I knew for damn sure no one who had permission from either of us.

Ahmet must have sensed my anger because he put his hand on mine, which did not go unnoticed by JoJo, who raised an eyebrow if you could call it that. It was more like a hooded ridge that came up over her right eye than an actual eyebrow because there wasn't a significant differentiation in the hair on that area of her forehead. She clearly was asking if something was going on with me and Ahmet, which, in the seriousness of the moment, seemed juvenile and funny. I shook my head at her as if to say "Stop!" and winked and she cocked her head just like Bif might and then smiled at me. It must have been JoJo's first time to see someone wink. As we sat in silence, we heard the voices once more, but they seemed to be moving away from us and after about ten minutes, we all sat up. Vance, Ahmet, and I stood and Bob followed. When JoJo started to stand, we all motioned for her to stay put. I went over to say goodbye. I barely had to lean over, she was so tall even in her sitting position. It was no wonder the two of them laid down during gunfire. It was probably safer down low. I suddenly felt afraid for them. How were they going to keep twin babies safe with crazy people roaming around the woods shooting guns day and night? And were the Crawleys trespassing again? That seemed unlikely given the restraining order, but if it wasn't them, then who could it be? And how, for the love of God, could I keep people off of my property once and for all? There was a lot to think about.

CHAPTER 22

Ahmet and I were walking through the forest on our two properties with an app open, trying to figure out property lines and mark them. I had called to see about having a surveyor come do it, but they were booked out for three months, and Bert told Ahmet about the app he used when he was showing properties. You can use it to see property lines and so we were now trekking through the woods between our two cabins, posting NO TRESPASSING, NO HUNTING, and TRESPASSERS WILL BE PROSECUTED signs. Neither of our properties had fences around them and so we could not simply post the signs on the fence, we were hammering them to trees. I loved the woods. It felt like a sanctuary, somehow holy in its very essence, but with just an edge of eerie added in. Everything felt different in the woods, the air held a weighty fragrance that as it filled my lungs felt like it was restoring some sort of lost wonder from my childhood. The writer in me wished I had paid attention when Grandma Goosey was identifying trees to me as a child, that I could identify even one tree surrounding me by name, but who knows if the same trees growing in Iowa grew here in southern Oklahoma. (Well, I guess plenty of people know. I, however, am not one of them.) All I knew is that even though there was a calm stillness and magic in the air, the forest was far from silent. Life hummed around us everywhere as birds called to one another, insects buzzed, and the occasional bunny rabbit or squirrel would zip past us. It felt wrong to defile it with these stupid signs and I hated doing it, but Bert said in order for us to prosecute whoever the hell these trespassers were that had been shooting yesterday during Ahmet's prenatal doctor visit to JoJo, we must clearly post trespassing is not allowed. I felt like I was drawing graffiti on the Mona Lisa, posting big, ugly signs throughout the beautiful forest. It actually felt worse than that, because even though it makes me seem uncultured, I honestly always felt the Mona Lisa was a tad bit over-rated.

"Maybe we should put up a fence." I pitched the idea again to Ahmet. It was ludicrous and totally impractical and would likely never happen, but I like to consider the "good fences make good neighbors" theory occasionally and had decided that it was true. "We could do it around both of our properties, but leave the line between our properties open to give the bigfoot more room to roam and hunt. At least it would keep these God-damn crazy lunatics off our properties." I hadn't been able to get the idea of a bigfoot preserve out of my mind, even though both Vance and Bert firmly seemed to think it was a terrible idea. But if I couldn't even keep strangers from roaming on my property shooting guns, then there was really no point in attempting to build a bigfoot sanctuary.

"Hmm," Ahmet just made a small neutral sound that was impossible to determine whether it was a show of support for or against the idea. He was studying his phone and then looking around him and then studying the app again. "This appears to be the property line between your place, my place, and the Dobsons." We had started at my cabin and walked along the border where my property meets with the Dobson land and were about to keep moving uphill and post signs on Ahmet's land. If I was looking at the app right, we weren't terribly far from Ahmet's cabin. He began hammering a sign into a tree. "Bert says the Dobsons live somewhere on the east coast. They inherited an enormous amount of property adjoining both your property and mine, and they seem to have no interest in selling it or doing anything with it. Locals know this and so probably feel safe coming here to hunt. As you can see, it would be super easy to walk off of their property and onto either of ours without realizing it."

"I want to buy it. Maybe Bert can convince them to sell to me. If I own it, then locals will be less likely to hunt on it and if a bigfoot preserve becomes more necessary, I'll already own the property for it." Ahmet was nodding.

"That actually makes a lot of sense, and if anyone could talk them into selling, it would be Bert."

"I'm going to talk to him about it next time I see him." I nodded resolutely. It felt good to make that decision. I had been toying with the idea ever since I found out that it was owned by people who wanted nothing to do with it. Ahmet finished hammering yet another sign to another tree, and my soul felt like it died a little bit with each bang of the hammer. A bonus if I bought the Dobson's place is that we could take down these blasted signs. Before the echo of the last blow faded, we both heard a crunching sound behind us and turned simultaneously to look. I thought I saw something move about thirty feet away from us, but the trees and vegetation were so thick, I couldn't be sure. Suddenly, the hairs stood up on the back of my neck. Something was there. Something was watching us and I wasn't getting any peace or love vibes to calm the crackling of fear racing through my nerves.

Even though Bert had talked me into buying a gun and then taught me how to use it when the Crawleys were giving me trouble, I rarely had it with me, and today was no exception. I wondered if Ahmet had one on him. I looked him over and decided it would have to be concealed if he did, and I determined it was highly unlikely. He seemed as "cityfied" (Bert's word, not mine) as I was about the need to carry weapons. I had fared just fine for years in New York City without one, so it was hard to wrap my head around why I needed one here, despite Bert's constant reminders of the dangers of the wild backwoods of Oklahoma. There was another sound, this time it came from about thirty feet away from us in another direction. It appeared to be circling us, keeping its distance. My heart literally leaped into my throat and fear gripped me. I grabbed Ahmet's arm, and he motioned for me to stay quiet, then he reached across with his free arm and patted the top of my hand to reassure me. He was watching the area the sound came from intently. Suddenly, all I could think of was having my heart physically ripped from my body by a balaclava-wearing crazy person. I started shaking. My heart felt like it was going to beat right out of my body of its own accord, doing the killer's work for them. The sound of it pulsed in my ears. I felt for sure Ahmet and whoever or whatever was out there could hear it, too. Another sound came. This time on the opposite side as before. It really felt like we were being circled, and I started feeling like I was going to hyperventilate. That was when Ahmet looked like he had suddenly remembered something and started talking loudly and animatedly.

"Hey there!" He stood tall and told me to hold the signs out with each arm. He held our hammers, one in each hand, puffed out his chest, and stood tall and erect. "We don't mean you any harm. You go your way and we will go ours." At this, he motioned for me to follow him and we made our way at a ninety-degree angle from where we last heard the sound. He continued to watch where the last sound came from as we walked calmly away. He started singing, "Knick-knack paddy wack, give your dog a bone. This old man came rolling home." I raised my eyebrows looking at him like he had lost his bloody mind, he smiled, nodded, and started in again with a look on his face that invited me to join him."

"This old man, he played two. He played knick-knack on my shoe with a knick-knack paddy whack, give your dog a bone. This old man came rolling home." We sang together as I wondered if he had actually lost his fucking mind. But again, he smiled at me and nodded reassuringly. We had probably moved about 100 feet away from where we had been standing as we finished up the third verse. He stopped, "You okay?" he asked me.

"I guess so, are you?"

"I'm fine." We stood together, listening. We didn't hear a sound. After a few moments of silence, Ahmet spoke. "Let's head back." He looked at his phone again and headed in a direction that seemed counterintuitive.

"Are you sure you're going the right way?" I asked, uncertainly.

"Yes, for my place. We're closer to mine than yours now and I don't know about you, but I want to be out of these woods as quickly as possible."

"Agreed." I said and followed. "Do I need to keep holding the signs up? Why did you tell me to do that, anyway?" I had a suspicion I knew, but wanted to hear his explanation.

"No, you should be able to carry them normally now. I was thinking, and I remembered that most advice upon encountering wild animals like bears or mountain lions tells you to look as large as you can. And to talk or sing to distinguish yourself as humans and not prey. I'm not sure what was watching us, but I just went with what I remembered. Whatever it was, seems to have lost interest in us and that was the goal. I am just grateful for that." The incline was getting steeper and steeper. Ahmet's place was up the mountain from mine. My breath was becoming a little labored. "You need to take a breather?" he asked.

"No, I'm good. It feels good to get my heart rate up. I have not been getting enough exercise since I've been here. In the city, I walked constantly but I seem to drive everywhere I go here and am not getting nearly enough steps in. You seem fine, though." I noticed Ahmet was not breathing heavily at all. "Do you work out?"

"I like to hike around my property, there's my trail now," he motioned ahead of him about forty feet and I could just make out a well-worn path and clearing up ahead. We continued to weave our way through the trees and brush to get to the path. "I had the same problem when I first moved here. I went from walking several miles a day to nothing, so I started hiking the property."

"That's a good idea. Have you had many encounters like we just had?"

"Not really. I often sing while I hike, though. Most sources tell you to be a noisy hiker if you want to avoid bears and such. Most wildlife wants to avoid you as much as you do them and, by being noisy, you give them a chance to avoid you so you don't have any unwelcome encounters."

"So, 'This Old Man' is one of your usual numbers?" I asked with a grin.

"No. I don't quite know where that came from. Nerves, I guess. I'm usually more of a Beatle's guy. Or I sing the Turkish songs my grandfather used to sing to me when I would visit him in the summers."

I could not help myself, "Oh, please sing one!" I asked and Ahmet hesitated and then began singing. If I had to guess, I would say it was a ballad or a sad folk song. The tune was melodic and catchy and when I started humming along, Ahmet glanced in my direction, flashed me a quick smile, but kept singing and moved in front of me to help break down the brush as we drew closer to his trail. I followed him onto the trail and up to his backyard. As we came into the clearing at the back of Ahmet's cabin, the biggest, fattest, yellow tomcat I have ever seen immediately greeted us. It had the most beautiful blue eyes. "Old Blue Eyes!" I realized. "I get it! Well, hello! You must be Frank," I said, reaching down and patting the head of the beast, who immediately started purring full tilt and winding himself through my legs in a figure-eight before collapsing to the ground and rolling to his back.

"Wow. He's usually skittish with strangers," Ahmet said, amused at Frank Sinatra's enthusiastic enjoyment of the belly rub I was giving him.

"Shoot!" I said aloud, suddenly remembering that we had started out from my place and that Ahmet had met me there. "Your car is at my place. We're going to have to walk back through the woods after all," I said. That is when Ahmet's face filled with a wicked grin.

"What?" I asked suspiciously, rising from the squat I had gone down into to give the big yellow tomcat a thorough rubdown.

"Oh, don't you worry. I've got another way to get you home," he smiled, and I followed him around the side of his cabin and watched as he punched some numbers into the keypad on his garage door frame. The door lifted open and to the side of the well-organized garage was a dirt bike. Ahmet smiled at me.

"Oh, no...I'm not riding that thing."

Ahmet shrugged. "It's this, or walk back through the woods and possibly get attacked by whatever that wild beast that was stalking us was." I groaned, he was right. As much as I did not relish the idea of riding on the back of what looked like a fifteen-year-old kid's dirt bike with Ahmet, I disliked the thought of being attacked by a bear, or worse, a serial killer even more.

"I guess you're right. This is better than that."

"What's wrong?" Amet asked. "Don't like motorcycles?"

"Nope. And I don't like whatever this is, either." I said with an ornery smile.

"Ahhh...burn. Hey! Are you saying this is not a proper motorcycle?" We both looked at the bike. If you were to look at our faces, you would assume we must be looking at entirely different objects, because my nose crinkled in distaste and Ahmet wore a sparkly look of little boy wonder on his face as we both took in the muddy, bright orange dirt bike standing before us.

"Is this dirt bike the realization of a childhood fantasy?" I asked, suddenly understanding the spark of wonder in his eyes. A laugh rumbled softly in his throat.

"How did you know?"

"You have that look of a kid on Christmas morning when you look at it."

"Well, that is a remarkably accurate vision, Ele. Are you maybe a little psychic yourself?"

I laughed. "Not that I know of. Why do you say that?"

Ahmet pulled down a helmet and held it out to me. "Because," he said with a smile. "I asked for this exact bike every year for Christmas from the time I was eleven to seventeen."

"You never got it?" I asked sadly, now feeling a little bad for him.

"Sure I did—when I was forty." He smiled and shrugged as he threw one leg over the bike and did that little thing with his hands and his heel that made the engine roar to life. I had very little knowledge of the workings of motorcycles. I had always had a bit of an irrational fear of them. "Get on behind me." He ordered. "But first, put the helmet on." I obeyed, pulling the hard round helmet over my head and then awkwardly throwing one leg over the back of the bike and lifting myself on behind him as I wrapped my arms around him, closed my eyes, and held on for dear life. I could feel the wind against my body as we wove our way down his road to the highway. His road wasn't any better than mine. Although our properties adjoined, his road dropped us off onto the highway on the other side of the mountain and at a quite higher elevation than mine. As we pulled onto the blacktop, I opened my eyes. It was beautiful. I loved this mountain I had purchased a little parcel of and the curvy tree-lined highway. I suddenly hoped very much to buy a much bigger parcel of this mountain. Ahmet turned his head and I could see that he was wearing a big smile.

"You okay?" He yelled into the wind as it stole away all but just a little of his voice so that I could barely hear the question.

"I'm good," I leaned forward and spoke to the backside of his ear and we headed down and around the twisty highway toward my place. When we'd almost reached my turnoff, we saw a truck with BILLINGS BILLBOARDS printed on the side of it pull onto the highway next to the property adjoining mine–the property I had just told Ahmet I wanted to purchase. The workers had apparently just finished posting up a new billboard. There hadn't been a billboard there before and it annoyed me to see one now, but if I found the mere presence of a billboard upsetting, that didn't compare with the boiling fire that was bubbling up in me as I looked up at the words before us. Ahmet pulled over to the side of the road just down a little and across from my turnoff. There, in huge letters, were the words nightmares are made of. "FUTURE HOME OF" in a big arch over the words "BIGFOOT HUNTING ADVENTURES!" We both sat staring dumbly at the billboard.

"I can NOT fucking believe it! I can't believe it. I just said I wanted to buy this property as a preserve. The Dobsons have sold to a fucking bigfoot safari hunting group. What the fucking hell?!" I had taken off the helmet and wanted to throw it at the sign, but refrained since it wasn't my helmet and I knew Ahmet wasn't the biggest fan of my angry outbursts. I pulled my phone out of my back pocket and swearing under my breath pulled up Bert's number so I could call him when I realized Ahmet was saying something over and over again under his breath and it wasn't the stream of obscenities that had been coming out of me.

"That's him," he said again and turned sideways on the bike. His hand was pointing up to the billboard, and I looked more closely. This one was a different design. In addition to the "FUTURE HOME OF BIGFOOT HUNTING ADVENTURES," it still had the bigfoot illustration with the crosshairs over his face, but in the background were three men in hunting attire, the two on each side were in pretty stereotypical hunting garb, with camo clothes and face paint on, but the one in the middle was big and muscle-bound and completely covered with a balaclava, goggles, and gloves over his camo gear. Oh my God! Could it really be the killer? I looked at the other two men closely, neither of them was Abner or Jeb Crawley and I couldn't imagine they wouldn't put themselves on the sign if this were their business. Ahmet was shaking his head, "Hang on!" he said over his shoulder and we took off again. When we passed my turnoff, I started to say something but figured Ahmet knew where he was going. He went straight into Oklachito to Bert's office, and both Bert and Vance's vehicles were parked out front. We got off the bike. I was so upset about the sign that I forgot entirely my fear of riding motorcycles.

We went in as Bert and Vance were just telling an older couple goodbye and Ahmet held the door for them as they left. "Well, to what do we owe this pleasure?" Bert asked good-naturedly. He looked the two of us up and down, and I realized we were looking a little rough around the edges. We were hot, sweaty, and dirty from trekking through the woods all afternoon hanging signs and add to that Ahmet's windblown hair from having given me his helmet and my sweaty helmet crushed hair and we were quite the sight.

"The fuckers bought the Dobson's land for the Bigfoot Hunting Adventures!" I spewed as Ahmet spilled his news simultaneously.

"I think there's a picture of the killer on a new billboard that just went up," Ahmet said somewhat distractedly as he sat down and started looking for Agent McGee's number on his phone. "I need to get a hold of the FBI as soon as possible."

"Wait, what?" Vance and Bert asked together. I explained what we had just seen on the highway coming down the mountain between Ahmet's road and mine.

"Let's go back out and take a look." Bert grabbed his hat and keys and looked at us, expecting us to follow, so we did. "I was just going to see if you could get the Dobsons to sell the land to me!" I exclaimed again angrily.

"Wait, what?" Bert said again, hopelessly confused. "Since when?"

"Since just a little bit before we saw the fucking sign," I said, exasperated. Why on earth was everything always one step forward, three steps back? I find a solution only to find another roadblock. Ahmet and I climbed in the backseat and Bert and Vance took the front. Ahmet was busy hitting redial on his phone as we pulled out.

"Agent McGee? Yeah, this is Ahmet Pamuk. I think I may have found the killer." I felt a little ashamed of myself. Of course, the possibility of the killer being found was of much higher priority than the sale of the land next to me. There was a long silence. "Yeah...Yeah. Well, not the actual killer, but a picture of him. Yeah...on a billboard." Another long pause. "No, I'm not joking. I'm completely on the up and up. Are you in Oklachito now? Okay, well, can we swing by the police station and you can follow us out to see what I'm talking about? We'll be there in about thirty seconds. I'm in an old Landrover with Mountainside Realty on the side of it. Okay, see you in a second." Ahmet ended his call. "Bert?"

"Already headed that way," Bert said, meeting eyes with Ahmet in the rearview mirror.

"You really think it could be a picture of the killer?"

"I would almost stake my life on it. I know that sounds crazy since he is completely covered, but it's the same exact outfit and the same exact body build. It looks just like the assailant I saw in both dreams. And there was something else–" We pulled into the parking lot of the police station and Agents McGee and Brothers were already opening the doors of their vehicle. Ahmet rolled down his window and had a brief exchange with Agent McGee, who said they would be right behind us.

"Why do you think the killer would be so stupid as to put a picture of himself up on a billboard?" Vance asked Ahmet as Bert drove out to the spot where Ahmet had told him to go.

I glanced behind us and the unmarked FBI vehicle was just about three car lengths behind us.

"You have to remember," said Ahmet. "The FBI hasn't revealed that Barnett was found at all, nevertheless alive, so the killer has no idea that there is a witness. And even though they discussed releasing a composite drawing of the killer from my dreams, they ultimately decided against it since, in essence, I had nothing to offer but a costume and body build. This guy, or woman," Ahmet glanced my way, giving acknowledgement to my female wrestler suspect. "Is clearly a sociopath and likely a narcissist. They are probably getting a real thrill by being so in the public's face without the public knowing who they are. It would be their ego's way of taking credit without actually getting caught. It's probably why they usually take the victim's heart. They want to be remembered for this."

"That makes sense," mused Vance. Vance was tapping away on his phone. "There is no record of the sale of Dobson's place in county records or anywhere online, Ele." Vance told me calmly. Despite the huge issue of the killer's picture, Vance was also investigating my concern, which surprised and pleased me.

"You think the Dobsons might be putting in the hunting park?" Vance asked Bert. Bert was already shaking his head.

"No, I really don't. I've talked to them every couple of years since I opened my real estate agency. Just checking in to make sure they don't want to sell. They have never shown any interest in doing anything with the place. They've also always assured me I would be the first to know if they decided to sell. It doesn't make sense. There has been no listing of the property by another agent and no word from the Dobsons but I will sure as hell be giving them a call just as soon as we get back!" I realized that Bert and Vance were boiling mad about the whole thing as well and somehow spreading the anger around helped mine to subside a bit. I wasn't proud of it, but it was true. If others were upset as well, I felt a little less of a need to keep my blood at full boil. I should probably really be in therapy, but thus far, excessive cussing and writing books about murder was keeping me afloat.

There was a really rough service road to the right just past the billboard and across the highway from it where Ahmet had stopped before. From that vantage point, we could see the billboard clearly when we got out of the car and looked back up the highway at it. Bert pulled onto the road and Agents McGee and Brothers pulled in right behind us. We all got out of the vehicles to look at the sign. Who the hell were these people? I wondered again to myself as I stared at the three hunters on the sign, focusing on the one in the middle, lost in my thoughts.

Ahmet had walked over to stand with the agents and was visiting with them, and Vance and Bert were listening quietly to the discussion. I walked over to where they were all standing with faces looking up at the sign. "I don't want to sound patronizing," Agent McGee was saying, "But this hardly feels like a viable suspect identification," he said, looking up at the billboard doubtfully.

"I know," Ahmet said. "It sounds crazy, but do you see how the top eyelet of the right boot is red?"

"Yeah–that's weird all right," McGee answered slowly and warily, his eyes squinting as they zeroed in on what Ahmet was showing him. I took a picture of the billboard and zoomed in on the right boot. Sure enough, one eyelet was red instead of black, like the rest of them.

"I've never mentioned this before in any statement because I forgot all about it until I saw this picture. But at one point when I was wrestling the assailant–er, when Barnett was wrestling the assailant, Barnett had his face right up against the killer's right boot and was trying to force him to the ground and I noticed the red eyelet. Just take a picture of this to Barnett and have him look at the whole thing closely and see if he doesn't remember it as well. I bet you anything he will." We were all quiet for a few moments, taking this new information in. "How's he doing?" Ahmet asked tentatively. "I mean, if it's okay for me to ask."

"Okay? We wouldn't have found him in time without your help. It's more than okay and he's more than okay. He's actually doing well. He wants to meet you."

"Me?" Ahmet seemed surprised.

"Yes, when he asked how we found him, we told him about you and he has been asking to meet you ever since. His mom has been very cooperative about not revealing any information about finding him to the public yet. They want to see the killer caught as much as we do, but it's only a matter of time before it somehow leaks out. We have him at a private facility and we were planning on releasing information to the press this evening that we had found him alive, but then we received your call. Agent Brothers, will you call in a stop on that? I'll call Barnett's mother and explain the situation. If this is really the guy, we don't want to spook him." Agent Brothers nodded and headed to the car to make the call, and Agent McGee shook Ahmet's hand and tipped his hat to me, Bert, and Vance, and then he took a picture of the billboard. "You all wouldn't happen to know the company that owns this billboard, would you?"

"Billings Billboards," Ahmet and I said in unison.

"I'll be calling them as well." He nodded his farewell and got back into his car with Agent Brothers and they headed to town.

CHAPTER 23

"Bob came to see me last night," Vance broke the silence as we headed back into town. I almost asked if they could drop me off so I wouldn't have to ride the dirt bike again, but decided to leave well enough alone. Vance's news surprised Bert.

"You didn't mention that,"

"Haven't had a chance. We've been going ninety to nothing today with clients," Vance answered, and Bert nodded in agreement.

Vance had turned slightly in the seat so he could see Ahmet better. "Bob told me he asked around about who saved Barnett and I don't know if you remember the older bigfoot who was there when Bob rescued Ele from the kidnapper–the big one who came to give Bob some blood when we thought Bob might need some in order to recover from his injuries he got saving Ele."

"How could I forget?" said Ahmet. Trying to figure out emergency bigfoot blood typing and if it was possible to safely perform blood transfusions on bigfoot without killing them is not something any conscientious doctor could forget. Thankfully, it hadn't come to that. Vance nodded.

"Well, that's who it was; the big guy—JoJo's dad—he was the one who saved Barnett."

"Hot damn!" Bert was grinning from ear to ear. "That old guy scared the shit out of us when we were kids, remember that, Vance?"

"Yep," Vance replied to Bert with a smile. "Anyway," he turned back to Ahmet. "I thought Barnett might want to know that he wasn't crazy. So if he asks, now you know. I'll let you decide what to do with that information." Ahmet nodded, and I sat quietly, smiling, taking it all in. After being rescued by Bob, any visions of bigfoot as vicious creatures had transformed in my mind completely. Although I knew they could be vicious, I had witnessed Bob's wrath against the kidnappers. I now couldn't help but think of the bigfoot in our area as guardians, our very own guardians of the forest, and I'll be damned if I was gonna let some chicken-shits hunt down our guardians.

"So what do you think it means that there is no recorded sale of the Dobson place online? Is it possible it just hasn't shown up yet?"

"Possible, but not very likely," Vance answered. "What it means is that there's still hope." He turned in his seat to look at me. "It means it's possible we could still talk the Dobsons out of whatever the hell is going on with their property." I nodded somberly.

"Now, I know you guys aren't too keen on my whole 'Bigfoot Preserve' idea, but I wanted to buy the Dobson land in case some kind of sanctuary ever becomes necessary. As a proactive move, it seems to me that things are changing fast. Circumstances are pushing the possibility of bigfoot being real to the forefront of people's minds. TV shows are popping up telling all sorts of tales and now with the idea of sasquatch murdering people, even though it will hopefully be proven false in the near future. The idea is now fixed in people's minds. People are starting to believe, which means some people are bound to believe the worst. I just thought that the Dobson place would make a hell of a preserve and if word got around to locals that I owned it, maybe they would stop hunting on it. After all, Bert, you told me everyone around these parts knew the owners live out west and would be none the wiser if they poached there." I heaved a sad and heavy sigh. "I can't believe it fell into the hands of those bastards on the billboard."

"We don't know anything for sure yet, Ele. I like where your head is, though. I think it's time we start thinking proactively. The Dobsons own about a thousand acres there, that's going to be a pretty chunk of change. Are you sure you want to try and buy it if nothing is in stone with this Bigfoot Hunting Adventure group? You may have to outbid them."

"I'm sure, Bert. Everyone's got a price. Help me steal it out from under them. Please. You could sell ice cubes in Alaska. Call them for me, will you? Don't let those bastards win."

"I'll see what I can do," Bert said. "If you're serious."

"I'm serious."

Bert chuckled, "Then I'll see what I can do about selling some snow cones to the Inuits."

By the time Ahmet and I were pulling up to my house on the dirt bike, I had nearly lost all my fear of it. I was sitting more relaxed behind him, no longer holding on for dear life with my eyes shut. I tilted my head back and watched the tree branches that stretched across the sky over the road. The trees that seemed to be embracing their sisters on the other side passed by in a blur above us. It was lovely. It was nearly five o'clock, and I knew Biffy would be desperate to get out of his crate and use the bathroom. My stomach growled, and I thought of the chicken salad with grapes and celery in my fridge and the store-bought container of croissants sitting on my counter. Ahmet followed me into the house and Biffy was so cute as he struggled to decide which was more important, loving on me and Ahmet or going outside to potty. I made the decision easy for him and ordered him out back to use the bathroom.

"You want a chicken salad croissant sandwich and some chips?" I asked Ahmet as I opened the fridge door. "I know you're going to need me to follow you in your jeep so you can get both vehicles home, but I am starving."

I had already poured tea into tall glasses of ice for us both without even asking. Ahmet hesitated, and I found myself yet again wondering what was going on in that head of his. "Yes." He smiled at me. "Thank you. You've been feeding me a lot lately. I'm sorry I've been around so much."

"Shut up," I said and saw Ahmet flinch ever so slightly at my brashness. I softened ever so slightly. "Don't be sorry, Ahmet. We are two friends trying to save a species of so-called mythical beasts from detection and certain extinction. You've helped me a ton in so many ways, the least I can do is feed you—besides, it's been nice not leading such a solitary existence. I'm an introvert and my work requires solitude, so it is easy for me to slip into self-imposed solitary confinement if I'm not careful." Ahmet laughed.

"Self-imposed solitary confinement. I guess you could say that is how I have lived my last decade." I laughed this time.

"You know, it's kind of surprising you are not weirder than you are." Ahmet looked surprised by this comment and then laughed.

"Weirder, huh? So I am weird. Just not as weird as you would expect."

"Exactly." I nodded, smiling at him. I handed him his plate with his sandwich, salt and pepper chips, and a little bunch of red grapes on it. He looked down and his stomach growled. I laughed. "I guess you were hungry, too." We took our plates to the deck out back where Bif was happily chasing butterflies.

"You make our little 5S group sound like we're superheroes," he said, and I raised an eyebrow at him as I took a big bite, clearly indicating with a single look that is exactly what I think. "Trying to save a species of so-called mythical beasts from detection and certain extinction?" he quoted me. "Don't you think that sounds a little dramatic?"

"Well, what would you say we're doing?"

Ahmet shrugged, "I don't know...being helpful?"

"Helping an old lady across the street, carrying groceries to the car for a person with a broken arm—those things are 'being helpful'. Setting up a triage unit in my backyard and risking your own safety in order to save a giant hairy creature that science says is mythical, with no concern for your own well-being is heroic." I countered with my eyebrows raised even higher, challenging him to continue disputing me.

"Who says I had no concern for my own well- being?" Ahmet looked at me with the slightest hint of a smile and shrugged, slowly taking another bite of his sandwich in that super chill way of his. He swallowed and took a long slow sip of his ice-cold tea.

"Well, you did it anyway, didn't you?" I said, exasperated. He shrugged again, his dimple betraying the fact that he was trying not to smile, and said, in a completely deadpan tone.

"Ok then. You can address me as Superman from now on, thank you." I burst out laughing and he took another bite, maintaining his deadpan demeanor with only the little wrinkles around his eyes twitching ever so slightly, and that one dimple giving him away. All the stress of the last few hours was unraveling in me. Bif, always interested in a good laugh, came running up to the deck to check things out and I watched as Ahmet broke off a bit of his sandwich and slipped it to him. This is what life is all about. These simple sweet moments.

"I wonder if the FBI has caught the guy yet?" I suddenly wondered aloud. Ahmet looked at his watch.

"It's only been an hour or two since we showed them the billboard, so I kinda doubt it." He smiled at me. "I hope this is it. That they find evidence. I'm not sure that a red eyelet is enough to even hold a guy on, but if they can figure out who the guy is from the sign company and search his place, maybe they will find some sort of physical evidence—"

"So, what are you going to tell Barnett?" I had been wondering this ever since Vance had revealed to us who had thrown the killer off of Barnett. Ahmet sighed and shook his head in contemplation.

"That—I do not know. This is quite the rabbit hole to fall down. He's just a kid. And people will think he is an absolute loon if he goes around saying bigfoot saved him, but that can be up to him whether he tells anyone. So if he asks me, I'll just tell him the truth. I probably won't bring it up unless he does, though."

"That seems like a good plan." We sat in silence, thinking about our day. I wondered what the hell it was we heard stalking us in the woods today, or if anything was stalking us at all. It could have been anything—a raccoon, a squirrel even (although I think it would have to be an obese one), a deer, a bigfoot, or even a serial killer. Ahmet interrupted my thoughts.

"So what exactly are you thinking with this preserve idea of yours? Are you going to post a big sign, 'Bigfoot Preservation Society'?"

"Of course not. It would be more of a secret undercover preserve, a sanctuary. But we could let Bob and JoJo and their community know that it was a safe place, and that others were welcome if their homes became compromised. More and more people are moving in around here and the big parcels of land are being split up all the time. Bert told me they have several investors who do this. It stands to reason that if someone owns a five, ten, or even twenty-acre track, they are more likely to come across the bigfoot on their property than they would if they owned 120, 500, or 1,000 acres. As the property becomes split up, roads and driveways go in, they cut the brush down for yards, and it becomes harder and harder for anything to hide. That may account for the growing number of sightings worldwide." Ahmet looked a little surprised. "Yes, I have been doing some research since joining 5S and I really do worry about the future of the creatures. It is a legitimate problem and while Vance and Bert don't seem to like the idea of official preserves, I think they may be starting to see the need for unofficial ones as the property that has been serving as the creature's homelands for millennia is slowly being parceled out."

"I like it."

"You do?"

"Yeah. I would feel much better if we could somehow ensure that strangers with guns and ill intentions are not wandering the woods around our homes."

"Me too." Biffy came running up, wagging his tail, and Ahmet rubbed his head.

"You ready to take me home?" he asked Biffy as he stood and started taking our dinner dishes into the house to wash them. Biffy just wiggled all over in delight.

"I guess we could do that," I said, picking up our tea glasses and following Ahmet inside. Before I could stop him, Ahmet had quickly done our dishes and was asking Biffy again if he was ready and the three of us headed out. Ahmet handed me the keys to his Jeep and Biffy and I climbed inside as Ahmet jumped on his dirt bike, pulling on the helmet he had let me wear during our ride together. As I followed him to his cabin, I couldn't stop thinking about Barnett and the fact that Agents McGee and Brothers were likely at this very moment tracking down the identity of the killer. I hoped Ahmet would take me with him when he went to see Barnett at the hospital, and I wondered if it would be rude to ask. I kind of didn't care. Ahmet was used to me by now imposing myself into this situation. Any hope of not being rude died as he watched me cuss and fight a police officer as they threw me into the cell next to him. Not one of my finer moments. Oh well. We had just pulled up to Ahmet's place, and he was punching in the number to his garage door so he could park the dirt bike. The door began opening, and he got back on the bike and drove it inside. I put the jeep in park and hopped out to move to the passenger side so he could drive me back home, of course Bif tried to jump out with me but the last thing I wanted was for him to go chasing down Frank Sinatra, they could make friends another day. I was about to climb back in on the passenger side when I heard his phone ring and I didn't want to miss a thing, so instead of getting in the jeep, I walked toward him.

He hit the button to answer his phone and then immediately hit the button to close the garage door and quickly slipped under it as it slowly lowered.

"Hello, Agent McGee." Silence. I moved closer, hoping to overhear. I had to move in pretty close, but it worked.

"—he was so excited about what you found. He really wants to meet you." I could hear Agent McGee's voice say through Ahmet's speaker.

"So I was right? He recognized the red eyelet?" Ahmet was excited and I could feel his breath on my cheek. I was inappropriately close, but damn it, I didn't want to miss anything. I looked away from him in case I perturbed him. All I cared about was hearing what Agent McGee would say next.

"Yes. He studied the picture closely and then gasped when he saw the red eyelet on the boot. He began telling me the exact same story you told me of wrestling with the attacker's leg. Listen, Barnett asked if you would come to see him. His mother asked if I would give you her number to set up a time, if you are willing."

"Of course, I'm willing! It would be an honor to meet with them."

"Okay then, you got a pen?" Ahmet was feeling around aimlessly as if he would somehow have a pen and paper on him. We were both still wearing the clothes we wore this morning when we were hiking through the woods.

"Have him text it to you," I whispered.

"Can you text it to me?" Ahmet asked.

"No problem. Listen, though, we have him at a secure location and until we've captured this guy, we do not want anyone to know his whereabouts or that we have even found him alive. I'll tell Barnett's mom to let us know what you all arrange, and Agent Brothers will pick you up at your place and transport you there." I made a little sound and Ahmet looked at me.

"Um...can—?"

"Ms. Carmichael is welcome as well." Agent McGee answered before Ahmet could even ask.

"Thank you, sir."

"Thank you, son. We appreciate all you've done. Your next move is to stay quiet about all of this and keep a low profile. Our next move is to arrest the suspect. You have a good evening." And with that, Agent McGee hung up. Ahmet looked at me. I couldn't quite read the look on his face. I was still standing far too close to him.

"You–are—"

"*Delightful?*" I asked hopefully.

"NOSY!" He laughed and stepped back, putting a more normal amount of personal space between us. "You are *so* nosy." I couldn't tell if he was okay with it or annoyed with me, so I just smiled and shrugged.

"What can I say? I like to know things." I heard the rumble of his chuckle as I went around to the passenger side and we climbed into each side of the jeep. Biffy was delighted to perch himself right in the middle between us, but before Ahmet could even get the vehicle into drive, his phone pinged.

"Call her!" I ordered excitedly. He sighed and started punching in numbers.

CHAPTER 24

The SUV they were using to transport us must be what they used to transport snitches or high-level criminals. The windows of the backseat were completely blacked out, not just like super darkly tinted, but like, we couldn't see a thing. And there was one of those roll down windows between the front and back that are in the fancy limousines of eighties sitcoms and movies, and as soon as Agent Brothers finished checking to make sure we were settled, she rolled it up so that we could not see where we were going. Ahmet looked nervous.

"Are you okay?" I asked. I ran to get us coffee before heading to Ahmet's and had arrived at his house just a few minutes before Agent Brothers showed up to pick us up and we hadn't had a chance to talk yet. We each had a "Coffee O'Clock" to-go cup in our hands and I watched as Ahmet took an anxious sip of his Americano.

"Just nervous. I don't really know why. It's been so long since I did this. I used to be a nervous wreck before going to see someone whose loved one had sent a message through me. I'm not even delivering a message, but it's still strange, you know. I thought when I moved here I had put all of this behind me."

I knew what he meant. I moved here trying to run from things too. Quite different things, but still. I nodded. "It's going to be okay, better than okay, Barnett can't wait to meet you. Ahmet, if it weren't for you and your gift, he would most likely not be alive." Ahmet gave me a sad smile and nodded. We sat in silence, repeatedly looking "out the window" out of habit, only to behold a black wall between us and the rest of the world. It didn't take as long as I thought it might, not quite an hour to wherever they were caring for Barnett. I felt the car drive up a ramp and wondered where the hell we were. Agent Brothers rolled down the window between the front and back.

"Alright, you two ready?" she asked, smiling back at us. I could see out the front window that we were inside a parking garage, but there were no signs showing what the parking garage was a part of. "Let's go." She opened her door, and we followed suit. It was nice to know that we could at least open our own doors. We weren't complete prisoners, even though the blackened windows made me feel that way. We followed her through an underground walkway and onto what seemed to be a private personnel elevator. The elevator door opened onto a large space that resembled an intensive care unit. We followed Agent Brothers to a desk where a nurse sat. I looked for clues as to where we were, the writer in me couldn't help myself, but there was nothing. The nurse's badge said only her name: Juanita. Juanita smiled warmly at Agent Brothers and spoke, smiling at Ahmet and me as she did.

"Barnett is so excited about this meeting." She rose from the desk and we followed her around the nurse's station to a room with interior glass walls that had curtains mostly pulled closed over them. I could see through the window where the curtain was open that the external walls of the building we were in were brick with windows along the tops of the room so that there was natural sunshine and light, but you could not see out. This was incredible. I was truly clueless where we were. I had never experienced anything quite like it. A woman about our age with a warm, generous smile stood up from the chair next to the bed and immediately embraced Ahmet.

"Thank you! Thank you!" She held Ahmet tightly. "Thank you for saving my boy," she said over and over again. I watched as Ahmet patted her back. He knew this pain. He knew what it was like to lose the ones most precious to you. He could only imagine the feeling of having that person restored to you. She pulled back from him, with a hand on each shoulder, and smiled at him once again. "I'm Jackie, Barnett's mother." She shook his hand and then turned to me and shook mine.

"I'm Elena Carmichael, a friend of Ahmet's," I smiled back at her warmly and then Ahmet, in that incredible way of humility that he has, spoke softly.

"I'm Ahmet Pamuk. It's an honor to meet you both." As he said this, he turned to the young man who was sitting in the bed with a large plastic collar around his neck, cradling his smiling face. He had his mother's smile. Barnett held his arms open to Ahmet.

"Bring it in, brother," he said, and Ahmet carefully leaned in to give Barnett a gentle hug.

"I am so–" Ahmet paused to get control of the emotions bubbling up from inside him, he gained composure and finished, "–happy to see you looking so good."

"Hey, thanks to you and a big hairy beast," Barnett said. And there it was.

"Barnett!" His mother said, kindly exasperated. "I think you were hallucinating, honey. Can you talk some sense into him, Ahmet?"

"I'm afraid not, ma'am," Ahmet answered seriously.

"Really?" Barnett got excited. "You saw him too?" Ahmet and I looked at each other nervously and Jackie did not miss a thing.

"Oh, sweet Jesus!" she said, shaking her head. Ahmet looked at her seriously and then back at Barnett.

"What I have to share, you cannot un-know, do you understand?" He asked nervously. "So...if you don't want to know, you should tell me now."

"Tell me!" said Barnett excitedly. "I can't unsee what I saw either, as much as mom wishes I could." Ahmet looked at Jackie to get her blessing before speaking. She looked him deep in the eyes for a long moment, seeming to suss out his intentions and whether she could trust him or not. He must have passed the test, because she finally nodded with resignation.

"First, do you mind telling me what you saw?" Ahmet asked. Barnett looked confused.

"I thought you saw everything I saw." His disappointment came over him like a shroud. He was worried Ahmet didn't have the answers he was seeking.

"I've seen many things," Ahmet spoke. "Both in my dreams and in my forest." It sounded mysterious, but it seemed to give Barnett the hope he was looking for. "But the last memory I share with you is when your neck was broken and you passed out, although your blackout must have been brief, I didn't wake back up with you."

Barnett nodded, suddenly understanding that Ahmet's vision did not include his rescue. "You see, I used to go fishing with my dad in the Kiamichis on the river. It was kinda our thing we did each summer before school started. And we were planning a trip to celebrate my graduation and going to college, but dad–" Barnett choked up and stopped talking and Jackie started.

"John passed away in March from a sudden heart attack," she finished for Barnett.

"I don't know, I just decided to do the trip on my own, spur of the moment. I was missing dad, and I wanted it to be a secret, you know, like our thing, me and dad–or at least me and my memories of dad, so I didn't tell mom I was going. Which, of course, I now know was a big mistake. Anyway, I went to one of our favorite spots and was fishing like we used to." His eyes had a happy glaze over them and he started chuckling. "Dad would always tell me bigfoot stories while we were fishing. And so I was used to getting the heebie-jeebies in the woods. I was always thinking someone was watching me, so when that feeling that someone was behind me came, I thought it was just my imagination, but when I turned and looked, he just sprung on me and I started fighting—" Ahmet nodded.

"I know. I was proud of you in my dream. You weren't going down easy."

"Damn straight!" Barnett said, and then looked sheepishly at his mother's raised eyebrow. "Anyway, there was a guy all covered head to toe in camo and then with a mask and goggles covering his face and gloves on his hands. Well, you know." Ahmet nodded. It was all exactly as he had seen it. "So we were wrestling, and I lost my footing and fell. That is when I got hold of his leg and was trying to take him down with me. That's when I was eyeball to eyelet with that single red eyelet and it was so strange that I couldn't help but take note, despite the desperateness of the situation. We wrestled until he finally got his hands on either side of my head and twisted. I must have blacked out at that point." Ahmet nodded that he did.

"That is the last thing I saw. So what happened when you came to?"

"I felt this sharp pain in the center of my chest and opened my eyes and the man was sitting on me pushing a knife down into me near the center of my chest and there was incredible pain and then I saw this huge creature grab the man from behind. His hands were huge and hairy, and I just caught that one glimpse of his face as he pulled the man off of me. That's when I felt another wave of pain from my neck and realized I was about to pass out from the pain again. I heard a loud thump and footsteps running and then I guess I passed out again." Barnett sat in silence. We all did. It was a truly unbelievable story. Jackie was wiping tears away when Barnett spoke again, this time with a voice filled with quiet desperation, "What was it? What rescued me?"

"Well," said Ahmet. "I don't know whether the bigfoot in your dad's stories was good or bad, but the ones I've encountered have been good or, at the very least, neutral. One rescued Ele several months back as well." Barnett suddenly looked at me with new interest. "The bigfoot who rescued you is one of the older ones in these woods as far as we know. He's about twelve feet tall and is starting to turn gray. I don't know if that is typical or not, but he is." Barnett was nodding as if that lined up with his memory. Jackie remained absolutely quiet during this whole discussion. I knew this had to be a lot for her to take in.

"I wonder if they've got the guy yet," Barnett mused.

"Me too," Ahmet answered. "I keep hoping to get a call or a text."

"You must be especially ready for this guy to be captured," I said to Barnett and Jackie. "They're not allowing you guys to reveal that Barnett's alive, are they?"

"Lordy, no," Jackie said, shaking her head. "And it's about killing me. I don't know if my sister will ever forgive me, but they were very clear that any information leaks could lead to the perpetrators escape. And I want them to put this guy away." I suddenly wondered whether they had any idea where they were either, or if they were as clueless as we were.

"So, do you know where we are?" I whispered. I hadn't seen Agent Brothers or the nurse since they left us with Barnett and his mother, but I was pretty certain I was not supposed to ask this question. Jackie laughed.

"Girl, I do not have the slightest," she said, lowering her voice as well.

"It's weird, isn't it? Not to know or be able to tell."

"Oh my God, it is SO weird," said Jackie conspiratorially. "I haven't left this floor since they first brought me here. They bring all our meals to us." I suddenly looked around the space and realized that there was a bed there for Jackie as well, and I could see that Jackie had been living there with Barnett. Of course, any mother would, but she actually had a better setup than one would in a regular hospital. "When they told me they had found him, they asked me to pack a bag and informed me that they would like to keep Barnett's discovery under wraps for a little while. Barnett's an only child, so it has worked out all right. It's just the two of us. Of course, my sister is texting non-stop because she is worried sick about Barnett and can tell something is fishy with my evasive answers. I keep 'missing' her calls because I know I won't be able to keep it from her if we actually talk. I hope they get this guy soon. We were about to be free–" she stopped herself, realizing it sounded like she was unhappy that Ahmet had made his discovery when he did. "Not that this isn't a good thing. I'm happy you saw the billboard when you did." Ahmet and Barnett were half listening and having a conversation of their own about Ahmet's gift and a little bit more about bigfoot. "I just hope they get the guy soon." We all nodded in agreement.

"We have an 'I Love Bigfoot Festival' coming up in less than a month!" I remembered suddenly realizing it was exactly the kind of thing Barnett might want to come to. "You guys should come if you're out of the hospital by then."

"I better be!" Barnett said excitedly. "I want to go, mom." It was kind of sweet seeing the young man yield to his mother, almost asking for permission. This, the same young man who had gone off on a secret hunting trip all on his own without telling her.

"If it will work with your classes, I don't see why not," Jackie said, smiling at her son. I had a feeling this kid could get away with anything for a little while after all of this. It was a good thing he seemed like a nice guy who hopefully wouldn't abuse it too much.

"You're still going to start at OU this semester?" Barnett looked surprised that Ahmet knew about his plans.

"Yeah, well, I'm still hoping to. Mom's pretty sure they will work with me, she used to be a counselor there. How did you—?"

"I looked you up as soon as I had the dream. I read all of your social media. All of my dreams end with the victim saying their names. After we–well, you blacked out, I heard 'I am Barnett Weathers.' It's bizarre, but it also makes my gift quite undeniable. I know things about people that I truly shouldn't. Typically, my dreams are of a person's last moments on earth." Jackie put her hand to her face and Barnett's color drained from his face a bit.

"That is why I thought you were dead," explained Ahmet. "I have to tell you, man. It was the best surprise of my life, finding out you were alive. And knowing that the details of the terrain from my dream helped them find you, it makes it all seem worth it. I hate it. I moved to Oklahoma trying to escape it. I have come to think of it as more of a curse than a gift, but I'm so happy it helped in your case." Ahmet shook his head as if to drag himself back to the original question. "When do your classes start?"

"They started Monday, I'm missing them. My fishing trip was supposed to be my private last hurrah before moving onto campus. Even though I may miss the first few weeks, mom's pretty sure that they will work with me. I've started reading all my textbooks so I won't be too far behind," he pointed to a stack of books on the nightstand next to his bed. "And as soon as they catch this guy and I can go public that I'm still alive, I can contact them and start getting my assignments to do in the hospital or at home until I'm well enough to be on campus."

"Wow. You're a tenacious kid." I said, impressed. "I would have probably just waited and started in the spring." Barnett shrugged and smiled at me. He had a sweetness to him that guys his age usually hide, if they have it at all. His mom put her hand on his head and kind of ruffed up his hair, while that same infectious grin spread across her face as well. These were two people who were keenly aware of the joy and privilege it is to be alive. My eyes suddenly started filling with tears and I blinked quickly, trying to get control of my emotions.

"I've been excited about college for half my life. I want to be a veterinarian and that takes so long I don't want to lose even a minute of time." I watched as Ahmet came to life at this information.

"A vet, huh? I'm a doctor! Veterinary medicine is an exciting field of study. Do you know yet what you want to do with it?"

"I'm not sure. I just love all things furry, so I suppose not an aquatic or herp vet. Not that those wouldn't be cool." Barnett said this as if to apologize for not loving all animals equally. It made Ahmet smile, and I suddenly remembered that if things had gone differently, Ahmet would have a son or daughter in college now. "But that's about as narrowed down as I've got it so far."

"Well, I know it's not quite the same, but if you need any help with any of your classes, feel free to call me. I don't know if I would be any help or not, but I would sure be happy to give it a shot."

"Thanks, man!" Barnett said excitedly. Joyce, who had been standing at the top of the bed by her son's shoulder, suddenly reached her hand out and placed it on Ahmet's arm.

"Yes, thank you so much. You don't know how much an offer like that means." She smiled at Ahmet and I watched as it seemed like the two held each other's gaze for just a moment too long, but maybe it was just my vivid imagination. I'm always thinking I see sparks between people and getting it wrong. Not that it was any of my concern, anyway.

"Hey," Barnett was suddenly very serious. "Do you think it would be possible for me to meet the bigfoot that saved me? So I could thank them? I know that seems weird, but I'm just really grateful to be alive and really fascinated that I wasn't hallucinating like everyone kept telling me I was. I knew it was real." He cast a quick glance at his mom when he said this, and she just smiled and shook her head.

"I'm still having a hard time believing it, but I trust you two," she said to Ahmet and I. "I'm not sure how I feel about Barnett meeting with the creature though."

"Well, you might not have much to worry about. I'm really not sure that would even be possible," Ahmet cautioned, but at the disappointed look on Barnett's face, he continued. "We have a few friends who are more connected to the creatures by far than I am. I'll tell them what you want to do and they can ask the creatures if it's possible."

"They can talk to them?" Barnett asked excitedly. Ahmet and I looked at one another, not quite sure how much to share.

"In a way," Ahmet finally said vaguely and I could tell Barnett wanted to know more, but he just nodded.

"Well, it means a lot to me for you to ask. Thank you, Ahmet. Thank you for everything." Barnett said sincerely. Just then, Agent Brothers came into the room followed by the nurse.

"I'm afraid it's time to take Barnett for some tests," Juanita said kindly. She must have been able to tell the visit had gone well. "But I'm sure you all would be welcome back anytime." Agent Brothers nodded. "Hopefully, however, Barnett will not need to be with us much longer." We all nodded in agreement and started our farewells, hugging and shaking hands with new friends who already felt like they could become old friends before any time at all.

CHAPTER 25

"I told my son last night," Nona said quietly. We were sitting together in her shop at my favorite table. We were the only ones there. Nona had a grown son with a man who was a kingpin in the music and club scene in Austin. He had nearly killed her with his beatings, which is why she eventually came here to start over. She said he was good to her until he wasn't and from what I can tell, that is too often the case. People with rage issues can often come across as the nicest guys you could ask for until something snaps. Thankfully, her son did not witness the abuse, as it usually occurred when he was with his grandparents. His father now managed his band, which was quite famous and often had songs in the top forty. When her son wasn't on tour, he was recording, so Nona rarely saw him. I hadn't met him yet, he'd had to cancel two visits to Nona since I lived here. It was one of the reasons she hired Chloe. She figured if her son's schedule didn't allow for him to come to see her, then she needed to find a little flexibility in her schedule so she could go see him. I knew she missed him terribly. I hadn't thought about how nervous she must be about telling a son in his twenties that he was about to be a big brother.

"How did he take it?" I asked. Nona looked up at me with that angelic face of hers and smiled warmly, her eyes brimming with tears.

"He was quiet for a second and then said all excitedly, 'Finally! I've been asking for a little brother or sister for almost twenty years now!'" Nona laughed. "I was so shocked. That is not how I thought he would respond. I thought it would embarrass him and he would tell me I was too old."

"Had you told him about Vance?"

"Yes, we talk at least once or twice a week, so he's face timed with me a Vance. He's actually a big fan of his music too because he grew up listening to it with me." Nona smiled.

"That's so sweet. So I guess your son was okay with you dating him."

"He was delighted! I guess I should have expected him to be supportive of Vance and me having a baby. He had the same response–'it's about time'—when I told him I was dating again." Nona paused, lost in her thoughts. "He's a good kid."

"How could he not be? He has you for a momma." She smiled again, I could tell only half of her was with me. Her thoughts lost with the ghosts of her past.

"Thank you," Nona replied just as Chloe and Abby came strolling in. Chloe liked to come in during the dead zone too. I wanted Nona to make money, but I also adored having the place to myself. "Hello, girls!" Nona's face lit up when she saw them. Chloe and Abby were so sweet when they found out Nona was expecting. There were both so excited.

"How are you feeling?" Chloe asked with concern.

"I feel great, thank you," said Nona, rising to help them.

"Stay put, woman!" Chloe ordered. "I've got it." Nona settled back down.

"Hey!" I said with sudden inspiration. "You want to run over and see Bert and Vance with me? I want to find out if Bert got a hold of the Dobsons yet. I know he has left several messages, but it's been a week now and I'm dying here." Nothing new had happened on the property next to mine since the sign had gone up, which was something at least. I think if developers were to come in, I would cry. We also hadn't heard a word from Agents McGee and Brothers about the man on the sign and they had made no announcements about Barnett, which I knew had to be getting old for him and his mother. They'd let Jackie tell her sister, though. She just had to swear her to secrecy. Ahmet was a nervous wreck waiting for news on the murderer's capture. The only good news was that nobody else had gone missing and no more murders reported. The encounter with bigfoot must have shaken him up.

Nona hesitated and then asked. "Chloe, if I give you all of today's tips, would you mind watching the shop while I run somewhere with Ele?"

"Of course, I'll watch the shop, but you don't have to give me all your tips. I don't mind watching the place." Chloe said, smiling.

"Thanks, Chloe." Nona carried our dishes to the sink, and I gathered my things into my bag and pulled the strap over my shoulder. It was a beautiful day, so we decided just to walk the couple of blocks over to Mountainside Realty. When we walked through the door, Vance immediately got up from his desk and came and wrapped his arms around Nona and gave her a quick kiss.

"Just the two I wanted to see," Bert said. He was sitting at his computer, tapping away. "Guess what I just got in an email?" The two of us looked at him blankly. I had no idea.

"Our ISPS Conference tickets!" The International Sasquatch Protection Society yearly conference was coming up this fall about a month after the 'I Love Bigfoot Festival' and we were all looking forward to it. It was going to be held in Ontario, Canada this year. Last year, they'd held it in the U.S.—in Washington state, and Vance and Bert had said it was a marvelously good time. I think they were kind of excited for ISPS Chapter #111 to have more than just the two of them attending this year.

"Oh, wow, that's exciting!" I said, a little surprised to find that I actually meant what I was saying. Bert nodded happily.

"So what are you two ladies doing coming in here this afternoon?" Vance asked.

"Well," I said. "I wanted to check and see if Bert had heard anything from the Dobsons. And I think Nona just wanted to see you." I winked at him, and the two of them embraced again. Like I've said before, I'd puke if it wasn't so cute and they weren't both so darn nice. There's so much shit in life, I think one of the small comforts is when two lovely humans find each other. Oddly, it's a comfort to more than just the two involved. It's like all those surrounding the couple are somehow a little buoyed and encouraged that good things do still happen, that true love does still sometimes prevail. But maybe that's just me getting all middle-aged-sappy on your ass.

"I have not," Bert replied. "But let's try 'em again since you're here." Bert picked up his landline, which I was surprised to see he still had, flipped through an old school Rolodex, and dialed the number he was reading off the card. He motioned for me to take the seat across from his desk, so I did. I could hear the faint ringing from the headset. Two rings, three. And then a surprise, "Hello, Bert!"

"Well, hello there. I was about to think you were ignoring me." Bert joked good-naturedly with the man who had answered on the other end.

"No. No. Nothing like that. It's just been a madhouse around here. I've been meaning to get you called back. Now, what is this you were saying in your message about someone claiming to have bought our property there?" The man must have a voice like Bert, one of those natural orator voices that project on their very own because even across the desk I could clearly hear him.

"You mean, you didn't already know? Well, I guess that makes sense. I was surprised you hadn't said anything to me."

"You know if we ever decide to sell, you'll be the first to know Bert."

"Well, someone just put a billboard up at your gate saying, 'Future Home of Bigfoot Hunting Adventures,'"

"Some crackpot, huh?" The voice came from the other side of the line. Bert shifted uncomfortably. That was the thing about knowing the truth, most people thought you were a crackpot if you revealed what you knew. It was interesting seeing Bert navigate this.

"Well, looks to be a liar, at the very least. You mean to tell me no one has even talked to you about purchasing your property?"

"No, and I need to get ahold of whoever put up the sign and see if they want to take it down of their own accord or if I need to get the law involved."

"Billings Billboards," Bert said. "I'll send you a picture of the sign and a link to their business site right now. Is this your cell number, Ron?" I watched as Bert pulled out the card from the Rolodex and scrawled another number on it.

"Thanks for reaching out, Bert. It's nice to know you're looking out for us."

"Well, there was one more thing, Ron. I know you don't have any reason to sell, but this whole thing has kind of shaken up your neighbor." Bert glanced at me and smiled. "I don't know if you know or not, but that famous author E. Carmichael bought the land next to you on the lower east side and she threw a fit when she saw the sign about a hunting business moving onto it. She would like the first option to buy and Ron," Bert lowered his voice all conspiratorially, which about made me laugh out loud watching his master salesmanship at work, "She's prepared to make a good offer sooner rather than later."

"Really?" Ron sounded impressed, which also made me giggle, but I had to keep quiet. I didn't want to mess up a master at work. "I did not know we had a new neighbor. I love those books. I didn't realize it was a woman who wrote them, though."

"Yep. E. stands for Elena. She's a right nice gal. I know that land has been in your family for years, but I can tell you, if you were to let it go to her, she'd do right with it."

"Hmm…" Ron seemed to actually be considering it. "Food for thought, Bert. Thanks for telling me, and thanks for letting me in on that other bit, I don't know what the hell is going on,

but I'm going to get to the bottom of it."

"Very good, Ron. I'll send you the picture of the sign they put up and a link to Billings Billboards as soon as we hang up. Thanks for your time, sir. And keep Ms. Carmichael's offer in mind, will you?"

"That I will do, Bert. You have a nice rest of your day."

"You too, friend." And they hung up. It was a bit amusing watching Bert and someone who seemed to be just as big of a salesman as he was out-doing each other in their "good-old-boy-ing".

"Well, that didn't sound so bad," I said, waiting for Bert's take on it.

"Not bad at all. Ele, you don't even know. He has never so much as let a breath pass before saying, 'Nope! Not for sale,' in the past. He might actually consider selling to you. It didn't hurt that he had read your books."

"I was happy to see you weren't above name-dropping," I said with a smile.

"Hell, no. Whatever will get me the sale. As long as it's honest." Bert smiled back. "That is crazy, though, that these assholes have put up a sign without buying the property or having any permission whatsoever."

"Maybe the sign company got the location wrong." Nona offered.

"Maybe." Bert mused. "Wouldn't be the first time. Remember when they put up that 'fill dirt wanted' sign over at Dalton's place, Vance?" Bert started laughing.

"Oh yeah, and people started dumping their dirt right in the middle of Dalton's driveway. Boy howdy! That pissed him off." Vance chuckled, remembering.

"Are we talking 'Indian-Taco-Eating-Champion', Dalton?" I asked.

"The one and only," said Bert.

"Maybe that's all this is. A misplaced sign. But it looks like it's got you a shot at buying the land," said Vance.

"I hope so. I know you guys don't think it's necessary, but I don't think setting up a bigfoot preserve would hurt one bit. Worst case, Bob, JoJo and their babies just have a little more much-needed privacy." Bert and Vance shrugged in deference. I was glad they were coming around to the idea. I was looking forward to asking around at the ISPS's convention. I couldn't be the only one wanting to do this. Maybe there were others I could talk to for advice.

"Well, I better get back. It's about closing time," said Nona. "Are we still on tomorrow to start setting up the festival grounds for next weekend?" Nona asked.

"Yes ma'am. Walt and Bart and I are going over to the campgrounds a little early, around 9am tomorrow, to see how things are looking. I hired the Tobey brothers to bush-hog everything down for us, so hopefully, they've got that all done. See you tomorrow–around ten?"

"Sounds good," I said, and Nona gave Vance one last peck on the cheek before we headed back to her shop.

CHAPTER 26

I climbed into bed with pruney toes from my long soak in an Epsom salt bath. I hadn't worked that hard physically since—well, maybe ever. It had taken all the freaking day, but we'd managed to get the whole campgrounds gridded out, blocked off, and marked with signs for next week's festival. Of course, I'm sure there would be a million other details to attend to this week, but the campgrounds were ready.

The new and improved "I Love Bigfoot Festival" would officially kick-off on Saturday morning, although campers would be setting up Friday night and of course, none of us could wait for the Saturday night event with free Indian tacos for all and the newly added "WHY I Love Bigfoot" stories by the campfire. Bert said that vendors and food trucks typically would start pouring in as early as Wednesday to stake out their spots, but no one was sure what to expect from this year's festival. With the "Sasquatch Serial Killer" headlines plaguing every newsfeed in the nation, maybe an "I Love Bigfoot Festival" was ill-informed. Maybe Dorothy and the Crawleys had this year wrapped up. Apparently, the presale of tickets for the event was down by half.

From my perspective, the fair committee had a strange way of doing things. They had a giant blank map of all the vendor booth spaces and the food truck spaces marked off with numbers, which was what I had spent most of my day helping to do, measuring and taping off booth spaces both indoors and out. But we didn't assign spots. It was a first-come, first-serve basis where the vendors simply staked their claim and then went and wrote their business name by the number on the map so that people could see where they were. Bert thought it made the most sense. No one could accuse us of favoritism, of always giving the same people the best spots, whoever was willing to show up the earliest got the best spot. They had, however, found it necessary to make the rule that no one was allowed to stake their claim before Wednesday at noon, because one year people were waiting for them to mark the campgrounds the weekend before the event which made it quite difficult to set things up and they'd all agreed then that was just a little bit ridiculous.

Bif and I were just climbing into bed. I had let him come with me today because I was trying to train him to stay right by my side when we were out in public and today seemed like a good safe place to practice since it would just be the planning committee and a few other volunteers there working. He couldn't cause too much trouble if he disobeyed. I definitely would not have made that decision if I had known what a grueling day it would be. But to Biffy's credit, he stayed right with me, even though I know he got nearly as tired as I did. He was a very good boy. I patted his head on his sweet spot and then pulled the covers up when my phone started buzzing. The room was dark except for a reading light on my nightstand and the glow of my phone that was now shining the name—AHMET.

"Hey," I answered.

"Hey," Ahmet replied softly. It had been several days since we had talked and even longer since we had seen each other in person. Ever since our whole "investigation" was relinquished to the FBI when Ahmet identified the killer on the billboard, we'd not had as much reason to see each other and upon hearing his voice, I realized that I missed him.

"We could have used your help today." I teased. "I am beat."

"I would have been happy to help, but the FBI asked me and Barnett to identify some things for them today."

"What? Wait, did they get him? What do you mean? Some things? Did they not catch the guy?"

"No, but they are letting Barnett come out of hiding, anyway. He needs to get back to class. He's even able to walk now, but he'll be wearing that brace for quite a while, I guess."

"What did they find that they needed you guys for?"

"Well, I guess this guy has been laying quite a web of deception. There was no official business filed with either the states of Oklahoma or Arkansas for this Bigfoot Hunting Adventures business that he has been advertising but the FBI tapped into his emails and they found out he has been leading hunting trips in Arkansas and even one on the Dobson property next to us. I think that may be what we heard that day when we were with JoJo and Bob. He hired Billings Billboards under a false name, so they have been chasing down clues nonstop since Barnett and I identified him on the billboard. A few days ago, they found his home. And Ele," Ahmet's cadence had gotten softer and slower as if the weight of each word became heavier as he spoke them. "He had the hearts of his victims in jars, so they've for sure got the right guy." This news made an audible gasp leave my body, and

I suddenly understood the heaviness I felt from Ahmet more clearly. "Now, all that is left for them to do is to find him. His name is Harvey Feinberg. He is ex-military, dishonorable discharge for some weird shit he did in Okinawa. Apparently, they could never fully connect him to some murders there, but they were able to tie him to enough stuff for a dishonorable discharge."

"Wow," It was a fairly lame response, but it was the word that naturally escaped my lips. Suddenly, something occurred to me, and from what must have seemed like nowhere, came a giggle. "You said 'shit'."

Ahmet let out a small burst of air in surprise and then chuckled softly, too. "I did? Hmm...yes, I guess I did."

"I'm rubbing off on you."

"No, that's not it. I was just quoting Agent McGee- he said shit." I could hear the smile in Ahmet's voice.

"You said 'shit' again," I whispered and Ahmet muttered something I couldn't understand and laughed. The somberness returned as it always does when dark topics were at hand.

"So, I'm confused, what did they need you two for?"

"His clothes were there, including the balaclava, the goggles, and the boots with the red eyelet. They asked us to take a look at those things. That was before they had found the hearts. Apparently, he had hid them behind a false wall in the cellar. Once they found those, it was over, but initially, it looked like they were going to have to go with our identification of the clothes and some dried blood they had found as their only evidence."

"Wow." Again, it was far too shallow of an expression for the circumstance, but regardless of the fact that words were my business, this was the one silly word that kept escaping my lips.

"Yeah, wow." Ahmet didn't seem to mind. "The blood ended up being Barnett's, so in the end, they hadn't needed us at all, but I'm glad they consulted us. I've been going crazy wondering about it all."

"So, what now?"

"That's what I asked them. They said they cannot in good conscience continue to keep the news of Barnett's survival a secret, but Barnett has agreed not to reveal that he saw anything, at least until they have him in custody. Unfortunately, they want to keep the 'Sasquatch Serial Killer' hype alive. The guy is clearly crazy, trying to fulfill his desire to kill and use it to fuel interest in this new business he is trying to get off the ground. That's another way they were able to track him down. Not for searching Barnett's name, but Harvey Feinberg was obsessed with searching for his moniker. He had the most searches for 'Sasquatch Serial Killer.' I told you the killer would be a narcissist. He's crazy, but he's no dummy. If people think sasquatch are killing humans, they will want to go out and hunt them. The FBI hopes that if he doesn't realize they are onto him, he may try to strike again."

"How is he not going to realize they are onto him if they have searched and seized his home?"

"I think except for the hearts and the clothes, they've put it all back as they found it. They watched the house for two days before going in and there was no sign of him. When they went in, he was not there and the clothes from Barnett's attack were on his laundry room floor. If he comes back, they will nab him. And if he doesn't, they have their suspicions on where his next attack might occur."

"Maybe he had to go to the hospital after the bigfoot threw him."

"Yeah, maybe. They've been looking and haven't found him so far, but that doesn't mean he didn't use a fake name or drive to another state to seek treatment. I think that is one trail they are following now and they have people searching the hospitals. He's either in a hospital and they're going to find him any day now or he is just lying low, waiting to see what happened with Barnett."

"Do they think Barnett is in danger? That he might come after him again?"

"They don't know for sure, so they are going to keep eyes on Barnett as well."

"Poor Joyce and Barnett." I sighed. "They have got to be so tired of all of this."

"Ele, they're going to get him. It's just a matter of time. Joyce and Barnett are committed to helping see that happen." Ahmet paused for a moment as if he was trying to decide whether to tell me the next bit. "I hate to tell you this, Ele, but they'll be talking to you all soon, anyway. They think there is a strong possibility he will try to strike next at the festival. Maybe even in the woods surrounding the campgrounds."

"What?!" Bif came up and started licking my cheek. I guess he could sense my alarm and wanted to make it better. "Holy fucking cannoli. That blows! This is my first 'Bigfoot Festival'. I just wanted to have fun." Like so very much of what came out of my mouth these days, this was a sentence I never in a million years would have expected to utter.

"I know, but maybe if it draws him out, they will catch him before any more damage is done."

"I hope so." I yawned, and Ahmet told me to sleep well. We hung up our phone and before I could even plug mine in, I was fast asleep.

CHAPTER 27

People were everywhere. According to Walt, numbers were way down, but I couldn't believe how many people were willing to drive to a podunk town in southeast Oklahoma to celebrate, of all things, BIGFOOT! And yet, here they all were, with big sappy smiles on their faces. All kinds of people in all kinds of sizes and shapes, colors, and credos. And more bigfoot t-shirts than I ever thought could possibly exist. Apparently, Bigfoot has been the hide and seek champion since 1776—just a little trivia for you there. He doesn't believe in you either, by the way, in case you were wondering. What stood out to me the most, though, was the lighthearted, happy demeanor of the people who were wandering the grounds. These were people who enjoyed believing. They really were the lovers. It made me smile along with them in spite of the high alert we were on at the possibility of the "Sasquatch Serial Killer" aka Harvey Feinberg, trying to strike again. We had hired extra security for this year's event, and I knew there were plainclothes agents amidst the crowd as well. If this Harvey bastard decided to strike, we would be ready.

I wondered aloud how things were sizing up at the enemy camp. Bert, of course, kept telling me to stop calling it that. I couldn't help it. I really wanted Dorothy and the Crawleys to fail miserably, so I told

Bert that while I respected him greatly, he was not the boss of me. He was quite thrilled, as you can imagine. We were all running around like chickens with our heads cut off trying to help handle the minutiae of strange little details that need dealing with at this kind of event. One booth that paid for electricity was having problems getting it to work, the toilet paper was already out on port-a-potty number 13 on the east end of the campgrounds, somehow, there were no bandaids at the south side first aid station, the first speaker at the conference portion of the event (the part that serious bigfoot enthusiasts could pay extra to attend) was not happy with the sound, and on and on the list went.

As I carried a box of bandaids into the giant metal building that looked like it was more used to hosting sheeps than peeps, good old-fashioned gospel music was blaring from the indoor stage, filling my ears with lyrics like none I had ever heard before. "Jesus was just a country boy—the first good old country boy, for there he lay in a bed of hay, Yippee Ay Oh Kai Yay!" I'd had very little exposure to gospel music in my life and while I couldn't say it was my new obsession, people were sure enjoying themselves and it seemed to me that the Crosby Crooners had drawn quite a crowd for a before noon performance. I couldn't shake my light-hearted delight at everything I saw and heard. Even though I was crazy busy, I kept an eye out for Ahmet. I knew it was entirely unlikely he would show up to something like this, but he had been going into the public more and more. When I mentioned this, he told me: "I was never an *actual* hermit, Ele. I just didn't know anyone or have much reason to hang about town. I'm not agoraphobic or anything."

So because of these words, I hoped he would come check this craziness out because I thought he would probably get as big of a kick out of it as I was. After I dropped off the band-aids and headed back to the makeshift office we had set up, I saw a news reporter up ahead on the path grabbing people to interview, so I ducked down a side path that led to the kiddie booths. I might be enjoying myself at the "I Love Bigfoot Festival", but I did not want to be seen on TV enjoying myself here.

I looked up and burst into laughter. The 'Bigfoot-Back Rides' were off to a great start. There was a man who was probably at least 6'5" dressed in a pretty shabby bigfoot costume, running around a pen with a four-year-old on his shoulders. The child was giggling uncontrollably and the whole thing was so cute, I pulled out my phone to take a picture and capture the moment. I watched as three other children took their turns and snapped a few more shots before the poor guy had to take a break. I hoped he was being paid well for this, then remembered he was a volunteer. Kids were running all over the place and I looked around. Someone was calling my name. I finally saw her, dressed to the nines in a cute dress that came in at the waist and flared out with a swoopy skirt with pockets, looking like some kind of mix between a fairy godmother and Miss Frizzle. And what was the fabric? It looked like a hounds tooth print, but not exactly, I couldn't quite make it out. Oh, my God! It was that famous image of the walking bigfoot who had been dubbed Patty, printed repeatedly so that it recreated the feel of hounds tooth and I couldn't help but laugh in delight.

"Matilda Finch!" I called out to my new librarian friend, who had a story-time booth set up with throw rugs and piles of pillows and stacks of bigfoot storybooks. I didn't know there were so many available. I clearly was not 'in the know.' on all things bigfoot. There was a sign that said, "Story-time Starts at the Top of Every Hour (Last Story- 6:00 pm)."

"How are things going?" I asked. Matilda gently guided a child back into the booth with their book.

"All the books have to stay in the Bigfoot Story Nook, dear." She said kindly, and the child plopped down on a pillow and started turning pages, eyes peeled to the page. "It's going great," she said. "I've been doing these fairs for nearly as long as they've existed." She looked around. "Small crowd, but everyone seems to be having a good time, which is all that really matters," Matilda answered. I looked around at all the children with tired-looking parents in tow and was again surprised to hear that this was a small turnout.

"Well, I better get moving. Have a great day!" I stopped, realizing it was my job to help take care of her. "Do you need anything?" I asked before leaving. Matilda lifted the tablecloth and checked her ice chest that was under the little display table that held her sign.

"Nope! I'm all stocked up on water and snacks." She smiled at me, "But thanks for asking." I headed to the office, going a back way in order to avoid any reporters who might still be lurking about interviewing people for their special interest stories.

The day was going smoothly. Bert and Vance were standing chatting and Nona came walking up from the other direction just as I did. Walt was still out making rounds and Bart was manning the Choctaw Nation's booth until 4:00, when he would come to be the man on board in our office. Even though Bart Longfeather was quite spry, Bert wouldn't let him be a runner since he was in his eighties. Bart kept saying we needed to buy a golf cart for him to drive around, and Walt kept vetoing it as an unnecessary expense. The last big purchase they had made had been for the walkie-talkies we were all wearing which Bart apparently loved to use as well so staying at the office and calling out orders to those of us on the ground was a good substitute for buzzing around on a golf cart. My dogs were barking, so I sat down and sent a quick text to Ahmet to see if he was coming. I sent the first picture I had taken of the laughing child on the back of bigfoot. And I added, "I can't believe you're missing this."

Just then, a frantic woman came up to the office counter. "We can't find our daughter!" She said, with tears streaming down her face. My heart literally leapt up into my throat. We all sprang to action. The child who was missing was only two years old. Her name was Alyssa, and she was last seen in the South Building where I had heard the gospel singing. The child's father had stayed in the building and was still searching. The woman texted Bert a picture, which he immediately sent out to all the volunteers to look for and the security service team was walking with the woman back to the building where the child had disappeared. While they were dealing with that, I was discreetly texting all the information to Agent McGee so his team on the ground would also be alert to what was going on. None of us wanted to think that the worst could be possible. Surely. Surely, for the love of God, this Harvey bastard wouldn't take a child. We had no reason to believe he was even on the grounds, so we all tried to keep this nightmare of a worst-case scenario out of our minds. And then things got worse. My phone buzzed, and I thought it was going to be Agent McGee again, but it was Ahmet responding to my text.

ELE! THAT IS HIM! THAT IS HARVEY!

He had somehow drawn a circle on the picture around the face of a man in the background of the photo of the three-year-old getting a bigfoot back ride, a man who was watching the children. Oh my God, he was right. It looked just like the photo the FBI had shown us of Harvey Feinberg.

SEND THAT TO AGENT MCGEE RIGHT NOW!

I was a step ahead of him as I had already taken a screenshot of the photo Ahmet had edited with the circle and sent it to Agent McGee along with the original picture. I was currently texting the explanation of when and where I had taken the photo. "Oh God, please!" I whispered and Nona looked at me, knowing I wasn't much of the praying type, and grabbed my hand. I told her everything, letting her read my messages with Ahmet.

"We've got to tell Vance and Bert," she said immediately. She called Vance, and I called Bert and asked if they could meet us back at the office, saying that it was urgent. They were making the rounds, looking for the child and checking in with each of the volunteers. They said they would be right with us. When they got to us, we discreetly took them to the side and told them everything, showing them the picture.

"Holy Mary, mother of God," Vance said under his breath. And Bert took off his hat and bent over.

"Agent McGee already knows. I sent him everything. I'm sure his team is doing everything they can," I said, trying to be encouraging, even though I felt anything but encouraged myself. About twenty minutes passed before we got the call from the security team, little Alyssa Thomas had been found. She'd crawled under a table with long tablecloths that reached the floor and had fallen fast asleep. She was safe. Nona and I started crying, and Bert and Vance were close to it. Just then, the second call came. This time from Agent McGee.

"Ele?"

"Yes," I said anxiously. My happy-go-lucky bigfoot festival day had turned into a nightmare that I had just woken up from, but my nerves had not yet been notified.

"We got him. Partly thanks to your picture—we have Harvey Feinberg in custody." I thought I was going to pass out with relief for a second. I sat down and Nona, Vance, and Bert looked at me with concern. I nodded to them, trying to let them know everything was okay. "Shortly after I sent out your picture, a few of our guys got eyes on him slipping off the grounds towards the woods. Agent Brothers and three other agents followed in close pursuit and apprehend him in the woods, but clearly, his plans were not good. He had camo gear, another balaclava, ski goggles, gloves, and a Bowie hunting knife with him in a backpack in the woods where he appears to have been camping. He also had a pickle jar."

At this news, I made a motion with my hand crossing my heart and I'm not even remotely Catholic. I just used to love it back when I was a kid in the eighties and would see nuns do it on tv shows. I used to do it all the time until my Aunt Becky told me to stop, that it was disrespectful to actual Catholics. It must have been a sacred moment because I hadn't done that since Aunt Becky had told me back then to cut it out. "Thanks, Ele! Tell your team there they can relax and enjoy the rest of the weekend." I hung up the phone and burst into tears as my three friends gathered around to comfort me, not realizing that these were the first real tears of joy I had experienced since being rescued by Bob and my own nightmare a few months back.

EPILOGUE

I was stuffed. The free Indian Tacos were a tremendous success and although the crowd was apparently small compared to usual, happiness flowed like the honey I had just poured onto a leftover piece of fry bread Nona and I had snagged from the kitchen. Nona told me fry bread was delicious with honey and when she and I found there were a few warm pieces left, we snitched them along with a cute little plastic bear full of honey. I watched Nona lick the honey off of her left hand and my eyes couldn't help but rest on the engagement ring Vance had given her when he proposed earlier that day, shortly after they took Harvey Feinberg into custody. He had dropped to one knee right there at the 'I Love Bigfoot Festival,' pulled a ring from his pocket and said he could not go through one more catastrophic event without her as his wife. It was weird and wonderful and kind of perfect, considering the wandering path their love had taken.

I was licking off the last of the sticky honey mess from my fingers when I saw Ahmet helping Barnett to the stage. Barnett didn't really need his help, he seemed to be doing fine maneuvering in the big plastic collar harness thing that came up around his cherub-like face and helped to protect his neck while it healed. Barnett beamed that same beautiful smile he'd worn when I first met him at the hospital.

Joyce was behind Ahmet and I caught her eye and waved at her to come and join us on our blanket, where we were sitting to the side of the campfire. We had a king-size comforter quilt all spread out on the grass and Bert, Matilda, Vance, Nona and I scooted over to make room for Joyce and Ahmet to join us. I couldn't believe my eyes. Barnett cleared his throat, and something about his presence brought a hush over the audience. I don't know if they realized who he was or not.

Joyce sat down between Nona and me and I quickly introduced them and Ahmet sat next to me on the edge of the comforter. I leaned over to him and whispered, "Oh my God! You brought Barnett! I'm so glad you guys came." I looked around at my little tribe. Nona's face was glowing like a beacon of light and love as she watched Barnett. Vance, who was holding her hand and stealing glances at her every few moments, looked like he could hardly believe his luck. Bert—sweet, kind Bert—had invited Matilda to sit with us and she was like a magical fairy, enjoying the storytelling like it was life itself. I looked at the two of them and I couldn't help wondering... Joyce was on one side of me, beaming up at her son expectantly. And Ahmet was on my other side, looking—at me—and smiling the warmest, loveliest smile.

PSA #30: Surround yourself with the kind ones, the shiny ones, the ones who choose to do the right thing even when it's tough, the ones who will laugh with you, and cry with you, and will stand beside you through thick and thin. Grab onto them. Make them your tribe. And love them.

(Look at me getting all sappy. I must be getting old. Oh well, I'm doing it in good company.)

The "WHY I Love Bigfoot" storytelling event went so much better than any of us expected. Bart Longfeather had kicked the evening off by telling his father's story of how one winter when Bart's grandfather was in bed fighting off death, a bigfoot had saved their lives by bringing a freshly killed deer to their doorstep for his family to eat when they were about to starve. He told it beautifully and added lots of details he'd left out the night he had briefly shared it with us at the planning committee. And now, it looked like Barnett would be the evening's finale.

"Hello," came Barnett's warm, rich voice. He could do audiobooks, I thought. "You guys probably don't know who I am, but my name is Barnett Weathers." The crowd literally gasped aloud. Everyone knew his name and was now understanding why he looked familiar, for his survival had been the top news story for the past few days. "You may be wondering why a victim of what the media are calling the 'Sasquatch Serial Killer' would stand before you at a storytelling event called 'WHY I Love Bigfoot,'" he flashed that big pearly grin at us, with his dimples at full tilt. "But, listen up!" He said and the crowd collectively leaned in. "Because I've got a story for you—"

About the Author

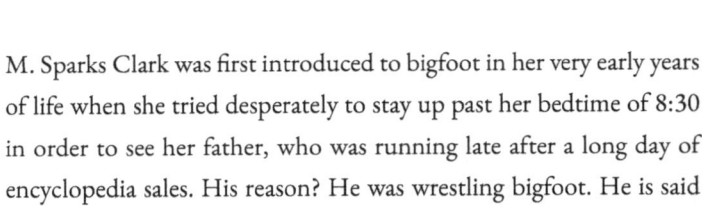

M. Sparks Clark was first introduced to bigfoot in her very early years of life when she tried desperately to stay up past her bedtime of 8:30 in order to see her father, who was running late after a long day of encyclopedia sales. His reason? He was wrestling bigfoot. He is said to have wrestled bears and mountain lions as well, but nothing quite captured the author's vivid imagination like bigfoot did.

M. Sparks Clark is a pen name Missy Hancock uses for the paranormal adventures she writes. "Sparks" in honor of her late mother whose feistiness lives on in the main character of the Ele Carmichael Novels and "Clark" for the above-mentioned bigfoot wrestler—her dad—who lives in the Kiamichi Mountains of Oklahoma and continues to have occasional encounters with the creatures.

Also By M. Sparks Clark

Bigfoot Watching Woman Watching Bigfoot-An Ele Carmichael Novel (Book 1)
Sasquatch Saves the Day!-An Ele Carmichael Novel (Book 3)—*Releases November 25, 2023*

Thank you so very much for reading this book. I hope it brought you a little joy and reprieve from everyday life and maybe a laugh or two! If you would like to keep tabs on new releases from M. Sparks Clark (and I so hope you do!), please follow me at msparksclark.com and sign up for free giveaways and my fairly infrequent newsletter. :) You can also follow me on instagram and tiktok: @msparksclarkbooks

www.ingramcontent.com/pod-product-compliance
Lightning Source LLC
LaVergne TN
LVHW041911070526
838199LV00051BA/2583